Similitude

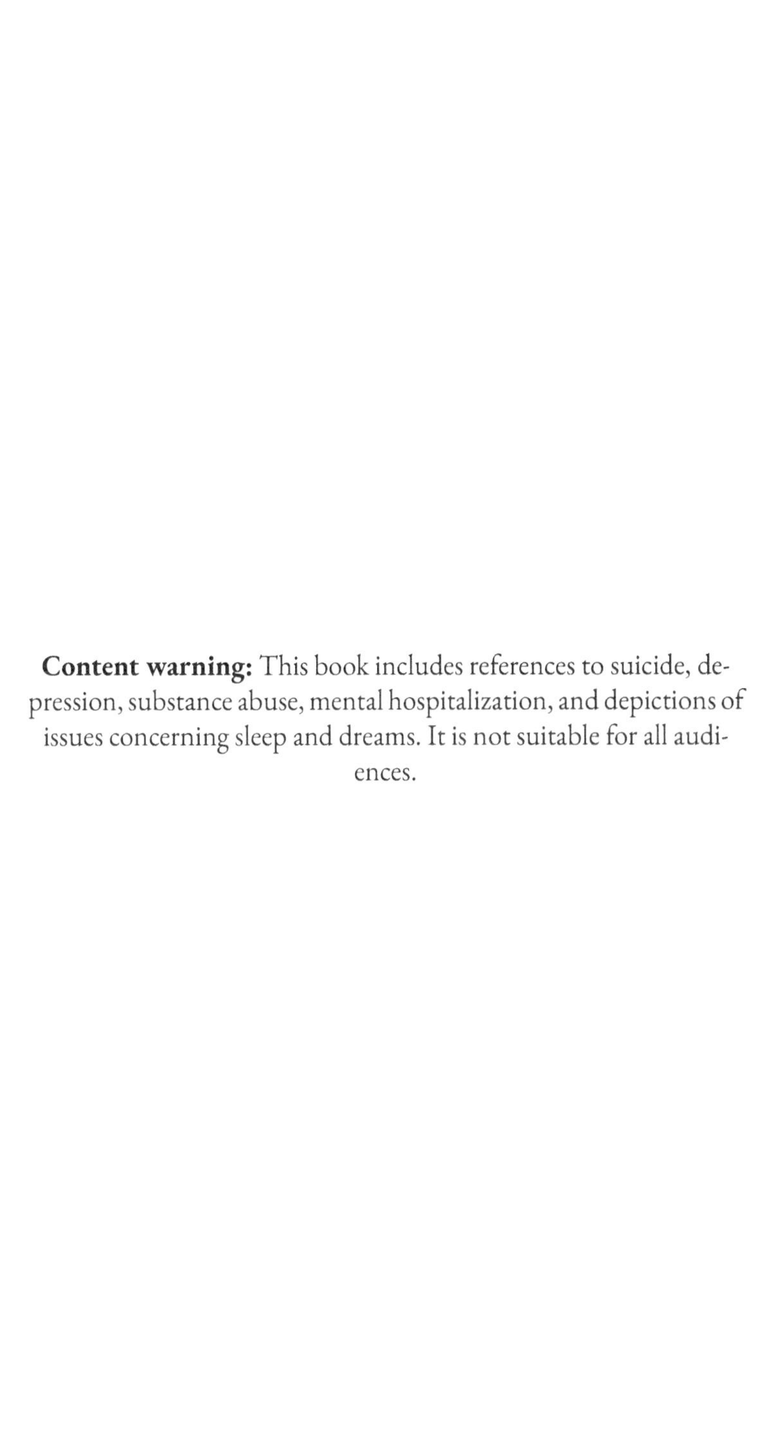

Content warning: This book includes references to suicide, depression, substance abuse, mental hospitalization, and depictions of issues concerning sleep and dreams. It is not suitable for all audiences.

Similitude
Shannen Greene

To those who ask.

Similitude
Shannen Greene

Part 1

One

Thursday, November 6, 2036, 3:32 PM.

I don't remember when the questions started.

As I stare at the notebook page full of bulleted questions in messy penmanship, each one concerning my past, a deep wave of void washes over me, and the words repeat themselves in my head: *I don't remember when this began. I don't remember when the questions started.*

My thoughts only become those sole words and my mind begins to block out the rest of my surroundings—the electronic ambiance that plays through my earbuds and the distinct sound of the San Francisco BART train's smooth travel along the rails—silenced. All that becomes clear now is the notebook page with a myriad of written questions, and the blank space that rests under every one of them. Because I cannot answer these questions, and I cannot answer the question that ponders when they began.

What made me forget?

That is one.

What was it like to live before adoption?

And another.

Why do I feel this way?

Why do I feel so numb?

I wish to understand every one of the questions that plague my mind; I wish to have an answer to each, but that wish seems far from attainable now. Sitting silently inside of this train car—visuals of the city of San Francisco that I've known my entire life passing by me through the grand, modern windows of the train—people, silent, commuting from work to home or from home to work; a sense of loneliness engulfs me sourcing from the notebook's page, and my hands grow cold in the pale air of the train car. That same void that rests under the written questions—it begins to become part of me. Initially, I figured that writing out my concerns would serve to help me understand and answer them; from a psychological and neurological perspective, that would make sense. It's why writing notes on paper in academia is effective. But now, staring at the notes of my mind, there's a distinct bleakness to it all.

I don't know.

I don't remember.

I write the words slowly on my paper in black pen.

I don't remember when the questions started.

But I wish to.

I part my eyes from the notebook page and to the outside view from the window beside me on the train, examining the city as it passes. Quick visions of advertisements and people with their eyes locked onto their sleek devices move by, and the train enters a dark tunnel as the rail by which it's moving on dips. Now, as I look outside of the window, all I see is the reflection of the inside of the train car and, therefore, myself.

I notice my knee is bouncing in an anxiety that I didn't physically pay attention to beforehand, and it only continues in a greater intensity at the realization. I see the notebook turned to a page full of questions that rests upon my lap, but most of all, I notice my own appearance. My straight, long black hair is tied up for ease of movement with subtle long bangs. I wear my glasses over my monolid eyes and my private school uniform: a white polo with my school's logo, dark gray straight pants, and a gray San Francisco sweatshirt for my own comfort.

But my face is blank with an emotion that I can hardly describe.

My mouth does not quiver in any enjoyment or sadness, my nose is straight and unbothered by any smell, my cheeks do not have any pink tint to them—my face is blank. And, though this is not uncommon by any means, the resemblance that it has to the notebook page that rests upon my lap stirs a pain within my stomach: an uneasiness. My stomach aches with the questions, my knee bounces with the lack of answers, and my breath quickens as I look at myself and notice my own resemblance to both those things. My mind, mirrored by a page void of answers—I feel void, myself.

I decide to close the notebook out of the knowledge that, if I leave it open, it will only torment me even more. From my gray smartphone, I increase through a screened surface the volume of the electronic ambiance that plays into my ears, allowing that sound and the smooth movement of the train car to lull me into a nap.

I wake up.

My eyes slowly open while the remaining senses of mine develop vividly and adapt to the scene. In that, I realize where I am—on the train, yes, but the atmosphere of it is undeniably desolate and the car lacks any illumination as does my outside view from the windows; it must be midnight with the pitch black sky that remains consistent with the quick movement of the train along the outskirts of San Francisco. I did not sleep long enough for the train to become this way—I'm inside of a dream.

As I sit in a blue window seat identical to the one I was initially sitting in, I watch through the windows the empty roads of San Francisco's outskirts from above. Although it's unrealistic for them to be empty, even at midnight, I can see the roads clearly as we pass above them; I notice the street signs, the trees, and the blank billboards that would typically display bright advertisements. Examining the train car itself, too, the displays inside are shut off and void of any bright screen. The smell of the inside of the train car is just as before: a smell of pale air that chills your skin. The sight would be comforting, until the train comes to a sudden halt and the car begins to shake, jolting me into a state of physically evident nervousness as my knee bounces and my hands tremble. Immediately, my eyes dart around the scene as if passengers would be reacting, but the visual of the empty train reminds me that there are no passengers but myself. A wave of dizziness encompasses me and sticks—the scene becomes somewhat blurry as the train cars sway back and forth over the railway high above the ground.

Expecting to hear something over the intercom, I try to keep composure, only to remind myself again: no human is present on this train aside from myself.

Loneliness.

The cars continue to sway and, with that, my knee continues to bounce aggressively and my head grows lighter in the increased dizziness. My mind plays quickly through images of my life: my mother, my school, and some memories that I haven't even encountered vaguely before. I wish to replay them inside of my head, but that wish dissipates as I hear a crack from beneath.

The scene warps into something completely unintelligible as—

I wake up.

Immediately, my body jolts aggressively as I felt it did inside of the dream. My heart pounds quickly and harshly, enough to hear it accompanied by a ringing in my ears, the drool on my left hand, the warmth of my cheek that I assume rested on that hand, and the trembling throughout my body that causes both my legs and hands to shake uncontrollably. The dizziness that I experienced throughout the dream—that same distinct dizziness—follows me into this reality, too. I wipe the drool onto my pant leg hurriedly as I notice the digital text displayed on a small screen attached to the train car's ceiling: Millbrae. The train is rapidly approaching the stop that I get off at—I need to compose myself before I leave.

I take the hair tie out of my hair and watch myself in the train window's reflection as I tie it back once more, patting down the frizz that followed my nap. I adjust my glasses and straighten my posture—*I need to rid myself of this dream.* Despite a desperate attempt to compose myself, my leg still shakes. I'm afraid I won't be able to stop it.

As the train reaches its stop, I quickly leave, carrying my black backpack after shoving the notebook inside of it. Leaving the station, I wait at the bus stop for the next bus to take me to my neighborhood. However, despite my quick movements from location to location, I can't stop thinking.

I need to stop thinking.

Images of the notebook page rid my brain, or the region responsible for mental imagery: the frontal-parietal control region. No matter the terminology, the image plays throughout my head and, with that, so does the dream that followed. The dark liminality of the train deep in the night: the detailed visions of the empty San Francisco highway from above, the displays both inside and outside of the train void of any images, the sudden jolt of the train and the swaying of its cars, the dizziness that followed, the quickly moving memories as the train faced derailment—

Stop thinking about this.

The fact that some of those memories—those vague, unrecoverable memories—were ones that I had never seen once before—

Get out of your head, Kaeda.

The city bus arrives, and I board, sitting at a window seat toward the back. During the bus ride, a few students from a nearby public school have a conversation about private schools, mentioning my own: GoldenPine. They talk about how the students are too preppy and the parents are all slaves to big tech, and I'm glad that I wore my gray sweatshirt over my uniform's polo.

I put in my earbuds once again and let the electronic ambiance play through them, attempting to relax my body following its dream inside of the train.

As the bus stops right outside of my neighborhood, I leave with my backpack and take out my earbuds to allow myself to hear the outside sounds. The wind rustles through the trees of orange leaves, some breaking off of their branches in death and falling to the ground.

Breaking off in death, falling to the ground.

No, stop it.

I sigh as I walk into my neighborhood. The houses here are small yet modern in their architecture—having a somewhat mid-century modern appearance that has been renovated to fit recent years. Alone, I would consider the houses to be interesting and even charming in their appearance, but they are all identical to one another. A neighborhood full of identical houses, each one's differences only stemming from the difference in "Welcome" mats, address numbers, and, occasionally, gardens—the sight is uneasy at times. I walk up to my house, and the automatic pathway lights increase in brightness as I do so. I unlock and open the door, walking inside to a familiar modern living room where no one sits. Down the hallway and into my bedroom at the left, I pass by the nearly empty shelves. From what I only briefly recall, these shelves used to have decorations.

I set my backpack full of academic textbooks, notebooks, and a laptop down onto my bedroom's carpeted floor, picking up one of the many textbooks, a notebook different from the one on the train, a case full of mechanical supplies, and my laptop. Sitting at my desk, I finish calculus homework days out from now as electronic ambiance plays into my ears, then psychology homework, then computer programming homework, then biology homework.

Shit, there's nothing left to do.

I study for a neuroscience course online, passing time once again. The course suddenly discusses memories and the hippocampus.

Memories.

My dream.

No, stop it. This means of passing time is supposed to silence these thoughts.

7:10 PM.

Through my earbuds, I hear a faint knock on my bedroom door. My adopted mother: Michelle Bynum. She tells me briefly that dinner is ready, another serving of pasta, and I put my equipment aside, walking to the kitchen and the small wooden dining table. My mother brings her laptop to the table and examines financial models for her job as we eat, saying nothing to one another again.

Dinner ends, and I work my day away once more. Now comes time for me to shower, where I'm alone with my thoughts. With this knowledge, I hurry through the shower, and study once more in my pajamas of an oversized white tee and black flannel pants until the clock hits 10:30 PM.

I should sleep now.

I lay down in my bed of gray sheets, shut off the lights, and attempt to fall asleep.

10:50 PM.

20 minutes of tossing and turning.

11:10 PM.

Another 20 minutes—tossing and turning.

11:30 PM.

A full hour since 10:30 PM—tossing. Turning. In my dark, small bedroom of only minimal white furniture, the digital alarm clock aside from my bed is the only source of illumination. Against my bedroom window over my desk with closed blinds, I notice the faint sounds of raindrops making contact with the glass, one by one.

I think of a dream I had last night where that same noise was present, then translating to the one I had on the train.

Stop.

Illuminated by the digital alarm clock is a jar of melatonin pills, half empty. I only recently bought this jar.

Do I take one?

No—you must learn to sleep without these, Kaeda.

But what if I just—

This is unhealthy and only enhances your dependence.

But I can't sleep if I don't take—

Please, stop it. Stop thinking about your dreams—stop thinking about your memories. Your questions. *Stop thinking.*

I can't stop thinking if I don't take a melatonin pill.

But—

I pick up the jar from my nightstand and pop a melatonin pill into my mouth accompanied by some water. After ten minutes, I fall asleep.

Two

I wake up.

As my senses gather, I start to notice where I am: a dark bedroom that is not my own. It's nighttime now, but I can still make out some details of the room: minimalistic flower wallpaper, photos of a family that is not mine, and gentle, childish art in frames. As I glance around, I notice another bed across from me: a child's single bed, where someone familiar stares at the ceiling. That person would be my sister, Ottie.

"Kaeda," she starts, rolling around her bed and finally looking at me. "Why am I always staying up late, tossing and turning, unable to fall asleep?" She hides under the covers and straightens out, frustrated. "It's like I'm tired, but it's so hard to go to bed!" she continues. "My mind runs and runs."

"I don't know how to help you," I answer through a younger version of myself, "I can't sleep, either."

Ottie looks back at me. "Yeah, but at least you do stuff when you're awake like this," she refutes. "Like reading books. With me, though, I just wait for my mind to shut up."

"It's not like I don't do that, too," I say. "I just sometimes make, I don't know, something out of not being able to sleep. That's why I read the books."

"But I can't pay attention like that," Ottie says in response.

"I'm sorry," I say, looking back at Ottie, who faces the window next to her bed in retaliation and pouts. My view of the scene and Ottie herself slowly dissolve into that of another one—the scene changes.

Beneath my legs which sit on a bench is a cool dew—touch is the first sense that I'm met with here. As my vision grows vivid, however, I realize where I am: my neighborhood—the identical small to medium modern houses all sit aside one another in rows beside the residential road without light in any windows. Familiar trees rustle in the wind which is quiet to me yet visibly harsh—sleek street lamps are dimly lit and I notice a bus stop along a sidewalk through the neighborhood trees: the bus stop I wait at each weekday morning to take me to Millbrae station. The sky is bleak and dark, with no late-night clouds to add a perceived depth to the scene. In terms of audible details, I hear not a single sound of human life either within or beyond the neighborhood: no electric cars, although they make little sound—no human discussions. It appears that, in this scene, only I am here—only I am sitting on this bench and pondering my surroundings. *Maybe this will change?*

As I glance around the scene once again with this question, I notice an element of intrigue that I hadn't before: a piece of notebook paper that appears to have words written on it, soaring through the harsh winds. Thankfully, I catch it in time and read its contents.

It barely has any.

Kaeda Bynum, ??/??/34

I'm waiting for a sign here. Genuinely, I am. I know that I'm not superstitious, but this altered reality that I'm living in is giving me no

That is the entire page.

A sharp pain pierces my stomach as I stare at the paper with an expression that, while I cannot see myself, I understand is blank.

"I'm waiting for a sign here. Genuinely, I am. I know that I'm not superstitious, but this altered reality that I'm living in is giving me no"

Clutching my stomach, I put the paper down on the sidewalk in front of me.

"I'm waiting for a sign here. Genuinely, I am. I know that I'm not superstitious, but this altered reality that I'm living in is giving me no"

Unlike how it did previously, the paper does not aggressively move through the air and become influenced by the wind—it only sits there, its words and the deep void that rests under them, staring at me.

"I'm waiting for a sign here. Genuinely, I am. I know that I'm not superstitious, but this altered reality that I'm living in is giving me no"

Like an unanswered question: a blank space under a burning, thought-provoking question—an absence of context. An absence of explanation. An absence of knowledge—an absence of understanding.

The dimly lit street lamps, along with the one beside me allowing me to read the notebook paper, flicker their lights. The sound of wind rustling through the San Francisco trees increases in volume and speed, though the paper is still solitary. It still pierces my pupils as I find myself unable to look away, despite the physical pain that its visual inflicts upon me.

"I'm waiting for a sign here.

Genuinely, I am.

I know that I'm not superstitious,

but this altered reality that I'm living in is giving me no"

I wake up.

3:52 AM

Shit.

3:52 AM—a loud ringing plays through one of my ears accompanied by my own pulse. I rest both my right pointer and middle finger on the left side of my neck to feel that same pulse against my fingers, breathing deeply: in and out, in and out.

Shhh, Kaeda.

3:52 AM—I move up on my bed to sit up slightly and rest my head against my bed's headboard without a move to my fingers and a change in my breathing. I look away from the digital alarm clock aside from my bed, closing my eyes.

I'm waiting for a sign here.

3:52 AM—I try to focus on the quiet whir of the A/C as it travels throughout my house to block out the constant repetition of *those words*.

Genuinely, I am.

3:53 AM—I open my eyes and check the clock. Maybe sitting in complete and utter visual blankness is making room for unnecessary thoughts of my dream. I move down my bed and move the gray bed sheets over me once more, resting my head on a pillow instead of a headboard.

Shhh, Kaeda.

I fall asleep.

I wake up.

As I stare up above, I notice what appears to be the bottom of a top bunk, along with movement in the mattress. A familiar voice calls from above: "Kaeda?" it says.

Ottie.

The scene dissolves, and I wake up.

4:06 AM

Why?

I fall asleep.

4:24 AM

4:39 AM

4:56 AM

5:02 AM

5:14 AM

5:26 AM

Aside from my digital alarm clock, reading these tormenting bright numbers of the early morning, I notice the jar of melatonin pills—its advertising effects being what is most illuminated on the jar.

No. I can't take melatonin pills this late in the morning—that would harm my academic performance for the rest of today.

I reject the thought and turn on the nightstand lamp beside me, sitting up in my bed.

It's not too early to do schoolwork for today, is it?

There must be some assignments for me to complete.

I grab my glasses and stand up from my bed, quickly stretching and yawning as I look at myself in the full-body mirror attached to my bedroom door. I see myself: I see the dark eye bags that rest under my eyes, I see the messy black hair atop my head, I see the paleness of my skin accompanied by pink sleep marks, I see my twisted pajamas from turning around in my sheets—I see an unexpressive facial expression, and it does not change.

Turning around, I sit at my desk and sort through the messily open textbooks and papers sprawled across the surface. This reveals my laptop's keyboard, and I wake the laptop to log into my school's online assignments portal to find a newly posted assignment for computer programming. I insert my earbuds connected to my smartphone and shuffle through tracks of electronic ambiance.

5:56 AM

Thirty minutes—I shut my laptop and shove the textbooks and notebooks on my desk into my school backpack, clearing the surface. Standing up, I dress in my GoldenPine school uniform with a zipped-up gray hoodie over the uniform's polo, hiding the school logo, and walk out into the kitchen with my backpack. To eat, I have a ham and cheese croissant and a can of 200mg espresso from the fridge. My mother sits at the end of the kitchen's island with a large glass of iced coffee, typing away on her laptop early in the morning with a view of work similar to my own. She looks at me and, surprisingly, speaks.

"Kaeda, I'm *very* unsure that you'll be able to continue attending GoldenPine," she tells me, not for the first time. I nod in understanding; what do I say to her?

"Living on a single income in this area has been horrible," she continues. "I love the school, you know I do, but I really doubt that you can keep attending it."

"I understand," I assure her.

"I hope it's okay with you," my mother finishes.

"It is."

As I prepare to leave the house, I glance at the nearly empty shelves along the house walls, only having a few small pictures of me and my mother, Michelle.

"Those shelves used to have a lot more photos on them," she comments from the kitchen, noticing me.

"I briefly remember," I answer. I do: there were more photos here on these shelves before my mother's ex-husband left her for a reason that I can't recall, even though that event occurred while I was living here after being adopted by the two of them: Michelle and Frank Bynum. Frank was part Japanese, and his subtle Japanese features carried onto my parents' late biological son, Cace. From a small photo in my mother's room, I can remember Cace's features although I never met him as he died before I was adopted: he had dark, straight hair and glasses, with an intellectual appearance. From what I've been told, I'm fully Japanese with Japanese facial features, have dark, straight hair and glasses, and have been told that I have a more intellectual appearance in how I present myself.

I theorize that, when Frank and my mother adopted me, they adopted me with the sole purpose of finding a child almost exactly like their late son. I haven't ever spoken with my mother about that, though.

"Yeah," my mother finishes blandly, returning to her work. I put on my plain white sneakers and leave the house, walking through my neighborhood to the city bus stop. During my short walk, I notice the bench along the sidewalk with the streetlamp directly beside it and, as the caffeine has not fully affected me yet, a stunning yet incredibly short-lived visual of a notebook paper on the ground. A hallucination—I shake my head, continue walking, and eventually board the bus at the stop, where I'm met with the usual crowd of people: two or three office workers commuting and one or two nearby public high school students who prefer a city bus over a school one. Sitting toward the back, I stare out the fogged bus window and silently observe the 6:30 AM stillness of San Francisco's outskirts. Leaving the bus after a quick ride, I sit and wait at Millbrae station shortly for the next train on a dew-covered sleek bench, a modern streetlight near me creating light through the bay area's thick fog.

No one speaks as they wait for the train's arrival; they only stare at their smartphones, glance around the station bleakly, listen to music through headphones or earbuds, or do a mixture of the three. The electronic ambience tracks from before continue to play through my earbuds—it's weird to comprehend as I don't consider them much, but I am one of these silent commuters.

The train arrives, and everyone boards, many of these passengers with large cups of coffee in their hands and seeming to carry themselves in a heavy, drained manner. I definitely believe I fit in the category of these commuters.

Sitting on the same window seat as yesterday afternoon coming home from GoldenPine, I look through the train car's window and out at Millbrae as the train quickly leaves the station, passing by rows of trees that you can only see the leaves of through the fog. It becomes redundant: the outside conditions, and a memory from yesterday crosses my mind.

The notebook page, full of questions.

Maybe a morning brain would be more effective in answering them—recalling those memories?

I open my backpack aside to reveal a myriad of notebooks, then pull out the one from yesterday which I know is not academic. The page's corner is creased to where I can easily open to the page, where I do so.

What made me forget?

I do not answer the question throughout the train ride. I stare blankly at the page with little to no understanding of every one of the questions written on it, stupidly thinking that maybe, *maybe* I am capable of answering them now. But, truly, what would have changed? I'm only caffeinated now and received little sleep.

What made me forget?

Please, quit begging the question this early in the morning.

What was it like to live before adoption?

I mark a bullet under that question.

Ottie—what was she like?

Energetic, creative, kind.

Those are such general traits.

What made me forget?

I mark a bullet under that question.

I wish to remember.

"I wish to remember."

Quietly sitting in the fast-moving train, I continue to stare at the page and silently, in my thoughts, repeat the words to myself.

"What made me forget?"

"I wish to remember."

It's not an answer, no, but it's something, at least. A goal: something to chase.

The train comes to a stop, and an automated voice plays through the train's speakers, announcing our arrival at the station. I shove the notebook quickly into my backpack and zip it, quit the bouncing of my knee, and leave the train car along with a few other passengers.

Quickly leaving the station, I arrive by a short walk at GoldenPine school's campus. I'm first met with an electrical sign within a sleek and modern structure to showcase each event at the school, the name "GoldenPine School" being proudly displayed above the sign of changing, high-quality images. Walking beyond this, I find the school's grand, modern, primarily outdoor campus through the bay area fog. Walking within the campus itself, the pathways from one building to another hold a beautiful symmetry, with benches aligned throughout the sidewalks and beautiful landscaping along each pathway. Within the mostly covered yet still outdoor main hallways are enormous posters and awards to boast the school's events and reputation, those awards being mostly academic. The students walking through the hallways themselves also carry this same pride for their school in wearing GoldenPine hoodies and owning GoldenPine merchandise, although they have a choice to wear whatever hoodie or boast whatever merchandise they please to.

Entering the buildings themselves, I quickly weave throughout the hallways to my first class: computer programming. Then to my second, then to my third, then to my fourth: college-level biology, where I'm informed by listening in on other students' conversations that there's a large three-person project today. I sit at my desk and, immediately, two students with whom I have not once had a genuine conversation tap my shoulder from behind.

"Hey, Kaeda?" one says. "You know that there's a project today, right?"

I nod.

"Could we both be your partner?" the student continues, pointing to their friend. "I heard it's a three-person project, and we've sat behind you the entire year."

"I guess so," I answer.

"Thank you so much!" the first one says. I turn around, and the two chat behind me, one praising the other for picking me. Shortly after, a group of two students with whom I've never talked either beside my table call my name:

"Kaeda!" one says, then points to their friend. "Could we both be your partners for the project?"

Before I can muster out an answer, the two students behind me with whom I've now been grouped aggressively respond, saying that I'm their partner already.

The class begins, and the teacher goes into detail about the project. It's due a few days from now.

"You finish the project organizer and we'll find photos," one of my group partners says from behind. I nod in silent agreement. The project organizer is a large part of the project—it's the entire project's outline. Finding photos is the easiest part of the entire thing and requires little to no focus or skill.

From behind, I can hear the two students talking with each other: a mundane conversation that continues throughout the entire class period, and I drown out the noise with my earbuds. After biology is lunch, and I walk outside of the building and into one of the school's courtyards with rows of dark green and yellow outdoor lunch tables. I sit at a lunch table and wait for two people: Juno and James Williams, the only two friends I have at this large 7th through 12th grade school. The two are twins whom I've known since last year, Juno being the first one I met in a poetry class that I had taken for credits. I found the class enjoyable yet never stuck with it, and Juno was enamored by the topic of poetry. She was easily the top of our class and took part in poetry competitions. To be a poet, though, you need to be intelligent to make certain analogies and form certain structures—Juno's very smart.

James is more involved in sports, playing varsity baseball, but loves very niche scientific topics like archaeology and astronomy, with an additional interest in philosophy as he's an active member of our school's philosophy club. James will invite other people to eat with us occasionally as he knows more people and, while they talk to me, I've never had a one-on-one deep conversation with any of them; I only truly talk to the Williams twins.

Out of a nearby building door, the two students walk out and sit at the table. Juno parts her black and brown box braids from her face and adjusts her round glasses as she sits on the dewy lunch table bench, placing down a generic light purple backpack with a keychain of an art piece. She wears a gray GoldenPine zip-up hoodie and the uniform dark gray pleated skirt, while James wears a black San Francisco Giants baseball hoodie and the uniform dark gray slacks. I take out the sandwich I had packed for myself as my lunch, and Juno doesn't seem to have anything—only revealing from her backpack a novel to read.

"Would you like some of this?" I ask Juno, eyeing both my sandwich and her absence of a lunch. Silently, Juno stops reading her novel, glances at me from across the table, and shakes her head "No".

"You sure?" I ask again quietly, after a pause. She still shakes her head, while James eats an insulated food jar full of pasta. He looks over at Juno and nudges her shoulder.

"C'mon, you were talking about how you felt hungry," he says to her. She looks back at him, somewhat sorrowful, and shakes her head again. "I'm okay," Juno mutters. "It's not important."

Trying to appear unaware of what is happening, I stare at my food. Still, the two are in my peripheral vision, and I can hear everything they say from the other side of the table.

"Is this about Will?" James quietly questions Juno. I had briefly heard about this: "Will" was a student that Juno had some minor crush on, asked out, and was rejected by. While the situation happened only two days ago and Juno still seemed down before them, James still asks, and I still listen.

"No, it's not about Will," Juno replies, almost mumbling. "I don't really want to talk about it, please let this go."

James subtly scoffs. "I will not put aside the fact that you're clearly feeling down," he refutes. He lowers the volume of his voice, but still to where I can hear him. "Does this have to do with Mom?"

Juno stares at her twin brother with both an annoyed and melancholy look on her face, lowering her eyelids and appearing somewhat "deadpan" yet still subconsciously frowning. "No," she mutters back. James backs away, but then studies her face again a minute later. He begins speaking again.

"I don't know what to tell you," James tells his sister, sighing. "Because I don't know what's up with you and it concerns me—"

"You don't need to tell me anything," Juno snaps, cutting off James. "This is my problem."

James gives no response, and Juno continues to read. I contemplate saying something for a moment regarding the book that she reads. *Would engaging her in a conversation, despite whether I'm good at that, help?*

I decide that I'll figure that out.

"What's the book about?" I ask Juno. She glances at me from the pages and subtly relaxes her gaze.

"It's some ..." Juno begins to answer, looking at the book's cover, "... mystery book. I've been told it's good. I don't know—I've just started reading it."

"How is it so far?" I continue to ask. Juno sighs and, from her expression, I can't tell if she's annoyed that I'm asking this, exhausted from the thought of giving a response, or both.

"It's pretty okay," Juno musters a response quietly.

"It sounds interesting."

"Yeah, I guess so," responds Juno, awkwardly. She stares down at the novel's pages once more, reading silently. Her brother, James, looks over at me whilst Juno absorbs her mind back into the book, mouthing something:

"I don't know why she's feeling this way."

I subtly shrug in return.

"Hey, Juno," James starts, "I had an idea for something that the three of us could do after school today."

Juno glances up from her book pages once again, eyelids low in annoyance at James and general exhaustion, or melancholy. I, too, look over at James, but with greater anticipation for what he'll say.

"I was thinking that we could—all of us—go to the nearby library after school and study," James clarifies. "You know, how we used to do that all the time."

Juno is the first to respond. "Why would we ..."

"We have a calculus test Monday—I thought it might be important," James answers. "Besides that, though, I miss going places after school, Juno."

"With *me*?" asks Juno, James nodding in response.

"No," Juno refutes. "Go out with your baseball team."

"They're not as in agreement about studying on Friday nights."

"And I am?"

"I'll go to the library," I chime in quietly. "But that's regardless of whether anybody is coming, I just find the place to be pleasant." I pause, momentarily wondering if I've made the conversation awkward. "Though, going with you all would be nice, as well."

Juno stays silent, and the deadpan expression on her face confuses me once more as to how she feels about what I say—confused as to whether she's annoyed with me.

"I think we should follow you, Kaeda," James comments, looking over at his twin sister, who shakes her head once more at him in refutation. The bell to dismiss students from lunch and warn of class returns rings, and James lets me know prior to leaving with Juno that he'll inform me of whether he and his sister will join me in the library.

The last three classes of the school day are like the others: solitary and productive. Thankfully, unlike fourth-period biology, there are no *group* projects in any of the other classes—only individual ones where two other students in my group don't receive a full grade for a project for which they only found mediocre images whilst I complete their actual work. During my second-to-last class period, however, I receive a text from James telling me he and Juno will join me in the library today and to meet them outside of the school's exit near a city bus stop.

After classes, Juno, James, and I meet as described, and Juno still keeps the same exhausted, melancholy expression and purposeful isolation from her twin brother. As we board the city bus to take us to the nearby library, she and James communicate little: James expressing audible concern for his sister and Juno typically being unresponsive. She says a few words to me about my class work, but they don't particularly build any interesting conversation or contain much enthusiasm.

The library has much peace, with rows upon rows of books displayed on modern shelves. The library's staircase is grand and modern, holding much depth in how simple yet significant it is. Upstairs, there are "study rooms" with tables and chairs in each and a beautiful window view of the nearby city. It rains outside, and that only makes the scene more peaceful. I have memories of this library and, while I don't stay as often as I used to, I think I'll start again.

As we pass through the library's modern entrance and walk up the extensive set of stairs to a study room, I notice uncomfortable gestures in Juno. She continuously looks down at her shoes and barely says a word to anyone, fiddling with her hoodie's drawstrings and slanting her eyebrows in a manner that only produces a melancholy expression. I refrain from asking her anything; I'm unsure of what to say.

Observing Juno with this undeniable sadness sets all surroundings *off*. The environment of the library, with its usual peaceful quietness, seems to suddenly turn to an uncomfortable silence. Studying with Juno in a way such as this is usually full of conversation, enthusiasm, or depth and focus. Today, in the library, there is nothing to what she says—and that is if she says anything at all. James mutters a few things, at first asking Juno more questions about her sad feelings, but gradually realizes that he'll receive nothing out of her—she's down. She acts like that of an individual with depression.

Juno writes the entire study session. She sits at the very end of the room table, preventing anyone from reading what she's writing—no studying, only writing—a complete and utter poet. In some ways, this is astounding and only beneficial. In others, this only enhances her negative feelings and sends her into a deeper spiral of melancholy. Her writing today, observed from how she behaved whilst in the act, seemed to only send her into that deeper spiral: that enhancement of her negative feelings.

"Juno?" I say, completing an assignment for a class. She glances at me, her journal in hand. Noticing that she doesn't have any laptop or study material aside from a pencil case, I ask the question: "Do you have anything to study for?"

She shakes her head "No", and James looks at his sister, confused. He joins in.

"We have a calculus test Monday, remember?" He reminds Juno, in the process of doing math problems. "Fifty points?"

Juno sighs. "Yeah, but it's Friday," she answers. "I don't need to do shit right now."

"Still, you should probably start early," he continues. "That's what you always tell me."

"I don't need to start anything," Juno refutes, cutting off her brother. "Maybe you do; you probably have a game tomorrow or something."

James softens his tone, expressing concern. "Really, what's wrong?" he asks. "You've been like this for a while now."

"It's nothing, James," Juno angrily responds from the end of the study table, portraying a deadpan expression toward her brother. She loosens up in her tone for a moment, "Or, it's nothing that concerns you. Continue studying; I'll be fine."

I can't figure Juno out the entire study session. It doesn't help with any of my studying, either. The entire time, I seem to only be studying her feelings. Why she feels this way, what caused her to feel this ... etcetera. The worst part is, however, I come to no conclusion. I can't make sense of Juno and her melancholy.

On the way home, I take the train from a nearby station and, eventually, the city bus. From the bus ride, I walk home. During these three commuting sessions, I listen to my electronic ambiance tracks and study my notes from my academic notebooks—I don't touch the other notebook; I can't overwhelm myself with my issues after trying to make sense of somebody else's.

I think of James' approach to Juno's sadness, and I see something that stirs within me a secondhand embarrassment. A constant asking of questions, a somewhat annoyance when Juno doesn't answer them entirely—I cringe at it. However, it makes sense. They are twins; they live together, go home together, eat together ... they are constantly around one another. For James, living with this observation that your twin sister is clearly not okay and not receiving much of an explanation for any of it must feel draining. It must be annoying; he must be fed up with the confusion it all causes. I agree—I hate the confusion caused by an absence of understanding or explanation of an issue that you're incredibly concerned about, although the issues at hand are different: one dealing with a sibling's depression and the other dealing with someone's own recollection of their past.

The short walk from the bus stop and to my house is calming—light rain falls from a cloudy, dark gray 6 PM sky and brings with it a sense of peace to my exhaustion. However, I would rather commute home with a sense of false calmness than a sense of genuine confusion and dread sourcing from a dream. Tiredly, I enter my house to find my mother sitting on the gray living room couch, silently typing away on her laptop with documents sprawled out across the nightstand without a word to greet me. She changes the area in which she works from home to add some uniqueness—some change of thought to the setting—I theorize, as I always find her working in a new place in the house. I set my backpack down in my bedroom and shortly change out of my uniform into loungewear, then walk shortly to the kitchen to grab a glass of water.

However, the scene as I enter the kitchen is far from mundane.

Sitting on the couch, my mother suddenly clenches her chest as she wails in pain, collapsing to the floor and hitting her head against the couch's armrest. This only causes her to wail in more pain as she struggles to breathe. *What the hell happened?*

As I glance at her face, I notice she appears abnormally pale and sweaty, and I start to sweat in my hands, as well.

"Help …" she struggles to whisper out of her shortness of breath, stopped by a wail in pain followed by gasps for breath. "Call 9-1-1."

Immediately, I rush for the home phone as best as I can—legs shaking. Picking it up with sweaty hands, I dial the three numbers: 9-1-1. Quickly, a dispatcher answers my call.

"9-1-1, what's your emergency?"

"Hello, my—my mother, Michelle Bynum, just fell to the ground in pain. She's—she's clenching her chest and gasping for air," I stutter, struggling to hold the phone steady. "This is a medical emergency."

The dispatcher informs me that the medical and fire departments are on their way, suspecting that what my mother is going through is cardiac arrest, then telling me to lay her on her back and open her airways, checking if she's breathing and performing CPR if not. I follow instructions hurriedly and, finally, ambulances and fire trucks arrive. The blinding lights of their vehicles shine through the large windows of the living room decorated with constantly moving raindrops. Upon entering my house, the medical officials quickly take my mother away on a stretcher as she continues to wail in pain, only briefly glancing at me as they rush together, bringing my mother into the ambulance. As I walk out of the house, one medical professional motions for me to join them in the ambulance, waving their hands at me. Before leaving with them, I lock the door and follow the medical team into the vehicle.

After a long drive, we arrive at the hospital, where the doctors immediately bring my mother on the stretcher into a room, whilst I stay in the waiting room until I'm called to see my mother. The hospital building's air is pale and cold, matching its surroundings;

the place is nearly empty considering the late time of day, aside from a few other visitors. It's desolate and dark outside; the rain is a calming quiet. If you were to erase the fact that everyone is undergoing incredible chaos at the moment, it would be very comforting.

Over the speaker, I hear a muffled voice speak with little emotion: a hospital worker. "Guest 'Kaeda' to room 139, thank you," they say, and I walk down the hallway to room 139, where I find my mother on a hospital bed. She glances at me directly with drowsy eyes—her face is as pale as it was when I had first seen her collapse. She asks that a doctor leave, saying that she has something important to tell me.

"What is it?" I ask. The entire time, my mom stares at the equipment they've hooked her up to, feeling it gently. She glares up at me with her tired, desolate eyes, and begins speaking.

"Kaeda, I'm not okay," she starts. Her expression almost seems regretful as I continue to study it, intrigued by what she may have to say to me. "I'm tired. I've been exhausted ever since my son died, and ever since the arguments between your former father started."

I glare at her, still with intrigue.

"Do you remember Frank?" she asks me. I nod my head.

"Briefly," I answer.

"That is right, you must not remember a lot," I hear my mom mumble. I arch my eyes at her in an increased feeling of intrigue; I have issues remembering the long-term past, and it seems to me as though I've been this way forever without a reason. Thinking back to the notebook page of unanswered questions—most concerning the long-term past—I decide I must dive deep into this. I need answers—does my mother have them?

"What do you mean by that?" I ask. "That 'I must not remember a lot'?"

"I mean I know you have some troubles with memory," she answers, "So you must only briefly remember Frank. But that's beside the point; I need to talk to you about him."

"Do you know why I have trouble with memory?" I persist, noticing my knee bouncing.

My mother pauses, looking up in thought as if she's attempting to recall a memory. "... no, I don't really," she answers. "But I've seen it affect you; I know that you have troubles with it."

"But how have you seen that?"

"Kaeda, it's nothing that can be changed," my mother continues. "But ..."

"I don't want you to stress over this," my mother says. "I understand you stress over many things—school is a good example. And stressing over your memories will not do good for you. I can explain to you what I know; maybe it can help you remember some things?"

I nod my head.

"Well, ever since my son's death, Frank was always on my ass about something," my mother begins. "Even when we adopted you, he still was on my ass about whatever he could find. I fell deep into depression, and it never seemed to get better, even when he left. In this time, Kaeda, I gave myself a will that states that, if I die, you'll go to live on with your biological sister, Ottie. Do you remember her at all?"

"Only somewhat," I answer. I notice immediately *why* she has a will—she considered suicide when Cace was dead and she was fighting with Frank while I had become a Bynum. That realization quickly hit me; quicker than any other connection I would typically make. Maybe it was something I had blocked out—something from the past I just now remembered?

"Oh, Kaeda ..." she sighs. "You know, you're just like Cace in how you say things—in how you look at me. You're just like him, except you lived."

Did you adopt me with the purpose of replacing him?

I decide not to ask that question.

The rest of our discussion mentions a few brief things about Frank and how the death of his son was incredibly difficult for him, causing numerous arguments between him and my mom. Though she told me she had "something important to tell me" beforehand, it appears my mother never really got to the point about anything particularly "new", only just that she had a will in case she passes stating that I'll be staying three hours away with Ottie and her adopted family. Maybe that is the important thing she needed to tell me—but why wouldn't she mention that with a doctor in the room?

Later, I'm informed that I must leave the room because of a few medical procedures that they must perform on my mom for information and recovery, so I wait outside in the waiting room with my laptop and academic notebooks to complete schoolwork, the rain picking up its pace and its sounds relaxing me in the process. Returning to the hospital room, I find my mom drifting into sleep and a hospital cot near the room's large window with scratchy sheets set by the doctors for me to sleep on.

I should make a note of my remembrance today in the notebook.

Sitting on the cot after brushing my teeth with a toothbrush and toothpaste that the hospital put in a plastic bag on my cot, I pull out the notebook without academic purpose from my backpack that I brought alongside me here, opening to the page of unanswered questions—only possibly progressive bullets under a select few of them. I shake my head as I look at them, reminding myself that I'm only here to make a note of a new remembrance—not to remember my lack of answers. Pulling out my pen, I write a new bullet under no question in particular:

Michelle was incredibly depressed because of Frank after their son's death—she considered suicide and made a will in the process.

Immediately after writing the note, I shut the notebook without time for the pen's ink to dry, shoving it into my backpack and laying down on my cot, my body turned toward the large window and its sheer white hospital curtains. My mother sleeps beside me on her bed, the sounds of medical technology surrounding her becoming an almost white noise to me accompanied by the whir of the air conditioning throughout the building. I hear little to no sounds from outside; the hospital campus is quiet and our view from the room is underwhelming, especially in the night with little to no illumination coming into the area. I try my hardest to regulate my breathing on the cot and inside of its scratchy sheets to attempt to fall asleep, but the attempt proves itself to be futile.

I don't want to dream.

Stressing about dreaming is often a source of my insomnia, although I realize that there is no period of sleep where I don't enter a dream unless I am sleeping for only a few minutes and unable to enter REM—rapid eye movement sleep. Though, sometimes I still have brief visions that could *lead* to a dream, yet still not being a full one.

Thinking about dreaming in a greater sense of rationality and explanation rather than anxiety about dreams themselves sends me drifting off into one—I fall asleep.

Three

Saturday, November 8, 2036, ?:?? AM.

I wake up.

Immediately, I sense the chilliness of the area, wherever I am, and a soft fabric laid over me in an attempt to rid myself of it. Once my vision develops, I find myself staring at the backrest of a familiar couch: the sleek gray couch of my living room. There have been only a few lights turned on which lay in the kitchen, but when you have a smaller house with a primarily open floor plan, a few lights illuminate the area enough for you to move around somewhat comfortably.

As I glimpse around my living room and set the blanket aside, another aspect of the scene occurs to me: noises. Loud noises; loud sounds of argumentative conversation from down the hallway and into my mother's bedroom.

Frank.

It's no surprise to me that my mind fixates on this subconsciously. The arguments between my mother and Frank, her ex-husband, or my previously adopted father. I still can't remember the reason he has no custody of me.

I walk around the house before I do so down the hallway, where the shelves that I'm easily familiar with decorating our walls appear with a striking difference. There are more decorations that sit on them: pictures. Though, as I move closer, it's then that I realize those pictures sit in cracked glass frames, some with a damage of greater severity than others.

And they all include Cace. Whether it be him alone, him with some academic club or award, or him with Michelle and Frank, every photo with a cracked frame includes him. Today, none of these photos exist on our shelves—few photos exist on our shelves at all. The photos that *do* exist, though, are only older photos of my mother and little to no photos of myself. These shelves I examine have even more souvenirs: ones that Frank must've owned.

I don't take too long looking at the photos as the argument grows louder, but I notice the demeanor that Cace Bynum holds—it's similar to mine. In each photo of him holding an award of some sort, he doesn't look very prideful—he moreover looks focused. He frowns in neutrality, though, when he smiles, it seems genuine. Though it makes him seem somewhat robotic, Cace is very well-kept in his appearance, and his features are much more Japanese than I remembered from what Michelle briefly showed me—like mine. I know why this family adopted me and, though I can't remember a lot from my earlier adoption years, it has always been very evident.

As the argument advances, I turn away from the shelves and move slightly down towards the hallway. It's muffled, but I can make out a few things:

"Why would you ever consider that?" says my mother. "It's wrong and I won't agree to it."

"Why? Why wouldn't you?" asks Frank. "How ... how sudden his death was. It's the right thing to do. Do you even love our son?"

"Of course I do!" my mother yells back. "And that's why I think that this isn't right! It's so complicated. Everything about (muffled) is so ... it's so wrong and I can't ..."

"Maybe you think it's complicated because you're too ignorant to understand it," Frank says, louder. "Because I sure as hell find it okay."

There's a pause in the conversation, and I hear faint sniffling from my mother.

"... Cace left for a reason," my mother states. "Whatever that reason was, it was his will. This is completely wrong and he never would have wanted it, especially with all of its (muffled)."

"Like what?" Frank refutes. "(Muffled)? Why would he want to think about those (muffled)?"

Each muffling of the words seems almost unintentional—like my brain is forcing it upon me. A sentence can be perfectly clear and loud enough for me to understand completely, yet a painful muffling or ringing of my ear will block it out.

"You want too much for our child," my mother says. "And I know that sounds like a horrible thing to say, but what if he left because of how stressed out he was? What if this is just another ..."

"You'll never understand!" Frank yells, seeming to have slammed a surface in frustration. "He was so *smart*. So driven; such a wonderful son." He sounds like he's tearing up. "And you don't get it at all. Shit, you weren't even involved."

"You know how horrible my issues are!" my mother cries. "Don't tell me that I wasn't there, or that I didn't love Cace. I loved him, and that's why I feel like this would just be another..."

For a reason unknown to me, an immeasurable and undeniable urge to knock on their door takes hold of me, causing a striking emptiness in my stomach.

Knock on the door.

My hand quivers, facing the door's surface.

Kaeda, knock on the door.

I do, and the scene changes.

I'm standing beneath a surface—a surface that appears to be another door. Except, this time, the door is wooden: a glossy wood which you'd find composing institutional building doors. There's a small window in front of me with closed blinds as if I was in a school or a hospital. As I try to grab its handle and turn it to leave wherever

I am, I notice the doorknob has changed: it's ligature resistant. It doesn't stick out in a way where you could … hang things on it.

The sight is strikingly medical, yet not seeming to be set in a general hospital but, rather, a mental one. As I turn around briefly, the scene quickly changes, existing for what I feel is less than a second. In that change, though, I can make out a very vague detail: I was in a bedroom, and it was very plain. What I see now, though, is almost entirely different.

A bedroom that is somewhat familiar sits in front of me, like the one that I had dreamed about only a day or so ago. It's a comfortable, family-oriented room, with a few gentle and childish decorations. There's a white bunk bed complex, a nightstand with an alarm clock, and a dresser, from what I can make out so far. The walls are painted light blue and there are string lights hung around the furniture. Sitting on the top bunk of the bunk bed is a familiar person who looks similar to me. My sister: Ottie. She seems to draw in a sketchbook and looks at me as I approach the bunk bed and take a seat on the lower bunk. As I walk toward the bed, I notice my younger self in the mirror next to the nightstand. I'm dressed in a young girl's gray striped pajama set.

"Kaeda," Ottie starts as I sit down, "There's a lot you don't really know."

"What do you mean?" I ask, in a higher-pitched voice.

"Like, about mom and dad. Our mom and dad," she responds. Ottie peers her head into my lower bunk for a moment. "I asked one of the foster siblings. They told me what happened, kind of."

"And that is?"

"Mom and Dad had us when they were teenagers," Ottie replies. "I don't really know how that works, but they gave us up for adoption because they couldn't handle it."

"You don't know how it works?" my younger self asks, somewhat in shock.

"No," Ottie says. "How do you know?"

"Science book."

"Oh, can I see?"

"No."

"Why not?"

"It's bad."

"Okay, well, anyway, Mom and Dad didn't like that they were so young and now we are here," Ottie adds. "So yeah. That's it."

"Wow," I say. "Do you think that they're still together?"

"I don't know," Ottie answers. "Maybe."

"Wouldn't they adopt us again, though?" I ask. "Like, take us back?"

"Maybe they died," Ottie says. My younger self shrugs in consideration.

"There really is a lot that you don't know, though," Ottie continues, with a more serious tone. "Like about *your* parents."

"What do you mean?" I ask, immediately.

"Like Frank and Michelle," Ottie says bluntly. "And Cace, who died by suicide."

What?

A looming feeling washes over me to both cause fear, then remind me that I am only dreaming; any occurrence of any obscurity is possible in my subconscious.

"Yeah, don't act surprised," Ottie says, almost reverting to her old, younger tone.

The scene disappears, and I wake up.

The hospital's setting is nothing less or more than indirectly eerie. The fluorescent lighting in each room, lined up throughout the hallway's ceilings in an inescapable pattern, makes the entire building and the experiences you'll have inside of it seem almost unreal. Here, there is a distinct detachment from reality—there is a transcendence of your regular life that follows you undeniably. Additionally, the cot I'm sleeping on is nothing but uncomfortable. The hospital's attempt at providing a sleeping space is painfully futile.

The element to tie the entire "eerie" description of the hospital together is the fact that, once I turn away from the hospital room's window after waking up, I'm immediately met with the sight of my mother in her hospital bed, hooked up to multiple large medical devices. They dig into her skin and pierce her veins, pumping liquids through her body while she feels the pain of the many needles in her hands—my own hands quiver coldly at the sight. Then, I hear a voice:

"Kaeda?" it says.

"Kaeda, are you awake?"

It's my mother. She makes no turns, disrupting none of the devices that she's connected to, whilst staring at the ceiling with dry, exhausted eyes and muttering words to me in a raspy morning voice. She sounds significantly more exhausted than usual, understandably.

"Yes," I whisper to her.

"Good," says my mother. "At least there's some time to talk before the doctors arrive again."

"What do you mean?" I ask.

"I mean the doctors will not be here until later—it's too early right now."

"No, I mean: what is negative about the doctors being here?"

"I wanted to talk to you."

"I know that, but why can't they be here when ..."

"I wanted to talk to you more about Cace, and stuff."

Cace.

Images of the living room. The living room, dead in the night, dead aside from the fact that faint noises of heated arguments from down the hallway bring the room to life. Heated arguments about Cace. Photo frames cracked, photos of Cace being the cracked ones. Discussions of Cace's death, ones that I'm still not entirely certain of their message.

"Cace?" I respond hesitantly. "What about Cace?"

"I wanted to talk to you about his ... passing," my mother clarifies. "And Frank and I. That entire situation—it must be so traumatizing for you, isn't it?"

There's an odd silence in the room.

"Can you remember it?"

Can you remember it?

"I don't think that I can," I respond. A pause follows the conversation once more as my mother says nothing.

"I'm sorry," I muster up an attempt to resolve my statement. As I look at my mother, she sighs—a face of regret and worry engulfing her.

"It's fine," consoles my mother; although, with her expression, I'm convinced I've gravely disappointed her. Her eyes wander around the room, searching for a response. "This world has problems. Too many of them to count. It's overwhelming how prevalent they are in our lives. I just feel that—"

She halts for a moment, noticing her trailing off in topic—something that, although I had little to no conversation with my mother, she had prior to her sickness, as well. Putting her hands to her head and slowly massaging her temples, she mutters in thought.

"No, that's not what I meant to ..."

She looks at me, somewhat surprised that I'm still paying attention.

"Cace: that was it," she says. "Cace was a wonderful, wonderful son. He was, Kaeda. He looked a lot like you—with his glasses and dark, straight hair. But these traits made me feel bad, in a sense. I felt like Frank and I were being unauthentic in how we treated you at times."

"Unauthentic?" I ask. "How so?"

"I felt like we treated you as if you were just ... Cace, but alive," my mother answers. "And that may not seem like a bad thing, but I don't know if we ever really registered the fact that you're—you're *not* that."

"A replacement for Cace?"

"Well, that's a bad way of putting it," my mother responds, slightly taken aback as she widens her eyes for a moment, then continues speaking again. "You were a remnant of Cace to Frank and I, I'd say. More to me, actually, but really to both of us. You only lived with Frank and me a few days or so before the arguments began."

How did he die?

The question pushes itself whilst in my mind. I want to ask her. I want to ask her so, so bad. Ottie's mention of it in the dream; the fragments of my cognitively-created film torture me while my mother brings up Cace, over, and over, and over again, yet never fully reaching a consensus about the whole topic. What is she trying to entail? What is she *thinking*?

I want to ask her the question.

But don't you already know the answer?

"... Cace left for a reason. Whatever that reason was, it was his will."

"... but what if he left because of how stressed out he was? What if this is just another..."

Didn't he leave himself?

I just need clarity.

I just need to ...

"How did Cace actually die?" I ask. Quickly, I notice that my question interrupted a topic my mother was talking about: a topic relating back to the adoption process. At first, upon hearing my question, I hear her turn her head to face me more directly with a look of silent shock plastered upon her face of exasperated expression and story-telling wrinkles as if she had just re-lived a terrifying memory. Actually, it's not "as if she had", it's that she is most likely being catapulted straight into the horrifying past concerning Cace and his death, whatever it is, right now. Soon after, she composes herself and her expressions, preparing a response to my question. Out of nervousness, I notice myself fidgeting with my fingers during the conversation, eager to hear an answer.

"He ... he left by his own will," my mother answers, lightly choking up on the words before composing herself once more. Her way of phrasing his death immediately reminds me of my dream and her entire choice of words throughout her argument with Frank: "It was his will" and "he left". She doesn't tackle the topic entirely. She beats around the bush, but it's clear enough that—

"He killed himself?" I ask, giving brief hesitation to the comment: a complete mistake caused solely by my mind running too quickly for me to keep up with it. A sense of immaturity overwhelms me as I quickly reflect on my responses, but that immaturity seems to follow me in my nervousness during the entire conversation, so I keep my same mindset. *Ask.*

My mother nods in response, choking up at times and quickly silencing it with a deep breath afterward.

"He left us."

An uncomfortable silence fills the room for a second time.

"I still don't understand why," my mother starts again. "He was incredible at everything. Maybe not at talking to people, yeah, but math and science and anything having to do with creativity or logic—he was a star. I loved him so much."

My mom looks around the room for a period of time, then back at me. She hesitates to say anything more than what she had already told me, even still choking up thinking about the experience. The time of silence where she only glances around, looking for a topic to take her mind off of her dead son, I'm thinking. Every glance she takes sparks a new question. I reflect on my dreams, where my mother and Frank argued continuously.

"Why would you ever consider that? It's wrong and I won't agree to it."

"Maybe you think it's complicated because you're too ignorant to understand it."

What was that?

I ask the question.

"What was it really that caused the arguments between you and Frank?" I wonder, looking back over at my mother. She quickly glances at me as I hit her with my question, beginning to think whilst looking down at her hands and muttering unintelligible sounds. After a pause in thought, my mother begins to answer.

"Frank and I argued about what seemed like everything after Cace's death, I think," my mother first responds. "A lot of arguments about what would happen to Cace—a lot of arguments about ..."

She doesn't finish her explanation.

"About?"

"... about your adoption," my mother finishes. "I'm sorry, I guess he just felt like we never really thought through adopting you."

Huh.

"It's okay," I quietly respond.

I decide to ask another question.

"But what do you mean by 'what would happen to Cace'?"

My mother diverts her eyes from mine, staring at her hands hooked to wires and muttering a series of repetitive unintelligible sounds once more. She pauses to think before giving an answer, avoiding any glance at me as if the topic was greatly controversial.

"It was ... familial," my mother answers, finally looking at me again and seeming to halt the nervousness. "Whether or not Cace would be buried—all of that."

"And was he buried?" I ask. At the question, my mother appears to freeze up again—looking anywhere but in my eyes and creating unintelligible sounds with her mouth redundantly. It seems to me that, in this avoidance of answering and recalling situations, my mother could have a developing issue with memory. Either that, or she's incredibly nervous about these topics for a reason that I don't understand.

She begins to answer.

"Well, Kaeda," she starts, "I don't—"

The knob of the hospital room door turns, and I can see a doctor opening the door. Looking in the same direction, I notice the clock reads 7:30 AM. The doctor starts off her entrance with a cheerful "hello!" and starts to ask my mother questions about how she's feeling while I back away from the situation, looking out the window and fidgeting with the uncomfortable sheets that the hospital gave me on my cot, which I leave as is in case I must stay here the next couple of nights. In my mother's responses to the lighthearted questions that the doctor asks her, questions that are slowly transitioning into ones regarding her health and the medical procedures, I notice a colossal weight lifted metaphorically from my mother's tone of speech. She feels less tense, less confined, and less unhappy—all the things she felt when I had been talking to her, specifically the things that she felt when I had been talking to her about Cace.

I spend the next few hours finishing up schoolwork on my laptop, occupying my time by completing projects and assignments due days from now. For lunch, I make my way down to the hospital cafe and buy myself a turkey sandwich. It's mediocre, and the environment is silent, though I see a large diversity of hospital patients or the families and loved ones of hospital patients. There's a husband there at the cafe, buying snacks for his wife in labor, an old woman with a medical provider assisting her, and a family worried about one of their members.

I wonder how these people go about their lives—what events occur in each of them and what significance each event holds in their lives. I wonder how they think—I wonder how they feel. I wonder how much they remember of their past. I wonder what their overarching goal, if there is one, in life is.

I wonder what their dreams are.

I blink my eyes quickly and repetitively for a few seconds, my eyes adjusting back to my surroundings instead of zoning out.

After lunch, I make my return to the room, until I'm stopped by a doctor I briefly recognize from yesterday. On his face is a look of concern. On mine is one, too.

"You're Michelle's daughter, yes?" the doctor checks as I approach the hospital room. "Michelle Bynum?"

I nod my head.

"It's unfortunate to tell you this as I know you hope to go back home soon but," he pauses. "Your mother has shown little signs of recovery. It's estimated that it'll be a week—or even over that—before you can return home with her."

I arch my eyebrows, subconsciously signaling that I want to know more.

"You'll stay with your sister," the doctor continues. "That's the will. But you're ... how old?"

"Seventeen," I reply. The doctor nods.

"You'll stay with your sister for the time being," the doctor repeats. "Laws don't allow minors to stay home alone for over three days."

Ottie.

I haven't contacted my sister in years. Truly, I can barely remember life as a foster child. I remember little of Ottie—I remember what has been indicated in dream sequences of living in a foster home, such as our personality differences. Ottie is far more energetic than I am yet very curious, similar to her sister. She enjoys drawing, I enjoy reading. She has rounder glasses and shorter, wavier hair than mine. We slept primarily in bunk beds as foster children, alternating families regularly.

But these are all simple details.

Who was Ottie in actuality?

"Your mother told me that her name was 'Ottilie Saito', but that you may know her as 'Ottie'," the doctor continues. "Is this true?"

I nod eagerly, though not trying to present myself as too keen.

"Alright," the doctor concludes. "It's too late now, and we still need to get back to the family, so you're expected to leave here tomorrow morning. Someone here will drive you home first where you can pack whatever you need. We have the address of the house; you'll take the subway there. The stop closest to the neighborhood is the last stop near San Jose. From there, you'll take the bus—it'll be a long ride. A colleague of mine is writing out a guide for you."

"Thank you," I respond.

The doctor nods, and I walk back to the room.

"You'll stay with your sister".

I don't know what I'll say to her. Sure, I remember a few simple details that may come up in conversation—that may be slightly helpful. But we were *children*—it's been years since we've seen each other, and those meetings with her are those of which I can hardly recall.

She appears frequently in my dreams—incredibly frequently. She's almost always in one of them and, in each one, the scene feels like a memory. I can remember them clearly. The one yesterday. There was one a few days ago. There has always been a dream of Ottie—it's incredibly rare for there to be a night without one.

As I open the door, I see my mother in the hospital room. She lay on the hospital bed as before, except with a tray of food at her side. Studying the wires inserted into her body, she looks up and notices me. Painting her face is an expression arguably communicating much more exhaustion than had before. Her eyes are bleak. Her face is pale. No, it's not solely exhaustion, she looks much more sick than how she did when I last came in contact with her, which was just this morning. *Is it stress? Or is she rapidly getting worse?*

"Hey, Kaeda," my mother sighs, motioning me closer to her hospital bed. A doctor is still in the room.

"I want to talk with you," my mother tells me. She looks away from me and toward the only doctor in the room who writes on a notepad, which I'm assuming from the looks of it is my brief "travel guide".

"Can you leave for a second?" my mother, exasperated, requests the doctor. "Maybe ten minutes or so?" They nod respectfully and make their way out of the room.

"I wanted to talk to you again," my mother repeats. "Because I don't know if I'll be here when it's time for you to come back."

I scoot back, wide-eyed.

"No, it's not meant to scare you," my mother says. "But I'm not well. You're going to go stay with Ottie. Did they tell you this?

I nod.

"Good," nods my mother, slowly. "Um, I wanted to speak about you."

"About *me*?"

"Yes, uh," my mother starts, "You're a wonderful daughter, Kaeda. You've always been a wonderful daughter. Even though we don't talk a lot, and I know that could be confusing because 'why would I adopt a daughter who I'll hardly talk to' and—"

My mother begins crying. A face of panic and melancholy—I'm unsure if she's accepting of her worsening conditions or scared. It escalates, she motions for me to move closer to her and puts her hand on my shoulder shakily. I can't remember the last time she did that, but it makes me both quiver and feel sad myself.

"Don't let them do it to me too, Kaeda," she sobs. "... If, if they talk you into something, don't let them do it. Please. Please don't let them do it to me."

My pulse quickens. "What do you mean?"

"Don't let them take me and ... and run experiments."

"But don't you have a will?"

My mother remains silent, immersing herself in her own sobs.

I look at my mother with a face of extreme confusion and concern. "Don't you have a–"

"Yes, I have a will, Kaeda," my mother answers in a series of sniffles. "But they don't—they don't care–"

The door opens. Immediately, my mother quiets herself and removes her hand from my shoulder. She yelps in pain after this, realizing how quickly she had just moved and instantly regretting it. The doctor from before the short-lived conversation returns.

"I heard noises that seemed to be painful," they say. "Are you alright, Michelle? What's wrong?"

"I'm fine," my mother responds, composing herself. "It's okay."

"Are you sure?"

"Yes."

The doctor stands there. My mother nods her head slowly once more.

"Yes, I'm okay."

Finally, the doctor leaves. The door shuts, and my mother sighs a sigh of exhaustion and relief simultaneously. I look back at her.

"If they ask me permission to donate your body parts to science, I'll refuse?"

"Yes," my mother responds. "Just—just don't let them do anything."

I nod an OK, but I want to ask why. I mean, in religious cases it's understandable, but, from what I know, my mother's not at all religious. Neither am I.

"Just curious, what's wrong about donating yourself to science?" I ask. "In some cases, it can be life-saving—"

"You don't know what happens to you there, Kaeda," my mom responds bluntly as if I had offended her. "You have no idea."

I tilt my head at her. "I'm sorry, I don't understand exactly what you're trying to say."

My mother stares at me with fierce, pale eyes. Her off-white face of exhaustion and terror wears a passionate message: *no matter what, I cannot let this one thing happen.*

"Just please don't let them do anything to me."

I nod a final agreement, still somewhat confused by her direct motivations for this. Her hands shake as if she's given that conversation all of her energy and, with the current state of health she lives in right now, I wouldn't be surprised if that was truthful.

My mother naps for the next few hours. Over that time, I wonder if those thoughts of hers were even coming from a logical place. Her state of health could actively drive her into a state of insanity. Though, I'll respect her wishes in the slight chance that I'm asked that question. She *has* a will, *why* wouldn't it be followed?

Dinner is solemn. My mother is still exhausted and doesn't look like she wants to communicate with me, for whatever reason. She repeats to herself phrases about Cace, about Frank, and some about me. They make little sense alone, but each one intrigues me enough to where I write them down on a small GoldenPine notebook I found in my bag that I had bought at the beginning of the year. They read:

They should have never done it.

They should have never done it. Why would they ever do it?

Please don't go. Please don't go.

Please don't go.

I'm going to miss it.

I miss him.

I miss him.

Cace left for a reason. Whatever that reason was, it was his will. This is completely wrong and he never would've wanted it, especially with all of its problems.

Please don't go, Frank.

I miss him.

I miss him.

I'm going to miss it.

Why to her?

Why to her?

It hurts me to know that this is all meaningless.

I'm sorry Kaeda.

Meaningless.

Meaningless.

Meaningless.

They should have never done it.

In and out of sleep, these were her repetitions. I hate reading them, but the eighth line sounds familiar.

Holy shit.

I heard it in my dream.

That was not only a dream. It was me, reliving a memory—my brain reciting a scene hidden deep in its subconsciousness to me while I sleep. And I hate moments when I come to this realization; though they are rare, they pain me each time for one reason and one reason only: which scenes of my dreams are memories, and which are nonsense? They're all vivid and somewhat realistic enough to where they could be either one.

The sense of a pulsing, undeniable headache swarms over me and doesn't leave at the thought of this recurring subject: dreams. I begin to massage my temples in a manner that is more aggressive than I intended for the action to be as a means of potentially helping myself—potentially ridding my mind of these thoughts through a physical act. I glance over at my backpack—*I wonder why I didn't simply decide to overwork myself as usual?* Right, there are no assignments left to be done.

I hate this.

The entirety of my time in the hospital has been nothing less or more than deteriorating. Thinking, thinking, thinking—thinking too frequently and about too much for anything to be comfortable. Conversations with my mother where each phrase that comes out of her mouth is so intriguing yet so vague and unable to be understood without context. But I can't ask for context, no—she doesn't respond. This loop is similar to that of my mind: a thought-provoking question or idea is introduced—so thought-provoking to where I'm unable to ignore it—but I cannot at all answer the question or elaborate on the idea. Because in my mind I lack context, especially concerning my memories.

The rest of the evening reminds me of a ticking clock. My mother continues moving in and out of naps, in and out of repetitive words, in and out of confusing conversation topics that last for a total of two minutes until she falls asleep again.

"Kaeda?" my mother starts. "Can you come here, please?"

My mother holds my hand. As expected, due to the medical wires she's connected to, she doesn't squeeze it. Rather, she just props it up onto her palm, as if it were a fragile artifact made of glass.

"I wish I could say more to you," she sighs. "I fear that I'm not well enough to, though, so I'd like to praise you for your curiosity."

I smile slightly. "Thank you."

"You'll go live with Ottie until I'm okay again," she tells me.

"I know."

"I'm tired, Kaeda. I'm tired."

I nod my head. "Me too."

Finally, my mother looks at me with brown, tired eyes, and says only a few words:

"Keep asking yourself questions, Kaeda."

I look down to the floor and manage a soft smile. "Thank you."

I try to let my mother's hand go, but she continues to hold it. Then I look back up at her.

Her EKG goes flat.

The long, terrifying sound of the machine—the extensive "beep"—becomes the only sound present in the room. The weight of my own head seems to have disappeared. My throat grows dry. My hand shakes. My hand holds my mother's—my dead mother's hand.

It does not leave mine.

Her eyes did not fully shut, and the thought that this face I am looking at is completely drained of all life horrifies me—I briefly notice the harsh trembling in my limbs. Sure, the dull, pale expression plastered upon her face for the past day after her cardiac arrest looked drained of its energy, but never of its life. The EKG machine would still display a heartbeat. I could still hear her breathing. She would still speak. That has all perished now.

That has all perished now.

I can't think. I can't think clearly enough to understand my surroundings, to decide on whether I expected this, or to compose myself. I sense the tears forming in my eyes and my face grows hot although the room is uncomfortably cold, I sense myself shaking, I sense my heart rate increase, and I sense my breath struggle. All senses to, more or less, distract me from the thoughts that I feel knock at the door of my mind—thoughts of death. Thoughts that I cannot register without noticing a deregistration of my own self.

Meaningless.

The doctors hurriedly enter the hospital room, one after the other. They ask me to back away, to move my cot, to leave where I am, but I don't seem to register a single one of their words—ignoring their loud requests as if the words were only white noise in a room where the only significant sound is that of my own thoughts. Like a statue, I sit there, holding Michelle's lifeless hand, staring at my mother's lifeless face. Michelle Bynum. What an interesting person, what a thoughtful mind, what a depressive life, all gone. Left.

This is only a body.

I hate death.

I hate it.

Meaningless.

Meaningless.

Meaningless.

I cannot tell if I am repeating the words to myself out loud or if I am only imagining them, I can barely register what I am hearing. That is what she said, over and over, without reason, and I can't process information efficiently enough to where I can determine whether those repetitions meant anything. Did she feel she would die? Is that why she repeated, "meaningless"? Did living lack meaning to her? I cannot ask her a single one of these questions—I will receive no response.

A doctor pulls my mother's hand away from mine forcefully. I subconsciously try gripping onto it, but I'm then shocked into reality. The noises aren't so muffled anymore, the requests of the doctors become those that my mind clearly registers and responds to, and the doctor who pulled my mother's hand away from mine holds an AED, preparing to attempt to restart my mother's heart. I move away from the scene. The image of my mom and her bleak, half-open, lifeless eyes lacks clarity as the doctors crowd around the hospital bed. An intimate viewing of my mother during and after her death becomes that of an outside viewer as a distance that I cannot control is created between my mother and I: a distance that is now completely permanent as I reflect on the fact that, after this night, I will live with my sister. My mother will become an insignificant part of my life—the conversations that only truly began yesterday about Frank and Cace have passed over. My mother becomes less of a "mother" to me, it only feels right to name her Michelle Bynum now, especially since this is what the doctors repeatedly yell as they attempt to revive her dead body.

"Michelle!" "Michelle Bynum!" "Are you there?"

There's no revival in her heartbeat—no end to the long beep of the EKG machine—as the doctors use an AED; this is truly it. A doctor approaches me hurriedly as I watch the scene from what is now the corner of the room.

"Did she show any signs of struggle before this?" They ask me, anxiety tormenting their facial expression. "Was she asleep? What did you see?"

"She said a few words to me," I respond. I lick a tear as it gradually rolls down my cheek, realizing that I was crying. "She seemed tired. Before, she had been napping and talking to me a bit … I didn't think that this would–"

"Alright, thank you, thank you," the doctor concludes, returning to their colleagues as they note down information. I wipe my tears away with my hands, and the bewildered look that I only now recognize had been very prevalent on my face vanishes, though the event to cause such a bewildered expression still plays inside of my head—over, and over, and over again.

"Keep asking yourself questions, Kaeda."

Like a dream sequence and its redundancy in my thoughts after waking from it.

Her EKG goes flat.

Her eyes did not fully shut.

The image of my mom and her bleak, half-open, lifeless eyes becomes less clear as the doctors crowd around the hospital bed.

Her eyes did not fully shut.

Her eyes did not fully shut.

Her eyes did not fully shut.

Be quiet, Kaeda. You cannot reverse your mother's death.

I know. But I hate the thought of the death itself.

I'm moved out of the room quickly after the death and transported to the empty waiting room. Upon my arrival here, a doctor I'm somewhat familiar with from my time with my mom approaches me:

"Kaeda Bynum?" he says. I nod my head, "Yes?"

"Is it by any chance known by you that your mother would have liked to undergo trials of scientific research following her death?" the doctor asks. "In these years, these kinds of trials are incredibly prevalent and I'd like to know if she'd–"

I respond immediately and in a more blunt tone than intended, as if programmed to do so.

"No," I blurt. "I mean, no to the—the research."

The doctor widens his eyes slightly as if taken aback by my response.

"Are you sure? This is a very growing field and many labs test on patients who have–"

"She didn't want any scientific research done on her body."

"None?"

"No scientific research."

"Oh, okay," the doctor concludes. "Thank you for your time, and I'm sorry for your loss."

I nod.

The rest of the night has an atmosphere that is making it incredibly difficult to fall asleep. The room my cot is set in is arid and off putting—the medical technology not being in use creates a scene of somewhat terrifying figures that only remind me of Michelle's death. How she looked, attached to all the complex devices that tried with so much effort to give her life. How she looked, when they failed to.

How she looked.

Her eyes did not fully shut.

I must be up for many hours, staring at the white curtains of the hospital room, replaying the haunting scene over and over again. Replaying the question concerning scientific research asked by the doctor that I never figured would occur when Michelle first mentioned it to me. How insane she looked and talked to me on the last day of her life. How insane I viewed her. But were those phrases and ideas truly phrases and ideas of insanity?

There's something so incredibly eerie in reflecting on the last questions and theories presented by a dead person. Though not considered important at the time, they become highly important in your mind after the person's death. I can't tell if I am insane for bearing in mind Michelle's questions, theories, conclusions, and topics that she had mentioned to me before her death, or simply logical. Her death is eating me up from the inside, especially while I'm trying to sleep. Thoughts of meeting Ottie again, or what will most likely feel like the first time when I truly don't remember enough about her, and how I'm going to adapt to my new environment keep me up.

I don't know what hour it is, but I eventually fall asleep after taking, with little illumination, a few melatonin pills.

Part 2

Four

Sunday, November 9, 2036, ?:?? AM.

I wake up.

The rumbling beneath me, one of the first things I notice, is indicative of an event largely familiar to me. I'm riding a train; the sound of a train's movement surrounds my ears before my vision adjusts and I can make out the details surrounding me. There is no sound of people, very little light—very little sign of any life. The train is empty and the outside sky is a cold, cloud-filled dark blue. Each of the advertisement screens is on from what it seems, but they display no advertisements; they only display a blank white screen. As I turn my body around, I see my mother, her body alive and presence almost terrifying me in that revival. She looks out the window then back at me, with longing, pale brown eyes.

"Mom?" I hear myself speak.

"Keep asking yourself questions, Kaeda," she mutters in response. The words feel so strikingly familiar, almost shaking me out of sub-consciousness. At the thought, the train shakes beneath me.

My mother leans back, relaxing in the subway train's seat. "I asked questions," she tells me. "I asked many. I asked *why*." She stops for a moment, gathering her emotions. "'Why, why would you let this happen?'" She imitates herself. "I asked Frank those things.

'Why? Why like this?'. It went nowhere. Meaningless, meaningless, meaningless."

My mother takes a deep breath. "Cace was a great son, he really was," she says. "What happened to him is a shame; it is. What happened to Frank was, too. Such a smart guy turned robotic: think of things, do things, interpret things in one way. No problems, right? Wrong. And Cace died and Cace lived; his sadness strikes me each day. Frank never really cared."

"You live today and you see things and you ask why they are the way they are," she continues. "And you battle between two things that seem to doom you: conforming to how you're directed to think and conforming to avoid conformity. There is no in-between."

My mother pauses. "You never let them have me, did you?" she asks.

"No."

"Thank you," says my mother. "Cace lived and died and lived and died again. Cace lived happily until he was sad, died sad, lived and died *sad*. I lived a feeling I don't know how to describe, died—never lived again."

I knit my eyebrows, both intrigued and confused. "Huh?"

"Keep asking questions, Kaeda."

As I turn back toward my mother in her seat, I realize that she's vanished from the scene entirely.

She's disappeared and left no trace but a gap in my mind, just as she did in the hospital. And the feeling pierces me—my stomach aches a sharp pain momentarily, then dissipates. The train travels at a quicker speed, and one of the advertisement screens begins to flicker its bright blue light until it finally displays text. I move away from the train seat and closer to the display to read it. It reads:

Your mind is filled with melancholy. You think so hard; you get so close to the answer, and you never, ever, find it.

The others flicker their lights:

Is it you? Is it you who causes all these problems with your mind? Or is it some unstoppable external force?

And small displays:

What do you remember of your sister? Why can't you remember—why can't you remember such a large part of your life?

Meaningless

Meaningless

Meaningless

Meaningless

A greater shaking of the train occurs. And I can't think. I can't move. I can't take any autonomy; my body becomes a statue, frozen in place, and I'm frustrated trying to get myself out of—

The train derails quickly, crashing to the ground.

The scene changes.

Surrounding me is a scene that I recognize: another foster home bedroom. Each one's room is so similar yet obviously different; they all have either two separate twin beds or a bunk bed complex, and almost all of them display photos of their family that they received through the same style of a photoshoot: the classic, loving, wealthy portrayal of a family. The furniture is almost always a white, sometimes wooden, color, inviting and peaceful. And not too far beside me as my young self lays on the bottom bunk of the foster room's bunk bed is my sister, Ottie, reading a book in her pajamas. It must be right after dinner; a calming sunset peeks through the bedroom's windows.

My sister notices my glancing at her, setting her eyes aside from the book pages.

"I should read more," she tells me. "This is cool."

"Which book?" I ask in a younger voice. I don't seem to have any control over my words.

Ottie shows me the cover. "I picked it up from the school library yesterday," she continues. "I thought the cover looked cool. And I like it."

"I love to read," I add. "Some books are very interesting."

"What genres?"

"Mystery and sci-fi."

"I thought so," Ottie comments. "I really didn't care for reading until now. I see you read books, and you like it, so I thought: 'why not'? And now I like to read. I want to draw more, too. I love drawing."

"You're a good artist."

"Do you think our parents were good at this stuff?" Ottie wonders. "Like drawing?"

"Probably," I say. "We are descendants of our parents—genetically, it would make sense that they would be good at drawing."

There's a pause in the conversation. The air has a homely, pleasant smell, and I think I'd like to stay here a while. Ottie relaxes as she opens the book again, then talks once more.

"Do you miss Michelle?" she asks me.

The air grows cold.

"What?" I ask.

"Do you miss Michelle?" Ottie repeats herself. "Your mom? Or have you forgotten about her, too?"

I pause and feel myself beginning to stutter.

"What about Cace?" she questions, cutting me off. "But, no, you don't remember him. Do you even remember what happened?"

I don't know how to respond.

I don't respond at all.

"Michelle was a sad mother," continues Ottie. "Always offset by something. She wishes you remembered. She feels, and she repeated it to herself, she feels that it's her fault you don't. She lived a sad life. I don't think she ever loved herself."

The air's coldness strikes me as though it's close to freezing my hands. I hold them to my body and try to find comfort in the sheets of the lower bunk that have now become as cold as the rest of the room, but my efforts are insignificant. The room becomes rapidly colder, causing me to experience slight shivers and sudden goosebumps.

"Don't hide from these questions you have," Ottie says. "Don't hide from what I'm trying to tell you."

"You're not supposed to say these things," I shiver.

"People aren't supposed to do anything," Ottie responds. "You weren't supposed to go through what you did. You aren't supposed to have these thoughts. I'm not supposed to say these things. Michelle wasn't supposed to die. Neither was Cace. We weren't even supposed to exist, if you think about it."

I turn away from Ottie and bury my face into the pillow of the bed in an attempt to block out the situation. But that's exactly what I *shouldn't* be doing: hiding from what she tries to tell me. It's not her, though. It's my mind. And it's speaking through Ottie.

"What are you going to do, Kaeda?" Ottie asks at last.

The scene changes.

It's a familiar night in a familiar living room, and one of the first things I notice are the sounds coming from down the nearby hall. Arguments between two people who have both, in one way or another, disappeared from my life: Michelle and Frank Bynum. I lay on the San Francisco house's living room couch, a known blanket over me as before. However, as I lift my head and glance around the area, I'm met with a sight of a person I have never truly met before.

Cace Bynum.

He looks so oddly similar to me; not genetically or in the features of his face, but in his expressions and presentation. He examines the shelves of the house, each with a picture of him in a shattered glass frame. The expression on Cace's face is inquisitive yet so strikingly disturbed. I mirror it as I'm met with his presence.

I call Cace's name, but there's no sound. He looks at me with a fearful expression plastered across his face. Am I mirroring his facial expressions, or is he mirroring mine?

It feels awfully as though I'm looking into my reflection.

"They're arguing about me," Cace tells me, regretfully. He pauses for a moment, glances at the cracked picture frames, and speaks again, "We look similar."

We do. I answer without sound once more.

"Why is that?" Cace wonders. He pauses again, waiting for a response yet not receiving one. "Did they choose you out of missing me?"

There's a silence that I can't break. I think Cace begins to understand that, and he studies the different photos of himself in cracked picture frames repeatedly.

"Why do they argue about me?" Cace inquires as if I'm able to give him an answer. "They should feel a weight off of their shoulders."

A weight?

"I was somewhat of a burden, and I think they knew it," Cace continues. "They didn't want to accept that, though. Becoming less and less happy with myself and more and more focused on problems I couldn't solve, I wanted none of it at all. Is that what they argue about? Me being a burden?"

Cace walks closer to the master bedroom door, where the sounds of arguing root from. I follow him out of curiosity and, as we move closer, the words of Michelle and Frank's argument become increasingly evident.

"Why would you ever consider that?" says my mother. "It's wrong and I won't agree to it."

"Why? Why wouldn't you?" asks Frank. "How ... how sudden his death was. It's the right thing to do. Do you even love our son?"

"Of course I do!" my mother yells back. "And that's why I think that this isn't right! It's so complicated. Everything about (muffled) is so ... it's so wrong and I can't ..."

"Maybe you think it's complicated because you're too ignorant to understand it," Frank says, louder. "Because I sure as hell find it okay."

The words are familiar to me; I can recall hearing them in a past dream that more than likely was a memory that crossed my mind while I slept. But, looking at Cace, he doesn't seem to be familiar with them at all—his facial expression resembles that of one I had seen earlier: inquisitive yet so strikingly disturbed. But his disturbance is very emphasized and his inquisitive expression fades as the argument continues. Then, he speaks with blank eyes, similar to Michelle's.

"I know what they talk about."

What?

"The complicated ... the 'thing to do' ..."

I want to shake Cace and make him think sensibly. He doesn't elaborate and, somehow, this mentioning of "complicated" and "thing to do" that refer to the argument causes a down-spiral of my thoughts. The scene grows colder, the lights become lower, and I shake my hands in a panic. I begin to forget that what I see is not reality, because it sure as hell feels like it.

"Open the door. Just–"

I open the door, and Cace disappears from my side. Beyond the room entrance is what I would expect reflecting on what I remember of the master bedroom, but Frank and Michelle appear different to me. Michelle sits on the bed in a hospital gown, with the IV device attached to her wrist and a face that seems to be just as exhausted and worn down as I last remember her—with desolate, brown eyes.

Her eyes did not fully shut.

I shake my head suddenly. Frank stands beside the bed in what appears to be work clothing and a face that I cannot make out the details of; my mind fills in his face with Cace's, just older.

"Kaeda?" My mother begins in a raspy voice, identical to the one she had whilst in the hospital, but it's odd to me; she never talked like that during the argument. "What are you doing here?"

I back away from the scene.

"Kaeda?" my mother calls again. With quick progression of the scene, her skin grows paler. Her face begins to droop greatly. Her eyelids sit low—her exhausted, bleak expression stares at me just as I had last seen it.

Her eyes
did not fully
I shut the door, and—

The scene changes.

I notice a familiar rumbling beneath my body, just as I had far earlier. Another train, still with no sound of people; very little light; very little sign of any life, but with somebody else beside me who looks out of one of the subway train car's many windows in a noticeably different way: with subtle excitement and a greater sense of wonder. The person is younger—with shorter, black, slightly wavy hair. They wear a royal blue hoodie, a pair of jeans, and glasses. Ottie.

Ottilie Saito.

My sister, again.

"Do you ever wonder what it's like?" she starts.

It?

"To live normally," Ottie clarifies as if I had verbally spoken. "Do you ever wonder what it would be like, just to live like happy people for a day or two?"

I hold back from a response.

"No, it's a mistake to even wonder that, because it's not possible," Ottie continues. "No one here is *really* happy. A sad life is lived, the life ends, and the sad life—lived again. Again and again and again. Over and over and over. Sadness."

What?

"What am I trying to tell you?" Ottie mirrors my questions. "That it's not really, I don't know, worth worrying about. Meaningless."

I hold back from a response once more.

"Meaningless, meaningless, meaningless," Ottie repeats. "I worry about a lot of things. You worry about a lot of things, too. What would it be like, to stop worrying for a day or two? To live like happy people, for a day or two?"

Ottie pauses and glances out the train window once more.

"Keep asking questions, Kaeda," she concludes. "I mean, isn't that all life is now?"

6:00 AM.

I wake up to a tapping on my shoulder. Turning around, I see a familiar doctor who had occasionally monitored Michelle room's at my side, backing away as I wake up.

"You leave to see your sister today," says the doctor. "Ottilie Saito is her name, is that right?"

I nod sleepily.

"Alright, good," the doctor continues. "There is breakfast provided at the desk in the corner over there," the doctor points. "In thirty minutes, another one of us will call you out of the room to drive you to your house, where you'll pack what you need and shower with as much time as you need to. Is that okay?"

I nod again.

"Alright, thank you."

The doctor leaves, abandoning me in the hospital room with only an absence of my mother: her deathbed. It lay there, coldly, just as she did following her death.

Her eyes did not fully shut.

As my eyes begin to zone out on the sight of the empty hospital bed, still with imprints of my mother's body in the thin, white sheets, my knee begins to shake against the cot aside from the bed. Slowly, at first, but picking up a pace—almost like the death of my own mother. Slowly, as she said her last words to me, as she held my hand, and quickly as I realized the haunting fact:

She would not let it go.

She was dead. She *is* dead. Images of death swarm my head as I continuously fix my eyes on the death bed.

Her eyes did not fully shut.

Stop it, Kaeda.

Stop thinking of *death.*

I take a deep breath and avoid any touch of the hospital bed.

For the next thirty minutes, I do as they told me to. I eat the breakfast that they provided to me, which is a simple meal of pancakes, bacon, and orange juice, as well as be sure to bring with me in my bag everything that they brought. Another doctor finds me at the end of those thirty minutes and drives me home simply in their car. As we approach my house, an odd feeling washes over me.

A bittersweetness, I'd call it.

Michelle and I live—or lived—here, though we rarely spoke to one another for reasons that I still don't fully understand. Was it the melancholy and dread of Michelle, of me, or of the both of us?

What was it that she went through? In full detail, what did my mother experience that left her so bleak and unavailable?

Looking outside of the car window and out onto the familiar San Francisco house that sits in front of me—identical to the surrounding ones—an undeniable urge to have complete knowledge of my mother's life shows itself in the violent bouncing of my knee. I would love to ask her these questions now, but I can't.

She's gone.

She's gone and I never had the chance to truly speak to her about everything—she's gone and left me with vague information about the past of both her and me. Something I wish to know greatly; my past has been a mystery to me that I've been aching to solve for as long as I can remember, only recently feeling myself get slightly closer in clarifying my questions on a notebook paper. But now I realize that, with enough time and conversations, Michelle could have been so, so beneficial in helping me recall my past.

I should have spoken to her more.

I should have reached out, maybe.

Why didn't I reach out?

The car parks in the driveway, and I'm reminded that I need to leave it in order for me to not waste this doctor's time.

This location is a harbor of many of my dreams, especially the one last night, yet never meant much to me at all considering how Michelle and Frank didn't involve themselves much in my life. After showering, brushing my teeth, and packing everything I find myself needing, I leave the house and once again enter the hospital staff's car.

But I don't shed a tear or speak a word to myself inside of the house. Instead, I find myself experiencing a confusing numbness with silent, distant melancholy: a melancholy that I'm afraid to express. And that's where the numbness appears.

I don't say anything to the doctor as I open the car door.

"I'm so sorry that this happened," the doctor says to me with a look of concern and sadness on her face. But I freeze at the comment—I freeze at the sympathy that she expresses to me, and I don't understand why.

I hold my luggage in my hand with my arms at my side, the car door open without a foot stepped inside by me. The chilling wind blows softly throughout the neighborhood trees and against my hair. The skin of my hands becomes cold.

Blankly and unintentionally, I stare at the doctor and finally attempt to form a response.

"It's okay—I'm okay," I answer, in a complete and utter lie.

Although I may not be sobbing to her face or choking up on my words, there is no truth to that statement. A painful stomach pain consumes me—a strong aching that only expresses my thoughts—those of which I can't comprehend—in physical form.

I'm okay.

No, I don't feel this.

No, I don't feel much at all.

The doctor drives me to the train station, the only location that has truly brought me a sense of familiarity, stronger than that of my own house. She leaves me with the guide written out for me yesterday, telling me where to go, and a hug goodbye, although I barely know her.

She says that she feels like I need it. Maybe not a hug from a stranger, but I think I agree with her.

The train station is not as busy as it may be on weekdays. The people silently commute from location to location, wherever they may be going. I silently commute—I guess that's what you'd call it—from a hospital to my twin-sister-whom-I-can-hardly-recall's town.

I guess I've always been a silent commuter.

I guess I've always been silent.

I wish I would have said something to Michelle. I wish I would have told her something—just talked to her about my day or how I was feeling. I wish I could have, as impossible as it may be in a logical sense, brought her out of her depression. I wish I could have done *something*.

I don't think I ever did *anything*.

But do I truly miss her, or do I just feel regret?

We never spoke.

Her death wasn't too unpredictable.

But her death was horrifying.

But I couldn't have done anything to prevent it.

But I could have made her life better.

But could I truly have?

I open my backpack—a necessary part of my luggage—and pull out the only non-academic notebook inside of it. I open to the page of questions, and my eyes immediately dart to two inquiries beside one another.

Why do I feel this way?

Why do I feel so numb?

I write a bullet under both:

My own mother's death doesn't change this fact.

I pause.

Numbness.

Does this make me a bad person?

I scribble the most recent question that is part of a bullet and begin to write a response to the scribble.

No, no—you're not a bad person for feeling numb.

I scribble out the statement of reassurance. This is a page of questions and their productive bulleted points that bring me closer to the answers.

I write another question down, apart from the bulleted point:
Why am I so obsessed with productivity?
I write a bullet under that question:
To forget about this page.
I scribble out the recent writing. It's nothing useful.

The station I see here, closer to San Francisco, is going to appear close to if not the same as the station near Ottie. Because we're at a stop closer to the general city of San Francisco, I won't need to make a transition stop; for the next two or so hours, the train ride of the train I'm close to boarding is the only one I'll need. From there, I take the bus and meet Ottie for what I reasonably predict will feel like the first time. She appears in my dreams constantly, sure, but I can't easily remember who she *truly* was.

I try my best to remember memories of the two of us as foster children that I could bring up and try even harder to block out the dreams, which I can't decipher from memories. I can't tell her I hardly remember any of our genuine memories—that would cause confusion and most likely sadness. *But, who is she now? How am I to predict that?*

A distinct knot in my stomach engulfs me.

The train ride ends. I'm far from the San Francisco area now, and most likely will be much further after the bus ride that the doctor had named to me as that of a long one. I pick up a coffee from a nearby cafe chain right outside the station; the weather here is just as foggy as it was in San Francisco—the November fog does not change.

The town scene is so different from that of the city, or even of the city outskirts. Everyone is quieter here, yet in a homely, less introverted sense. The posters displayed at the bus stops—particularly the one I'm waiting at—mention local businesses and school opportunities rather than general advertisements. I board the bus once it arrives and find a seat in the back, staring out the window as the fogged town I've never visited until now passes by. Further into the bus ride, I watch the cars on the highway and, finally, another town whose few stops have one which I'll leave from. During the bus ride, I notice a few citizens looking at me with concern since I carry a large suitcase and a duffel bag. *Shouldn't I be coming from an airport shuttle?* They must ask themselves that question.

Furthermore, only a few stops away from the one I'll be getting off at, a group of local teenagers board the bus. At first, I don't think much of it, but I do get around to listening to their conversation out of curiosity and the noticeable strong facial expressions within the group.

"No, but seriously, do you guys know where Amani went?" one teen asks their friends.

Another one replies. "Beau said he saw her in a class a few days ago, I don't know what your concern is."

"Yeah, but that was a few *days* ago," the teen responds. "She's usually always around. And she hasn't been picking up her phone."

"Maybe it's another Sasha situation."

"No one gives a shit about that, though," the teen blurts, which gets a few strong responses from the group who appear to have very different ideas. "But Amani? She's always talking to people. There was supposed to be a party and we couldn't even invite her because she was 'gone'. Why?"

"I don't know, maybe she got her phone taken away or something?"

The teen scoffs. "Maybe, but that doesn't explain her missing school."

"Doesn't Amani seem like the type of person to skip, though?"

"You're making excuses. Amani's never out. She's not even that bad of a student—she'd know when to cut the act and not harm her chance of getting into college."

"It's not much to worry about."

"Yes, it is," the teen refutes. "When someone randomly stops showing up to school and doesn't say shit to anyone, it sounds like a missing person. Does anyone have her parents' contact?"

"You think we're going to talk to her parents?"

The bus arrives at my stop. The conversation crosses my mind slightly as I leave, and I'm intrigued enough to where I wish I could hear more, but that is all unimportant now. As I leave the bus and take my hefty luggage with me, a neighborhood of contemporary-style modern townhomes that all look similar to one another sits in front of me, making itself clear through the fogged atmosphere. Each of the townhomes has sleek, large windows, discrete porches and garages, and well-kept yet identical green gardens. I tread with my baggage along the neighborhood sidewalk until I reach the number of the townhome that was given to me on a small note: 1053. Townhome unit 1053: it looks identical to the rest. Approaching the front door and walking up the small set of concrete stairs to bring me there, a pit of nervousness in my stomach swells up within me.

I take a deep breath and ring the doorbell, and that ringing is accompanied by sounds of much human life inside of the townhome, rustling and making something out of their chaotic feelings that I seem to be able to sense from here. A thin, petite, forty-or-so-year-old woman with dark brown curly hair and a Star of David necklace answers in loungewear. She smiles politely, yet keeps a nervous expression that shows not only on her face but in her entire body language.

"Welcome!" she chimes, studying me and then my luggage with a slightly surprised face. "Kaeda Saito?"

"Bynum, but yes," I correct her quietly.

"Oh, right," the woman says. "You look so similar to Ottie! Come in, you have a bunk prepared for you!" She pauses for a moment as I walk inside, looking visibly mistaken. "I forgot to tell you: my name is Janice Weizmann. I'm Ottie's legal guardian and have been since she was fifteen. I have a son who lives with me here who is Ottie's age, and that's Beau Weizmann. After you pack, I have a few papers that I'll need you to sign between you and the nearby high school to get you all set."

"Thank you," I say, picking up my luggage in preparation to go upstairs. "Where's Ottie?"

"Oh, she's upstairs," the woman, or Janice, answers hurriedly, closing the door behind me. She lowers her volume to a whisper. "She's a little nervous today, knowing that you'll be here and such. But it's okay–you seem like a great sister!"

I nod, smiling awkwardly, and walk upstairs with my luggage. Janice catches my attention one last time:

"You'll be sharing a bedroom with Ottie, like I said, in a bunk bed. She asked for one when we first adopted her a little over a year ago because it reminded her of you. Isn't that nice?"

I nod. "It's very nice."

"Oh, and Beau is upstairs in his room, too," Janice continues. "He was just finishing up some schoolwork. He'll get around to talking to you!"

I continue to nod with an unintentionally awkward demeanor and finally reach the second level of the townhome. Nearby is a closed bedroom door with three small colorful flower stickers decorating the front of it feeling, oddly enough, like a hug to me. Like a warm embrace. They're so familiar; so lighthearted—they're out of a foster home dream scene of mine—before it turns confusing. I knock on the bedroom door. A voice speaks from inside.

"Kaeda?" it says. A voice identical to Ottie's in my dream, yet more mature. Still higher-pitched than mine, yet still similar.

"Yes?" I answer.

"Oh my god," the voice mutters in distinct eagerness. "Come in, please."

I open the bedroom door and am met with a very familiar person, sitting at a white computer desk with textbooks and sketchbooks sprawled across it.

Ottie.

Ottilie Saito.

Ottie Saito.

My sister. She still looks so much like her younger self.

Her black hair is a little shorter than shoulder length and very familiarly wavy. Her bangs are of a similar style. She still has her round-ish transparently-brown glasses and wears another hoodie this time—a red hoodie naming a local high school—and purple sweatpants with mismatching printed socks. Her nails are chipping away a blue paint. Her face is just as similar to mine as I remember it.

"My sister," Ottie whispers in awe. "I missed you. I missed—"

Not finishing her sentence, Ottie runs up to hug me. The embrace is warm—a vague visual of us as children, presumably from a dream, quickly crosses my mind. Though this encounter feels more like meeting a new person than it does reuniting with a twin sister, although that's how it should feel, I notice my body slightly relaxing in the hug—then how tense I was beforehand with no realization of it.

Ottie then begins to cry whilst in the hug, and it doesn't end. She's sobbing, it seems. I tense up again.

"I never thought I would see you again," my sister chokes up. "I didn't ever think that ..."

In the same stance as before, I stay in the hug with Ottie, allowing her to cry yet not feeling the desire to cry myself, and then feeling slightly bad about that absence of feeling. After a few seconds, the hug breaks, and Ottie returns to her desk chair. She looks ridden with curiosity as if there are many questions she wishes to ask me. I also notice her attempting to hold them back, which confuses me, but I don't mention it.

Ottie attempts to ask me one question on her mind. "Are—are you okay? I mean—" she pauses. "I mean, what happened? How did you feel? How *do* you feel? What—what's happened for the past five years? I have so many things to ask, I don't know how to ask them all, I just ..."

"It's okay," I attempt to reassure my sister awkwardly.

"Are you going to Redworth?" Ottie asks randomly.

"Is that the school closest to here?"

Ottie nods quickly.

"Then yes."

"Oh, that's great," Ottie says. "I don't really have too many people to talk to, so it's cool that you're going to the same school. I don't know what to say. I really don't know how to act in this situation."

I ask a stupid question.

"Why do you think that is?"

"I mean … I just never thought I'd see you again, so it's kind of weird for me, I guess. I don't really know, I just kind of—"

Ottie stops speaking.

"You have to meet Beau," Ottie says, changing the subject. "He's technically my brother, I guess, and he goes to Redworth, but knows more people than I do."

In the conversation, every single detail of Ottie's dialogue: her body language, her tones, and her ways of story-telling, in a sense, are identical to how they have been briefly displayed in my dreams—dreams that I hesitate to mention and decide not to yet. Ottie brings up another topic briefly.

"I hope you're feeling alright after what happened last night," Ottie comments in a change of subject to the conversation, and my mind, prior to reflecting on last night itself, quickly plays a vague image of a familiar dream sequence including Ottie and me where a young version of her would speak to me a comment completely out-of-the-blue. But then I think of my mother—I think of her death.

The image of my mom and her bleak, half-open, lifeless eyes becomes less clear as the doctors crowd around the hospital bed.

Her eyes did not fully shut.

I shake my head slightly, only shortly noticing that Ottie finds this to be concerning. *Stop thinking. Stop thinking of death.*

"I've been trying to recover," I tell Ottie, truth to the comment. Maybe I haven't been exactly *trying*—actively making the effort to become mentally and emotionally *recovered*—however I've been, well—

Well, I don't know if there's full truth to the comment. Then again, I don't know what is fully truthful of how I've been feeling after last night.

As the conversation comes to an end and I unpack all that I brought in my luggage for as long as it takes, which totals around an hour, Janice orders takeout. Beau finally approaches me once lunch arrives, and he looks similar to his mom, unsurprisingly. Dark brown hair except less curly, a defined facial complexion, a thinner build, and a Star of David necklace. He first appears to me with a messy appearance: frizzy wavy hair, eye bags, and wearing a Redworth band t-shirt that I'd assume is one he slept in. He looks almost half-asleep and holds a glass of water in his hands as he walks downstairs.

"Good morning," Beau says.

"I thought you were finishing up your essay?" Janice responds with suspicion.

"I was, and then I fell asleep," Beau answers. He glances over at me. "Kaeda Saito?"

I open my mouth instinctually to correct the last name, then halt myself.

There is no one left in the "Bynum" family. Who would I be—Kaeda Bynum—with no "Bynum" mother, father, or sibling?

I can't stay attached to a family that consists of nobody but my own self. Then again, was I ever truly attached to the Bynums?

I give Beau a nod, not correcting the last name this time. Kaeda Saito—Kaeda Bynum Saito.

"Woah, Ottie's been speaking about you since she first lived here. *The* Kaeda Saito. You look so similar to her, yet so different."

"What's your essay about?" I ask, unintentionally breaking away from the subject.

"Oh, it's for a research class," Beau responds. "It's on dreams. I chose the topic."

Dreams.

Janice scoffs lightly, then glances at me, as if we have the same idea. "He's *way* too into this," she quietly tells me. Confused about why that's negative, I ignore her opinion and continue to ask about the essay.

"What about dreams exactly?" I wonder.

"Vivid dreams and why people may have them," Beau answers with slight hesitation, potentially trying to avoid the topic, though I'm not sure why—it captivates my attention entirely. "I don't know, it's just something I thought would work. Anyway—"

"That's really interesting," I comment.

Beau laughs. "Yeah, sometimes talking about it makes me nervous, though."

"He's been dreaming vividly for a while now, that's why," Ottie chimes in blatantly while eating. Beau looks at her, annoyed, and mouths something along the lines of "You didn't have to tell her yet."

"Come *on*, Kaeda *understands*," Ottie says excitedly in response to Beau. "I have a *very* smart and understanding twin sister."

As I finish up lunch, I head back into Ottie's room, which is technically also my room now. Sitting down on my lower bunk bed, Ottie follows me and sits at her desk chair once again. I recognize a weird urge to start the conversation about Beau's essay, and a lack of awkwardness about it as Ottie's here. Maybe because she's a large part of those dreams, it only feels right to let her know about them.

"Beau's essay seems very intriguing," I say. "Vivid dreams? And you said that he has them a lot, right?"

"Yeah, they've been an issue for him for a while now," Ottie answers. "He and Janice get into petty arguments about it because his mind runs and Janice finds it all stupid. I think they're cool, don't get me wrong, but they're a lot to deal with. I don't know what he has."

"They must be incredibly vivid to be such a problem, then."Ottie sighs. "Yeah, they are."

I wait for a bit to introduce my connection to the whole topic, then finally speak.

"I have very vivid dreams, too," I tell Ottie. "They hint at a lot of things: memories, you ..."

I stop myself. I don't want to talk about anything "Bynum" yet—I still don't think I can coherently comprehend that topic, let alone explain it.

"What do you remember of me?" asks Ottie. A question that creates a piercing feeling deep inside my body—a question that makes my heart rate increase. A question that I have been asking myself for as long as I can remember, not even setting aside the time that Ottie and I lived in foster homes because, even then, I don't remember the majority of my thoughts and feelings. I stutter in my answer.

"I remember how we used to live in different foster homes, and that you would ..." I pause, "... you would draw a lot and ask me about my books."

"Well, yeah, but those are pretty basic details," says Ottie. "Say, do you remember the time—"

"I don't remember a lot."

Ottie halts her thought. A look of subtle devastation slowly falls upon her face, and it feels as though I'm looking into a mirror with her expressions and facial features.

"Oh."

"Yeah, I'm sorry, I just—"

"No, no! It's okay, we can put this back together," Ottie cuts me off, still with devastated eyes and now a forced smile and optimism. She picks up the pace of her speaking.

"It's fun to make new memories with someone, don't you think? You don't really need to have them there already. But do you remember all the different things we kept in our bedroom? From all the places we went? I still have a few things, I could bring them out to you, you know." Ottie looks through storage containers in her small bedroom closet, rummaging through different souvenirs and photographs to show me.

"My memories appear in my dreams a lot," I tell her through her rummaging.

She pauses.

"You appear in them frequently," I continue.

"But you can't think of them when conscious?" Ottie asks me.

"... No."

Ottie turns her head towards me. "That's a lot like Beau."

"Really?"

"Did you have a concussion?" she asks me.

"No, I don't think so," I respond. "Did he?"

"No, actually," Ottie answers. "Which is why this is weird. Because I got two weird cases living in my house. You can't really remember me much, you have weird dreams, Beau has weird dreams ... I don't really talk to Janice, but she's weird, too."

I refrain from saying anything. Ottie grows a look of worry across her face.

You're not ... upset that I called you a 'weird case', right?" asks Ottie. "God, this must be

why you can't remember things like I can. I'm irrational all too often. I can't even think."

"No, it's okay," I reassure Ottie. Her nervousness still appears to cling to her, causing expressions of worry and hurried body language indicating that something is wrong. "I don't think that you need to explain."

A deep pit swells in my stomach—I'm lying to Ottie in telling her it's okay. Really, I'm trying to make sense of the conversation. I understand the disappointment and almost detachment from reality that Ottie appears to feel as she realizes that I don't remember our past as she does. I understand her feelings yet, still, I can't entirely grasp the way in which she acts towards me. I understand that her nervousness and jitteriness are because this day is the first day in which she's talked to me in years, though I still feel like something is deeply off: something that I cannot rationalize. And I hate feeling something without being able to rationalize that feeling.

"But why don't you remember?" Ottie repeats to me, setting aside the items she rummaged for in her closet. "That's the only thing I needed to reassure myself that you were still there."

"That I was still there?"

"I ... I can't think right now, I really can't," Ottie repeats. "It may be better if I stayed quiet. I'm sorry Kaeda. I'm just a little shocked at this. Please forgive me."

"It's okay."

"Thank you, Kaeda."

Ottie comes closer to me and brings me into an embrace. I do what I can to best comfort her, but the moment is still somewhat awkward.

I may just need to adjust to having a sister—I may just need to adjust to having someone there for me.

The next few hours are somewhat eventful, somewhat not. Janice brings me downstairs occasionally to talk to me about my enrollment at Redworth High School and what I'll need to do once I go there tomorrow morning, and each of her words are awfully cheery to where it becomes uncomfortable. Aside from that, I have small conversations with Ottie as she completes assignments for school. Dinner is takeout, and I learn Janice cannot effectively cook through subtle conversation during that time. Nothing really happens, but Beau does reveal to the dinner table that he's trying to obtain more research for his essay on vivid dreams, and Ottie spontaneously suggests that I become a subject of research, and I don't oblige as it seems interesting. Now, I sit on a plastic garden chair on the balcony of the Weizmann and Saito townhome, looking at the rest of the townhomes identical to this one in the misty northern California dusk. The sky is less of an orange, but more of a dark, melancholy blue: a color I've always liked. Beau walks out onto the balcony with a bar of dark chocolate and a notepad.

"So, Ottie tells me you have experience with vivid dreams, right?" he begins.

"Yes," I answer.

"What exactly?" Beau asks.

I hesitate to speak, realizing that it's the first time I've ever opened up completely—or am beginning to open up completely—about these vivid dreams of mine. I didn't once speak to Ottie about my confusing feeling—or lack thereof—regarding my mother's death. I left her on a simple note. I didn't open up completely to my *own twin sister.*

How well will I be able to open up to a person I only met today about the complex question that is my vivid dreams?

Though, I do realize that it's needed for research, so I respond.

"I always seem to remember my dreams entirely," I tell Beau. "There has never been a night, from what I can remember, where I haven't remembered a dream. And, in my dreams, I often see things that—I guess you could say—connect to another dream, no matter how far along it's been since I've had said dream. I don't really know, I just ..."

"Interesting."

"... And the dreams, most of the time, aren't obscure or completely impossible," I continue, the awkward feeling alleviating. "Yeah, they have some unrealistic element to them a large portion of the time, but they typically hint at a memory of some sort. But I can't really remember the memory normally. It just feels like I'm reliving one, and a vivid one at that, as I dream about it. And I can tell it's a memory because I've asked people involved and they–"

Beau stops writing. I realize that I've over shared.

"I'm sorry, was that too much?" I ask. "I figure that, if its research, I may just—"

"No, no, that's fine," Beau says. "I just have a few questions."

I wait.

"Do these dreams sometimes have people you don't really 'know' per se or remember as a large part of them?" Beau asks. "Or, it doesn't really *have* to be a person, but a 'something'? Like a place or a thing? But it's not minor—it appears a lot and repeats itself. Do you ever have that?"

A few things come to mind.

"Yes," I answer.

I notice Beau not writing anything from here.

"Like what?" Beau follows up. I hesitate to answer, but if it's for research—which I'm starting to doubt that this specific part is now—I will.

"Different memories related to my foster homes and adoption."

"That's really interesting," Beau says. "But you didn't remember them at all, right? It's completely unfamiliar to you aside from those dreams?"

I nod.

"Me too," adds Beau.

I tilt my head out of intrigue.

"And what is that 'thing' that you don't remember?" I ask.

"I don't really know if I can tell you," he says. "I've only actually known you for about a day."

"I've told you about mine, though."

"Yeah, but that's research."

"What is significant about the specifics of my recurring dream element that I can't remember to the research?"

Beau considers the question, then laughs. "I'll admit, I was just curious."

"So what is it that you see in your dreams?"

"An unnamed girl," Beau answers. "I remember the details of her face more vividly each day. She's my best friend and girlfriend, but she only appears in my dreams. It's weird, because the more something appears in your dreams, the more it's supposed to resemble a memory, right? But I can't remember this girl at all. I don't remember any time we spent together–nothing. Yet she's in every single one of my dreams."

"Interesting."

"Yeah. I think I'm done with my research now," Beau nods. "Thank you, Kaeda, and whenever you go to bed: goodnight."

The short-lived conversation ends at that, and Beau leaves the balcony. For the next hour or two, a few things happen that are considerably uneventful. Janice hands me my Redworth schedule, I shower, have a snack of fruit, and brush my teeth. As I walk back into Ottie's room in my pajamas, I see her napping on her top bunk. She wakes up as I lay down on the bottom bunk due to the noise below her.

"Kaeda?" Ottie quietly says.

"Yes?"

"How was the Beau conversation?"

"Interesting, just a little short-lived."

"I'm sorry for being rude about you not remembering things earlier."

"It's okay."

"That's nice to hear," Ottie says. "Sleep well, anyway."

"Thank you," I return. I open my mouth to say something about how I truly feel about Michelle's death—though I close my mouth. The incident with Michelle is an issue that has received a solution—one that I still don't know how to grasp: *death*.

I cannot keep thinking about an issue with a solution, and I cannot keep thinking about the solution itself.

I don't tell Ottie about how I truly feel.

"Sleep well," I return.

After thirty minutes of tossing and turning in thinking about dreams, I drift away into one.

Five

I wake up.

A misty coolness of the air is the first thing I can feel. It seeps into my skin: a cold moisture, causing the hairs of my body to rise, and my eyes begin to open.

An empty playground area in the night. The fog is thick enough to where you cannot see beyond the actual playground and the surrounding benches, but thin enough to where that central area is visible. I know that I'm reflecting on some childhood memory, whatever it may be, and that gives me a slight sense of comfort.

Comfort, yet eeriness in that the area is completely void of life and what lies beyond the thick fog that surrounds this place is completely unknown to me.

I begin to walk around the area, hoping to explore it, then to notice a person sitting at one of the surrounding benches and a faint cry that is not subtle; it wails and wails as if the source is in pain. My legs tremble, my hands grow sweaty without influence from the mist of the air, and my view of the dream grows weaker in a feeling of deep panic. But then I notice who the person is, and the feelings become mixed.

Ottie. Ottie, in her pajamas, as I had just recently seen her, wails in pain, although there seems to be nothing physically harming her.

As I move closer, she starts to notice me, and I recognize her clinging to something the size of a notebook. When my vision adjusts to the area, I realize what she clings to: a manila folder. A file, of some sort. She continues to cry, wailing—her face disturbed and depressed.

"Ottie?"

She continues to cry—a face I can't erase from my mind.

"Ottie?" I repeat.

Ottie musters out quiet words. "I can't, I can't, I ..."

"What?"

"No, no, no," cries Ottie. "I can't take it. Please, this wasn't what I wanted. I can't ..."

She clings to the file in her hands and against her chest with more force. "Why did this have to happen, Kaeda?" Ottie wails. "Why is this all that is left? Where have you gone?"

Where have you gone.

The fog closes in on my visibility of the scene and the air grows cooler. My ability to rationalize my surroundings depletes, and the panic that Ottie seems to feel begins to feed onto me as well. A raindrop lands on my head; it rains. The rain picks up its pace at a rapid speed, soaking Ottie and I as well as the file she so desperately clings onto.

"Kaeda, I miss you, I miss you Kaeda, I—"

The file slips out of Ottie's hands. I attempt to pick it up—*what in here could be so significant to her?*

"No, please–"

I wake up.

"*Where have you gone?*".

It's the first thing that I remember of the dream. "*Where have you gone?*".

A cry for help.

I cannot help but shake the feeling—however early it may be in the unlit bedroom only illuminated by the window blinds' shining of the sky's dark blue hues—that I have caused this great despair within Ottie. This great disappointment and terrifying realization that I am not who she expected; I do not remember and connect with experiences as a child with Ottie as she does or had expected me to. *But what have I done to cause this?* I highly doubt that I will be able to fall back asleep, regardless of whether I need the rest, because of these significant questions and worries within me that always, *always* result from *the dreams*.

The vivid dreams.

The dreams Beau asked me about last evening on the balcony and gave a confusing yet intriguing response to—the dreams where he practically stopped in his tracks as I opened up about them as if he had looked into a mirror and seen himself. Because I firmly believe that is what happened.

I am now far too amped up to continue laying here, and I'm far too hungry to put the idea of going downstairs away. Weirdly, though, the hallway light is dimly lit as I exit the room slowly and wrapped in a blue blanket that lay with me on the lower bunk. I continue walking, beginning to hear very faint arguing.

Am I still in a dream?

No, this is not the Bynum house.

I can feel the coldness of the wooden flooring beneath my feet and each quiet step I take down the staircase, though that doesn't mean much given the vividness of my dreams. As I step foot on the first floor, I notice Beau and Janice sitting at the small kitchen table, mouths moving. Noticing me, Janice has a slightly mortified look on her face. However, Beau seems relieved.

I apologize. "Sorry if I interrupted—"

"Kaeda," Beau's mom greets me, with a change in the tone of her voice from the tone that I had briefly heard a moment ago: a hostile one. "Why are you up so early, dear?"

"I just was hungry," I respond softly. "I'm sorry if I interrupted anything."

"No, please sit," Beau suggests, his voice slightly hoarse. His mom, Janice, looks at him, confused by his suggestion.

I take a seat at the table. Though I'm slightly confused by why exactly they'd be arguing this early, involving myself seems interesting.

Beau's mom takes a sip of coffee, then speaks. "I've been told that your—"

"Did you have a weirdly vivid dream right before this?" Beau immediately asks. "Not only 'weird', but experienced something incredibly 'off'?"

It then occurs to me: what Ottie told me about. How Janice and Beau *get into petty arguments about Beau's vivid dreams because his mind runs and Janice finds it all stupid.*

I nod. "I did."

"See?"

"Beau," Janice starts, "You're over-exaggerating this situation. Everyone has 'silly dreams'."

"They aren't 'silly'," Beau debates, portraying images and connections rapidly with his hands. "They're anything but 'silly'. They're extremely vivid—they leave a painful, growing wound inside of your mind and it doesn't go away. And you wonder what it is, why it's there—whether it's infected. And, if it's infected, *what* infected it, *why* couldn't I notice the infection in time ..."

"That's a perfect way of explaining it," I whisper. He was less expressive last evening—maybe it's that he's tired and therefore doesn't filter himself.

"Exactly."

"You're talking too loud, Beau," Janice comments, whispering.

"But why does that matter if what I'm saying is important?" Beau reasons in return. "If Ottie were to wake up and find us here, wouldn't you think that she'd want to know about this? In fact, maybe it's best if she *were* to wake up."

"Beau," Beau's mom continues, "No one wants to hear about the weird dreams that you have."

"You don't," Beau refutes. "But maybe it's best if you do."

"Beau!"

"I'm sorry! I'm sorry," Beau hurriedly apologizes. "But think about it. It just appears: anything remotely concerning or important that I tell you about, you disregard it."

"I want to hear about the dreams," I tell them. I typically avoid conflict, but maybe my restlessness is blurring the lines between what I should and shouldn't say.

"No, no, you don't, Kaeda," Janice laughs.

I pause before responding. "... I do."

"These are *teenage boy* dreams he speaks about," Janice attempts to inform me as if Beau was referencing dreams that were nonsensical or hypersexual. It's clear that he's talking about vivid dreams, given that he mentioned mine.

"I know," I reply, "and that doesn't necessarily make a difference."

Beau's mom looks at the two of us, disappointed, and it confuses me. Beau is expressing his vivid dreams, why is his mom disappointed?

"My visions take place in Arizona," Beau starts. "Y'know, how you and I used to live there, Mom. But I can hardly remember anything; it's all in fragments. And as soon as it seems like I have a grasp on something in my mind, it disappears, and I end up in a strange, unknown reality. From there, everything just down-spirals."

I nod. Everything he's mentioned is something I can relate to.

What happened to Beau?

"I'm very, very sorry to hear that," Janice says. "I ... really, I don't know how this happened."

I look at Beau, and then at Janice as she takes another sip of her coffee, finally setting it down on one of her heated coasters.

"I don't either," Beau responds in a quieter tone. "It's not your fault. Really, I don't know whose 'fault' it is."

Glancing at Janice, it appears she'd have something to say—her eyes scanning the area. But, no, she simply takes another sip of coffee, staying silent.

"I'm sorry that you have to hear all of this, Kaeda," she finally says, looking at me. Her eyes of much exhaustion zone out deeply into the scene. In a way, they look bleak, yet by studying them, you can tell just how full of thought they are—whatever the thoughts that run through her mind may be of. It seems that she'll never share them.

"I need to breathe," Beau sighs, leaving the kitchen table. He walks outside onto the balcony, leaving a small portion of the sliding door open. Janice continues to stay silent yet, every time I look at her, she glances back at me as if she wishes to tell me something. I say nothing, but contemplate leaving the table and following Beau out to the balcony in hopes of a conversation. Eventually, I decide in favor of the idea and step outside onto the balcony, where Beau sits on the same garden chair as he did before, with the same subtly exhausted expression on his face. He glances at me as I take a seat on the other empty garden chair.

"What did you dream about last night?" Beau asks with little change in facial expression.

"Ottie," I respond. "I remember her panicking, clinging onto some manila folder—a file. She kept on saying confusing things to me that I assume stem from my lack of remembrance towards my childhood, and therefore her."

"But I assume you can remember what she said, right?"

"Yes," I tell Beau. "'Where have you gone?' was something she said to me."

"Wow," Beau responds. "And what else?"

"'Why did this have to happen, Kaeda?' was one," I continue. "And 'Why is this all that is left?'."

"But you said you had trouble remembering her?"

"I have trouble remembering my childhood and, in turn, her, yes."

"But you dream about her still?"

"That was the only way I could truly remember her for much of my life. At least from—"

"From what you can remember, yeah."

There's a pause in the conversation—it's as though I'm speaking to a version of myself.

"It's weird, actually. With this 'girl' in my dreams, it is the *exact same* way," Beau continues. "I don't know her name, yet I know what she looks like, how she speaks, what she says, what she wears; she appears so vividly in my dreams, yet I don't have any real recollection of who she is outside of those dreams. How did you learn Ottie's name; or did you know beforehand?"

"I don't know, actually."

"This is so *weird*. I can't sleep properly because of these dreams and how incredibly vivid they are, and my mom ignores every single one of my concerns," Beau continues. "She ignores every concern. She just drinks or smokes it away—that has been her way of self-medicating for every single problem since we moved to California and adopted Ottie."

"She drinks and smokes?"

"She's kept it exclusive to the middle of the night ever since she heard about you coming here," Beau tells me. "But, trust me, if you're here for long enough, she will begin to do it mid-day again despite her remote job."

"That's sad."

"A lot of things are," Beau keeps on. "It's sad that I dream so frequently of a person—of a lover—of a best friend whom I have no contact with or recollection of aside from my subconscious state. It's sad that you can't remember your childhood as much as Ottie wished. A lot of things are *sad*."

I focus my eyes on the 6 AM view in front of me for a moment. A misty, mysterious, blue fogged sky that has yet to disappear after many days of experiencing it; a quiet neighborhood aside from a neighbor walking their dog along the sidewalk; gardens and townhouses identical to one another with only a few differences per balcony, such as wind chimes or flowers. The view is calming when you dissociate it from the conversation's topic—then it only becomes a view of much anxiety and anticipation. Anticipation for an answer in a bleak, quiet environment; an environment where that answer rarely arrives. Beau speaks again.

"There's someone who seems to be missing at Redworth," Beau starts. "Amani Sanchez. She's in our class, actually, and I'm unsure if she's been fully reported as missing or not, but some people I talk to haven't heard from her or seen her in a while. I saw her in a class of mine a few days ago, but it's been a while since then."

"I think I've heard of this," I tell Beau. "On the town bus, on my way over here yesterday morning; I heard some kids talking about this person. And—thinking of it now—they mentioned your name."

"They said nothing bad about me, did they?"

"No, just that you saw her a few days ago as you said."

"Well, they got that notice late, then."

"Yeah, I guess."

"Kaeda, do you know what this also shows?" Beau starts with another idea. "This recollection you have shows that your memory is not, well, shit. And that this isn't a problem that you've always had: your lack of remembrance of your childhood—all of that. This is something *in the past*. And it's to be solved *in the now*."

"That's true," I respond. "That's very true—you've been thinking about this for a while."

"Haven't you?"

"Well, yes," I respond. "I have, but I guess I've been shoving away my questions—or trying to at least—only until recently. For a while, I found the questions overbearing and deteriorating; I tried to set them aside and focus on academics."

"You're an overachiever."

"I mean, if that is what that tells you, I guess."

"Don't shove away your questions."

"I've been getting better at that."

There's a pause in the conversation.

"We'll just have to keep on analyzing these things," Beau speaks. "Maybe over-analyzing them. Maybe that process, as crazy as it sounds, is how we'll understand our dreams."

"It doesn't sound crazy," I add. "What's crazy to me is *what* we're supposed to analyze. Delving into this just convinces me I'll go insane."

"You've already gone insane," Beau points out. "You know this. Now, I don't think that you've gone *clinically* insane, no, but other people assume that you have."

"Other people have never viewed me as normal."

"I know that," Beau agrees. "But that doesn't mean bad. You think a lot; Ottie's told me before and I can see it myself, and I'm calling you out on it. It might just be your ability to think—and to think deeply at that—that will help you understand yourself."

"Huh," I respond, "You're right."

"But no, you know this information," Beau goes on. "You've always known it. You've always known about your questions, no matter how harmful they've been—no matter whether you've tried to ignore them. You don't really feel comfortable telling other people about these questions because you think you're crazy. But you're not the only one like this, Kaeda."

"And you must know all this because you've felt similarly, or feel similarly."

"Exactly, exactly."

It sprinkles rain, and the sky grows brighter. As I get up from the garden chair and leave the balcony, I remember something that Michelle said to me.

What she said to me right before she died—what she said right before I tried to let go of her lifeless hand then to realize that she was *gone*. Death: a painful thought—one that I can hardly comprehend—but I remember what Michelle said to me.

It stuck with me since, those words:

"Keep asking yourself questions, Kaeda."

There's no time more suited for this memory—although painful—than right now.

I take the next forty to fifty minutes getting dressed, having a quick breakfast, and leaving the townhome, where I follow Ottie and Beau to the nearest stop sign where the Redworth school bus will pick the three of us up. I'm knowledgeable that I went to public school off and on as a kid with Ottie, but I haven't been recently and can hardly remember what attending was like when I was younger. Not having to wear a uniform leaves me dressing in comfortable black straight pants, a white t-shirt, a gray zip-up hoodie, and my casual white sneakers.

The fogged view of the northern California town through the school bus windows is calming, unlike the actual environment of the school bus. Ottie sits next to me as we both individually listen to music, and Beau sits a seat in front of us next to nobody else.

The Redworth High School campus hasn't been renovated since the 90s, it seems, while referencing the teachings of an architecture class I took back at GoldenPine. It has a somewhat modern design, yet nothing unlike many public schools. The surroundings of the campus aren't very populated; only a few students sit around on the benches outside the school entrances, some individually and some in groups. Ottie tells me that Redworth isn't very good in terms of athletics and is mediocre in academics; she says it's an underwhelming high school. By the looks of it, I agree with her.

As I walk shortly around the campus to find the main entrance of the building with both Beau and Ottie, I notice that it's not only the school that is apparently underwhelming; it's the people, as well. I don't know if it's the weather, but typically, I would find students talking to one another in groups with somewhat of an energetic disposition, despite their differences in personality or interest. While I was never one of those students, I don't find that here. Everyone seems to be individualistic, going about their days with a neutral—sometimes melancholy—appearance. I may just be hyper-observant of this, though.

I attend the first half of my classes, which briefly introduce me to each of them. Unfortunately, I don't have many classes with either Beau or Ottie, which is especially because all our interests are so different: Beau takes the band and applied physics or engineering elective classes primarily, Ottie takes many art and writing classes, and I take computer science and psychology electives. One class I have in common with Beau, however, is his college-level research class in which he writes about vivid dreams for a project. Ottie and I have a similar advanced writing class. My last class before lunch, though, is college-level psychology, where I sit next to someone near the back corner of the room who recently came back from a long break from school, as the students in the classroom's front mentioned in a conversation I overheard. Sasha is her name.

"Class, we have a new student today," the class's teacher, Mr. Padilla, says. He looks over at me. "Everyone, this is Kaeda Bynum. Kaeda, can you tell us where you come from and what you enjoy doing?"

"I come from GoldenPine School in San Francisco and I enjoy writing," I say blankly. It's obvious that I don't want to respond.

"Thank you, Kaeda!" Mr. Padilla says. He doesn't introduce Sasha, the girl next to me, although she recently came back from a long break, but she introduces herself to me.

"Why'd you come here from GoldenPine?" Sasha asks, pushing back her dyed-yellowish orange hair with clear brunette roots. "I've heard that's a beautiful school."

I debate on giving her the real reason, so I give her a half-truth, instead.

"I moved back with my sister, Ottie Saito, if you know her."

"I've briefly heard. She was in an art class I had last year. You *do* look like her; are you two twins?"

I nod.

"Why were you away from her at first?"

"I was adopted."

"But what about your parents?" Sasha asks. "Wouldn't you be staying with...." She pauses after making sense of the situation. "I'm sorry, that must not be a pleasant topic."

"It's not, but I'm ..."

I don't finish the response.

"But you're?" Sasha ponders at my lack of an answer.

"I'm—I'm trying not to think about it much," I tell her, truthfully. I'm trying not to think about it much.

I can't think about it at all. What is "Bynum" is gone—there's nothing I can do about that reality.

There's a pause in the conversation.

"Did I hear you had a long break from school?"

"Yeah, you did. And that's true—I just came back after two months or so of being out."

"Why were you out?"

At the question, Sasha seems almost dismayed. Her blue eyes widen, she looks around nervously—she doesn't know how to respond.

"It's okay, you don't have to tell me," I answer. "I understand."

"No, no, I can," Sasha refutes. "I can tell you. Can I follow you to lunch?"

"Sure, but is it alright if my sister and her technical sibling join?"

"Who's the sibling?"

"Beau Weizmann."

"Oh, yeah, sure," Sasha says. "That kid's about as weird as I am."

"What do you mean?"

"He's smart and creative, not to call myself that, but that makes a 'weird person'," Sasha answers. "I was kinda friends with him for a bit, but things fell off in our old friend group. That was late middle school and early freshman year—it doesn't matter now."

The conversation goes on throughout the class and until when we both walk down to an outdoor spot Ottie and Beau told us to meet at for lunch. Sasha talks about people at Redworth and I talk about GoldenPine, Juno, and James. The fog has cleared slightly, and the air is still misty and cool. The four of us, Beau, Sasha, Ottie, and I, all eat mediocre free school lunches whilst sitting at an outdoor table.

Beau looks over at Sasha. "I heard you were out for … what, two months before today; is that true?"

Sasha nods. I can tell that the topic still makes her nervous as she bounces her leg violently as she did during class when this same topic was introduced.

"Why were you out?" asks Beau, but then notices hesitation to answer as she begins to stutter and bounce her leg even more. "You don't have to ..."

"No, no," Sasha interrupts. "It's fine, I'll tell you." She sighs. "For a couple of weeks I was hospitalized."

"Oh shit," Beau comments, chewing his sandwich. He waits for a moment. "What happened?"

I mutter a few things. "Injured, or ...?"

"Not necessarily *injured*," Sasha responds. "There *was* an actual hospital involved, but ..." She pauses. "I don't know if that's necessary to talk about."

"Oh, you don't have to," Beau replies in reassurance. "I mean, it's intriguing, but ..."

"I *could* though," Sasha continues awkwardly. "As long as you wouldn't tell anyone. It's not disturbing—at least I don't think so."

"Is this psychological?" Ottie questions, tapping at her yellow canvas sneakers.

"Well, yes," Sasha answers. She straightens out in her posture, changing conversation topics. "Today has been weird; it's been really odd coming back to this building. I can't pay a lot of attention; I've been in my head."

"That makes sense, though," I add. "You were out for a while."

"Yeah, I guess so," Sasha continues. I can tell that her nervousness is worsening. "You may not understand. Or—sorry—maybe you do. I've had an issue with being quick to assume and do things; I've been trying to work on it."

"No, you're fine," I reassure her.

Across from me, I notice Beau's deep thinking about the situation. He eyes each of the three of us, then looks back at his tray of school lunch. The cycle continues, yet each time, each visual interpretation of the situation appears to affect his facial expressions and body language differently; he's confused by Sasha. I don't blame him, though I wonder if this hesitation to respond and nervousness is for a reason—and a large one at that.

Sasha finishes her turkey sandwich. "Everything has felt off recently," she repeats. "And I'm only halfway through the day. These things can't keep on plaguing my mind."

"These 'things'?" Beau asks for clarification.

"I think I can really best describe them as when you feel as if everything else around you is almost just ... insignificant?" Sasha answers. "And you feel like you should be somewhere else—doing something else. But then everyone wants to *keep* you from doing that." She pauses. "It may be because of me. My approaches to things annoy people, I feel."

"I understand what you mean by that," Ottie chimes in.

Sasha nods in consideration, then speaks again. "When I approach things where I'm trying to chase something, like an idea—a question—I don't know, it annoys people."

"What do you want to chase?" Beau asks. Is he feeling the same way regarding his essay and Janice?

"It's not clear anymore," Sasha answers. "And I wouldn't want to leave school for another couple of weeks again, so it's probably best that I don't chase it—whatever it is."

Beau looks at Sasha, concerned. "'Chasing something' is the cause of your leaving?"

"Yes," answers Sasha, "That's part of it."

Although Sasha is providing us with a multitude of responses, I still get the sense that she's not elaborating on them to the extent that she could be. And I get that; I don't expect descriptive responses and elaboration from a person whom I've only met today. But this introduction of ideas and feelings, specifically the feeling as though there's something "more" and something to "chase", are all sending me down a downward spiral of my own thoughts and interpretations. I don't fully understand it; I don't fully understand what Sasha is attempting to communicate, although I wish to.

Sasha continues to eat the rest of the food on her tray, and I can see in her eyes that the topic is further bothering her, although there is no discussion of it for a temporary period. I had imagined that the topic's bothersome elements were primarily internal a few moments ago, but they've started expressing themselves externally, meaning they most likely just now are *truly* ingraining themselves into her mind. After she stops eating, she blinks her eyes rapidly a few times in an attempt to clear her thoughts and pick up the pace of the moment.

"So, um ..." Sasha starts hesitantly, "Kaeda, you've only recently started going here, right?" She was already aware of my background—it's clear she's only asking me this to the conversation topic around.

My eyes shoot over to Sasha as she says my name. "Yeah," I respond.

"Funny," Sasha responds, "They only brought me back to this school today. Things have changed since I was last here."

"I wouldn't know," I say.

"Yeah, you wouldn't." Sasha sighs, her face falling into her propped up hands, looking at the clouded, gray sky for a moment. "Sorry."

Sasha's reluctance to even answer worries me.

She wraps herself in her purple hoodie. "Anyway, uh ..."

"Are you at all okay with talking about your hospitalization?" Beau asks, looking up from his tray table. His eyes appear to be genuinely invested, and it takes Sasha by surprise. "If you aren't, that's, you know, fine—"

"It's okay, I can," Sasha sighs. She begins to fidget with her shoelace. "I was at a mental institution. It's for a complicated reason—no psychosis or anything."

"And you were there for two months?" Beau asks.

"That wasn't the only place I went to," Sasha answers. "I was also hospitalized for a coma that resulted from a chemical imbalance. The coma was the reason for my mental hospitalization."

Beau's eyebrows knit. "How do those two work?"

"It's really, *really* complex," Sasha replies. "I don't know if I can say anything."

"Oh, man," Ottie adds, "That's odd."

"It was very weird," Sasha says. "It still is."

I look down at my shoes and think. A mental institution. *Huh.*

I think back to my dreams, yet then feel selfish in doing so. A mental institution. Hospitalized for two months, generally hospitalized at first. A mental institution afterward. *For what reason?* I don't know.

I'd feel bad asking.

I don't think I'll ask.

I still get the sense that there's something I need to ask Sasha, though. It might ask for the reason, but I can't do that. She's already stated that she doesn't know whether she can say anything.

How secretive is this entire situation?

Ottie continues to eat her food. She looks drained, staring and picking at the tray of food while looking at the sky with reluctance to speak to me for a reason that I think relates to my dream. The people sitting in this little circle we've created, I've noticed, look *miserable.*

And, by that, I'm referring to emotional states.

They look *drained.*

I wonder if I'm only an addition to the entire theme. Eventually, the lunch bell rings. The rest of my classes pass quickly—I'm only thinking about going back to the townhouse and laying down. I seem to have feelings of exhaustion and confusion, and if I think about my feelings anymore, I'm afraid that I'll lose my mind in questions.

The dismissal bell rings, shocking me out of my long period of zoning out in the last class of today. Raindrops that grow in intensity hit the building's windows. Beau and Ottie walk back to the bus with me as the raindrops hit the hood of my hoodie.

As we take the bus home, Beau naps and Ottie zones out with her headphones in. The surrounding students on the bus seem to do the same. I just watch as the town goes by in the window: the foggy, deep surroundings; the raindrops. The people. The lack of interaction between them.

Is it just my mind and hyper observance, or are they experiencing this same emptiness, too?

We get off the bus, Ottie, Beau, and I. Beau says a few words whilst Ottie seems to just be lost in thought. And, me? I don't know where I stand.

In the townhouse, I sit with Ottie in her room on the lower bunk while we both finish school assignments. She asks me of my opinions on Redworth High School, to which I tell her that I generally like it but have concerns about the lack of emotion shown in the people there, and she agrees with me in a sense that she takes five minutes explaining because it's difficult to pinpoint why exactly our surroundings feel off. She begins to talk about Sasha.

"There's something more to her, I'm telling you."

"I agree."

"A mental institution," Ottie starts. "Going from a general hospital to a mental hospital—how? Brain surgery? Witness of a hospital death? I don't understand what she means."

"Me neither."

Ottie pauses, closing a textbook of hers. "Things used to be a lot better when we were children," she tells me. "Though you may not remember it, it's very true. Everything was brighter and more vivid. Going from foster home to foster home was no issue; I had you, and that was all that I needed."

Ottie chokes up, holding in a soft cry. "I'm happy that I never lost you, Kaeda," Ottie tells me. "I'm happy that you never left permanently."

"I'm here for you," I reassure my sister, finding my tone awkward right after the fact.

"And that makes me thrilled, I promise," Ottie continues. "Even if you may not remember your childhood and our times together all that much, you're still here, and you're still Kaeda Saito. And I love my sister."

Ottie leaves her desk chair, walking up to me. She pulls me into a hug gently.

"Thank you for never leaving permanently."

I nod, then open my mouth to say something. Forgetting what that "something" is, I halt myself. I'm unsure of how to respond in these scenarios.

After finishing school assignments, dinner arrives and the townhouse residents eat Italian takeout at the circular kitchen table. Beau joins us at dinner about five minutes late after Janice had to wake him up. He's visibly exhausted.

"This kid doesn't sleep at night and ends up sleeping all day," Janice chimes. "You're nocturnal, Beau."

"No, no, I'm not," Beau refutes, "It's just that I wake up in the middle of the night."

"Dark room?" mocks Janice.

"No—dreams."

"Often, I wake up in the middle of the night because of those," I add, preventing Janice from insulting her son further.

After dinner, Beau showers and quickly falls back asleep in his room. I shower afterward and Ottie follows. After my shower, I walk downstairs to grab a glass of water, where I find Janice on the balcony of the townhouse, smoking with what appears to be a half-empty bottle of alcohol by her side. I don't intervene, and make my way upstairs, where I lay on the lower bunk in the dimly lit bedroom while Ottie sketches in her sketchbook. The night is quiet.

I fall asleep to the sound of Ottie's pencil marks above me.

Six

Tuesday, November 11, 2036, ?:?? AM.

I wake up.

Raindrops and a misty view of the outdoors are all I see through the window I find myself staring at. I sense a movement from below whilst I'm sitting down—I'm on a bus; it's about evening, I think. The cloud-filled sky seems to darken as portrayed by my view of it through the window; blue-hued tones surround my view.

The scene is peaceful—peaceful and quiet.

But it feels awfully as though that peace won't last.

The rest of the bus is darker—only illuminated by the light outside of the bus that shines through the windows. The raindrops that hit the bus window pick up their pace, increasing in volume. I don't know where I'm headed, but, wherever that place may be, I've brought nothing to accompany myself. There's no one here to accompany me, either.

The bus and its surroundings are uneventful and therefore calming, but can be perceived as ominous in their dark emptiness. We halt as the bus approaches a bus stop, opening its doors afterward, where someone enters. I can't see exactly who it is at first, and my pulse plays quickly in my ears, but their face soon becomes clear to me.

The individual who entered the bus is Sasha, and she carries a heavy, large backpack, struggling to make it inside as she fights the weight of her luggage. As she enters, I notice a hospital bracelet around her wrist. Under her eyes hangs dark eye bags—there's a distinct strong exhaustion plastered upon her face. She takes a seat behind me, dropping her luggage immediately; with that follows a loud "thud" and slight shaking of the bus.

"Oh, God ..." whispers Sasha in exhaustion. I glance over at her, and she looks back. "So damn heavy," she clarifies as if I may have been unaware.

I contemplate saying something to her, but I don't have to worry about that—Sasha says something to me instead.

"Do you take this bus often?" She asks me, still catching her breath. With the comment, my eyes wander the bus—a generic, city bus.

"I ... don't know," I respond.

"The last time I took this bus was a time that I don't quite remember," Sasha responds. "I couldn't even *tell* you what I remember if I wanted to."

"How so?" I ask. In my mind begs another question, though I don't speak it aloud.

Have you forgotten it all, as well?

"No, but I'm pretty sure that I know someone who has," Sasha responds with knowledge of my unspoken question. "Forgotten it all, I mean. I can't tell you because it's 'private information'."

"'Private information'?" I ask further. "How?"

"That's the thing," Sasha responds. "I don't know. Where are you getting off?"

I hesitate to answer.

"Uh ..."

"You're weird," Sasha goes on. "I'm weird. You don't understand the number of times that I've been told that I'm 'weird'. But, I can see it in you, too. You have a potential similar to my own, don't you?"

What is she saying?

The bus starts to rattle as if riding over a bumpy road.

"You're looking at me," Sasha notices, with a change in mood. "You're ... you're looking at me weirdly; I've seen that before. I've seen someone look at me, just like that, a long time ago."

The illumination the bus receives from outside dims.

"You've lost it, haven't you," Sasha speculates. "Look, I don't know how to differentiate what is real from what is not anymore."

"Lost it?" I ask, confused.

"You're slowly losing your mind," Sasha elaborates. "With questions. And I get that; often, I feel that is what is happening to me—in the hospital, especially. Being unconscious yet so painfully conscious was weird."

I tilt my head in further confusion. "I don't ..."

"You're right," Sasha continues. "This information doesn't apply to you. You'd know by now if it did."

What?

"What it really is, Kaeda," Sasha concludes, "You have questions you feel you need answers to, or you know you need answers to. What I can provide you with is kind of up in the air right now."

Before I have time to process any of the information that Sasha had just told me, the sky continues to darken, growing in desolation at a rapid pace, and the rain increases in intensity; it becomes louder each millisecond that I'm inside of here.

Louder, louder, louder.

I can't hear myself think. I can't hear—

"I'd suggest that you get out of here," Sasha tells me, raising her voice to overcome the sound of the rain. My surroundings begin warping into one another as I grow in dizziness and lose vision intensely. Nothing that surrounds me is intelligible anymore; each detail is impossible to make out. Right as my visions become the pinnacle of a blurred and overstimulating disaster, I can hear Sasha faintly yell as if she's been greatly injured.

A screech of *pain*. She wails; she wails and—

The dream ends.

My eyes open, and my body twitches. The room is hardly illuminated, only so by the dark, narrow blue hues barely shining through the blinds of the window. I haven't gathered the energy to roll on my side and look at the digital clock beside the bunk bed, but it's evident that it's nowhere near the time that I should be awake. However, I know one thing: with my current mental state, I cannot fall back asleep.

I notice the rapid pulse of my heart, traveling to different parts of my body as I lay silently awake in the quiet darkness. My dream has shocked me awake—I cannot help but acknowledge it. For a moment, I find a distinct disconnection from my own physical self. My hands appear unfamiliar to me. My body quivers in a cold sweat; my mouth is unbelievably dry.

The discomfort does not last long, however. As my hearing begins to properly return, the sound of raindrops hitting the window like faint firecrackers comforts my ears. Deciding that I've gained enough energy to move, I grab a cup of room temperature water from the nightstand aside from the bunk bed that I remember bringing here last night, and drinking it feels extremely refreshing. I finish the entire cup in a short amount of time. I turn to the digital clock:

5:04 AM

I lay back down, warming myself in the twin bed sheets as my arms grow goosebumps in the chilling temperature of the townhouse.

As I lay quietly, however, I hear a sound from above me on Ottie's bunk bed: a quiet sniffling, followed by a slight shake in the mattress as if she were crying.

Ottie's not asleep.

I don't want to call her name or ask her anything directly, so I move around the lower bunk mattress nonsensically and make noises to ignite concern within her, checking on the lower bunk. But it doesn't work, and I decide to whisper Ottie's name as if I'm asking her something, laying still on my bunk from below.

"Ottie?"

She doesn't reply, but the faint sound of rapid breathing in a sob from above stops.

"... Ottie?" I repeat. In my chest grows an ache, then a quick feeling of déjà vu—this has happened before.

"Are you okay?" I ask her.

"Why are you up," she asks blankly, as if she's upset at me.

"I can't fall back ..."

Ottie walks down the stairs of the top bunk to mine and sits on my bunk across from me. Though I can't see much of the rest of the room, the dim blue light from the window and its open blinds shines upon her face. The veins of her eyes are a deep red, creating absorption in the rest of the white of her eyes. Those same eyes are incredibly teary with deep eye bags hanging under them. There's a clear sense of exhaustion plastered upon her face. Her glasses are gone. Her hair is a mess. She looks sick, and not at all comfortable.

Her resemblance to me has never been more evident than it is now.

I look at her once more. The atmosphere of the room—the dim, blue lighting, the darkness of the hallway, and the sound of rain tapping against the window at a fast pace—only add to her melancholy appearance.

"Ottie ..." I start, hesitantly. I keep my voice at a low, quiet tone. "What's wrong?"

Ottie sniffles quietly as if she was holding in a sob. She tries to open her mouth to speak for a moment, but her voice only lets out a shaking crack, and she sniffles again. I look at the rest of the room, then back towards her. Her hands shake in complete anxiety. She tries to spit out quiet words again.

"I ..."

Her eyes rapidly travel to different places across the room, yet they still appear deadened in exhaustion. Her mouth quivers and her jaw tightens with deep nervousness.

"I can't ..." Ottie tries, her words coming out shakily. At the end of every word she attempts to speak sits a *crack*. A painful halt—a realization that you cannot go on. If you were to do so, you'd break down into a painful sob.

"I had a bad …" she tries again, cracking in between each word. She sniffles and her breathing rate increases both audibly and visibly.

She finally spits it out.

"I had a bad dream."

I widen my eyes at her. "What happened?"

In an attempt to breathe deeply, Ottie shakes and lets out a cracking sigh. "It wasn't …" she continues. "I saw things that …"

"What … what did you see?" I ask quietly with concern, the feeling of ache in my chest piercing me. "You can tell me—it's okay."

"I can't …" Ottie responds, her eyes swelling up with tears. "I can't … no, no, I can't tell …"

She continues to struggle.

"Kaeda, I …"

"They …"

"*Kaeda* …"

"I had a bad dream," Ottie repeats, this time more direct, still shaking at each breath taken. "A weird, *weird* dream."

"What happened?" I ask again.

"No, no …" Ottie quivers while speaking. "There were things … things from when we were kids. When you were adopted, and—"

"I can't," Ottie cuts herself off, shaking her leg violently against the bed's mattress. "Don't mind it, Kaeda. No more."

I repeat her name. "Ottie?"

"The caretakers," Ottie adds, misty-eyed. "They were bad, *bad* people. I'm sorry, I don't know if I can …"

Tears continue to build inside of her eyes and she continuously apologizes while rocking back and forth on the bed in extreme anxiety. An expression of concern on my face intensifies each time. Ottie's terrified, whether it be of the dream or something else that I can't decipher just yet. But the sight of it all deeply worries me. The amount of pain she appears to be in terrifies me. My throat closes in on itself in a shared nervousness after watching my sister struggle to think straight, and I take a silent gulp.

Ottie lets out a sob.

A quiet yet telling sob. Tears stream down her face. With every advancement in her melancholic break, my eyes start to tear up as well, but my facial expression does not change. I sit completely still, looking at my sister, as her face represents a clear helplessness. The mannerisms that she has in her painful sadness are strikingly similar to what I can remember of mine. All movements she makes—all the quivers that she lets out during her words—her way of dealing with the situation … each indicates that she is not at all in control of her thoughts and emotions.

My sister.

"K–Kaeda …" Ottie manages to crack out of herself. "Kaeda, I …"

"Ottie?" I ask again gently. "What happened in this dream?"

"It was a bad dream," Ottie responds swiftly. "You … no, you don't want to know."

I gulp down my questions, as hard as it may be. Ottie's tears hit her yellow graphic tee as well as the lower bunk's sheets. They stream down her cheeks in a quick manner, similar to the raindrops on the bus windows. They dry her eyelashes and eyes alike. And, with all of this, whenever she isn't speaking or attempting to—moving her eyes around the room in nervousness—her eyes convey absolute bleak *dread*.

"I feel terrible," Ottie tells me, quaking. "Kaeda, I felt so much pain; *I was so alone.*"

I look at her with intrigue following her response, indirectly encouraging her to continue in her thoughts.

"I couldn't think," Ottie continues. "I didn't … no, it wasn't true."

"What wasn't true?" I ask. "Ottie, you can tell me; it's okay."

"No …" Ottie cries. "You wouldn't want to know, I can't …"

"*Ottie?*"

"I can't tell you now," Ottie responds rapidly. "I couldn't believe any of it, and you wouldn't either. We should leave it alone."

"Any of *what*?"

Ottie gulps, shaking. Her hand moves back and forth in uncontrollable quivers as her leg bounces against the bed's frame. She visibly tries to calm herself, but it makes everything worse; she fidgets with the ends of the bedsheets.

I look at her, concerned again. "What is it I wouldn't want to know?"

"They—they told me ..."

"Who?" I question. I receive no response.

"They told me that you were ..."

She pauses again.

"They—they—"

Ottie struggles painfully.

"They told me—they told me that you were *dead*, Kaeda."

I look at her face with piercing confusion.

"*What?*"

"I don't know why."

"Who told you?" I ask.

"The caretakers."

"In the dream?" I ask.

"I mean, not just in the dream."

I tilt my head. "When did they tell you that I was ..."

"When you left," Ottie responds. "When you got adopted, and—and I wanted to see you, after a few years they told me that you were ... that you were *dead*."

I knit my eyebrows. "Why would they ever ..."

"Exactly," Ottie agrees. "It ruined me, and I couldn't believe any of it at all. You're alive. They were so rude to even ... why would they even—"

Ottie pauses, gathering her emotions.

"They must've hated me," Ottie concludes. "That *ruined* me. For a year I had gone mad. I was in denial. I haven't even told Beau and his mom. The caretakers—they hated me, so much, they told me that my own sister was dead just because I wanted to visit you and had questions. It's terrible."

"Holy shit," I say, concerned. "That's horrible."

"I couldn't fathom any of it," Ottie continues. "I couldn't ... I lost my mind. I lost *myself*. I can't go back to that time."

"I'm so sorry, Ottie."

"I don't know what I'll do."

The expression across Ottie's face seeps into my mind, producing inside of my mind a memory that I know I won't let go of although I may wish to. Her painful look of melancholy: her fingers clutched around the bed sheets as a way of fidgeting as her mind operates at an incomprehensible speed with incomprehensible nervousness. Her eyes, with a similar shape to mine: dry and weary. Her hair a mess. Her nose scrunching up occasionally in a sniffle to refrain herself from sobbing. Her mouth quivering at every painful realization that forms inside her mind.

Her.

A feeling of terror swells up inside of me, causing nausea within my stomach. Although I had very little knowledge of the memories between Ottie and I as children, causing much distress in her, I still felt and currently feel as though I have known her for years. I loved and love her like a sister, although she was never all that present in my memories. Not in the grounded ones, at least. Only in my dreams was she there.

And that thought leaves me wondering:

Is Beau experiencing the same thing?

I want to hug Ottie. The desire for me to do that is rarely present in my mind; she'll typically be the one to hug me, but seeing her like this, as her sister—it's all blurry. It all feels so *weird*. Her face, her mannerisms, her thoughts; they all resemble mine in one way or an-other as I continue to study them. The way she reacts to experiences such as this one—similar to me.

But I've never been told that my sister was dead, just for her to *not* be. And dealing with that *silently*. Sure, she's revealing it now, but she could have revealed that on Sunday as she met me. She could've revealed that to Beau and Janice when she first was adopted by them. The fact that she waited—the fact that she kept this inside, bottling it up—it only further resembles my actions and thoughts.

I love Ottie as a sister. I love her as a friend: an old friend with whom I parted due to a complicated situation.

And I give her a hug.

For a moment, I feel the shocked quake of her body. But that moment is brief, and she accepts quickly and holds me tightly in the hug. Her arms squeeze—somehow comfortably—around me. Her head rests against my shoulder. At every muffled sound of her sobs, she squeezes tighter. I continue to hug her, staring toward the wall against the lower bunk that we both sit on. Finally, I let my head rest on her shoulder as well, fully embracing the hug.

I've missed my sister. I've missed her subconsciously.

I've missed Ottie.

I've missed her, *subconsciously.*

She pulls out of the hug, wiping her tears on her shirt which is many sizes too large for her. I prefer the same sizes of clothing; It fits more comfortably.

"I'm so happy that I have you, Kaeda," Ottie concludes, sniffling between words. "You're a great sister, although you may not realize it."

"Thank you," I answer. "And the same applies to you."

The dim, blue light from the early morning surroundings shines onto her face once more through the window blinds. It's non-blinding. It's a comfortable light. However, it's sorrowful.

It's a familiar light.

It's a familiar scene.

A familiar setting.

A familiar sibling.

Knowing I will not be able to sleep for the rest of the morning, I leave the bedroom to make my way down to the townhome kitchen. Ottie decides to stay in her room, laying on her bed. On my way to the kitchen, I find Beau, laying down on the sofa with a blanket over him, napping. Though, because of the creaks made whilst I walk down the stairs, he wakes and notices me. I don't bother him and toast a bagel for breakfast, still within eye and earshot of him. He sits up, rubbing his eyes and yawning. I try not to question why exactly he fell asleep on the sofa in the first place—something new yet intriguing always appears to be with him, although I've only known Beau since Sunday.

"Kaeda, something *very* weird has been happening," Beau slowly says with a hoarse voice, still waking up yet already full of thought. "I can't shake these dreams. I can't ..."

I look over at him, arching my eyes in interest.

"I can't get that girl out of my brain," He admits, sighing. "She's only in my dreams, yeah, but she's in *every single one* of them. And those dreams are vivid. It's not even just an attraction to her, it's more of a complete ... intrigue. I'm intrigued by her personality. Yet I don't know who she is. I'd never seen her before. But I feel like ..."

He catches his breath, leaning back on the sofa.

"I feel like I *have*."

"Weird." I comment. "Is this the same—"

"Darker skin, defined nose, piercing green eyes," Beau describes swiftly. "Shorter black hair with bangs."

"And she's unnamed?" I ask. "She's never mentioned her name?"

"I know that she has," Beau responds, "But I can't recall what it was. I remember everything about her *but* her name. All provided to me in the dream, yet that's the thing that passes over."

"It's always the *one detail* that matters the most," I say. "The one piece left of the puzzle: that's what disappears. That's what can't be found. Yet everything else—all of those other seemingly insignificant details—bleed into every thought formed by your mind. Those details are eerie—those details signify the unknown."

And I'd like to know so much.

Beau looks at me, slightly shocked, as I am at myself for speaking my mind. "You know exactly what I'm saying," he says.

"Janice thinks I'm crazy," Beau continues, shaking his head. "She thinks *we're* crazy, really—we have similar experiences with dreams—but mostly me since I'm her son. It's understandable, I get it. She won't listen to me. Yet I feel as though it's all coming together, slowly, maybe, but—"

Beau stops himself.

"I'm losing it," He finally says, stiffening his hands.

As I take my plate to the sofa chair near where he sits, his eyes reek of dread, yet bounce across the room in anxiety. The blue 5 AM lighting of the windows decorates the townhouse living room with almost melancholic anguish, and studying his face almost adds to that. His pale purple eye bags almost make him appear as though he's bruised. But he doesn't add to his thoughts, he simply plops down onto the couch of the living room once more, sinking in exhaustion. All I can do is observe.

He clicks his lips, creating various, quiet sounds; but they aren't enthusiastic. His breathing is heavy and sorrowful; he's sighing between each sound. Paying attention to these details further emphasizes the struggles of people. Recently, with Beau, I've noticed that our dilemmas aren't all that different. On the surface they may seem like such, but, digging deeper, it's clear that they aren't.

The uncanny similarity of almost everything that appears inside of my mind—that's what lies at the heart of my dilemma.

I hear a person walk down the stairs, approaching the living room.

"You two?" Janice sighs, making her way down the stairs. "What are you doing up this early?"

I start. "I'm just—"

"Go to sleep," Janice demands, still half-asleep. "Go to sleep, now."

The two of us walk upstairs, Beau leaving the couch blanket and sleepily heading to his room. I find Ottie in her bedroom, still laying on her bunk bed, still looking at the ceiling. I lay at the bed beneath hers as usual. My eyes aren't tired—neither is my mind. I have to go to school today. Weirdly enough, I don't care to go to school today.

No one is sleeping; I hear a loud typing of a clack-y keyboard in the room beside mine as I face the wall laying down, lost in thought that I cannot make out. Lost in thought—thinking about what? I don't know, but it forms a pit in my stomach that I know is not hunger.

There's a giant void; there's something missing. And whatever's missing appears to be incomprehensible.

6:34 AM

Is the time at which it feels safe to walk into the kitchen whilst Janice sits on the couch. She assumes I had fallen asleep, and she assumes this same thing for Beau and Ottie when, in reality, the three of us were wide awake the entire time.

Janice almost seems to dead-eye Beau as he walks in, annoyed by his presence as she was yesterday morning during their argument. But I take Beau's side, and I don't understand why his mom doesn't. I don't understand *why* she doesn't care for what he has to say when it's all so interesting and holds great importance.

I grab a cold can of coffee and granola bar, setting them down on the round kitchen table as Beau finishes an energy drink, tapping against the glass of the table rapidly. He tries to speak, but every word he attempts to say is cut off by his mom, who wishes to change the topic. But her topics are uninteresting and unimportant whereas Beau's topics are intriguing and relevant.

Throughout the rest of the morning, Ottie remains silent. She's been dead silent ever since the conversation we had about my supposed "death", and I don't blame her for it.

Dead, Kaeda, the words repeat inside my mind. *They told me you were dead.*

Ottie's caretakers eventually grew so weary of her chaos to the point where they lied to her about her own sister's death completely to get her to shut up. That's what we assume had happened; that's what makes sense. *Yet it doesn't.* You'd have to be severely messed up to lie to someone about their sister's death in order for them to stay quiet.

That can't be the only reason they told Ottie that.

A misunderstanding?

After getting dressed, the three of us, Beau, Ottie, and I leave the townhouse and wait at the nearest stop sign for the school bus while carrying our backpacks. Ottie's is yellow, consisting of small yet meaningful keychains and pins from different sources, mine is black with a San Francisco keychain, and Beau's is a deep red color with a small pin from Band. Given the time of day, it's quiet outside. Dark, deep blue skies remain full of clouds. A light rain accompanies us. It's an empty yet beautiful sight.

As the bus halts to a stop near us, we take our turns entering and take seats, mine being next to Ottie's with the window seat and Beau sitting in front of us. Nobody seems to say anything. Eventually, we arrive at Redworth High School.

"I hate this place," Beau mutters under his breath as we walk toward the entrance. "Sky looks cool today, though."

I nod my head, staring up at the dark, low clouds while gentle raindrops fall upon my shoulders.

The next few periods, until fourth, are mediocre as usual. As I enter fourth period, I'm met with Sasha sitting in the same seat as before. I sit at the desk next to her.

Meeting Sasha once again after the dream I had last night involving her ignites confusion yet intrigue within me, and I can't help but think to myself that there's much more to this girl.

"I think I'm ready to clarify everything during lunch." Sasha tells me right before class starts. She says nothing following this for the entire class period—we only focus on assignments. But I still wonder; my knee bounces in anticipation to know what her clarifications are. As class ends, the two of us follow one another to the same spot outside as usual and take a seat at the outdoor bench with Ottie and Beau.

"I want to skip these next few classes," Ottie says, exhausted. "I can't seem to focus at all."

"Sleep through them, maybe," Beau suggests.

"I can't sleep, that's the thing," Ottie says, taking a bite out of her school food.

Sasha takes a sip of water out of a bottle. She stretches, taking a deep breath before speaking. "Man," she starts, "Right out of leaving the hospital, I'm already doing something that the doctors told me not to do."

"What?" Ottie questions, "Talking to us?"

Sasha nods. "Yeah," she answers, "Talking about my experience not necessarily *in* but *out* of the coma." Sasha pulls out two hospital bracelets from her blue backpack's front pocket, pointing to one. "From the general hospital while I was in a coma," she says, then points to the other. "And the mental hospital."

I lean in to get a closer look at the two. Beau and Ottie do the same.

"Anyway," Sasha continues, putting the bracelets away. "I need you three to promise me something."

I tilt my head.

"I need you all to promise me that you won't take this information and tell everyone and their mother," Sasha continues. "I need you to promise me that you won't run around with what I tell you and let the entire world know."

"As long as the information you're telling us is truthful," chimes in Beau.

"I promise you, it's what I heard and what I can remember," Sasha answers. She finishes her tray of school food, pushing it away from her as she speaks once more.

"Alright," Sasha starts, "Because my coma was vegetative, I could hear everything around me without being able to see or react to any of it. The doctors didn't know this because there was absolutely zero physical reaction to their touch or the noises they would make, but my brain was active enough where I could hear my surroundings, dream, visualize, and remember most of it."

Beau reacts visually with concern. "That must've felt insanely weird."

"Yeah," Sasha responds, "It did. But, however, I remember hearing something from the doctors. It wasn't a dream—I could differentiate authentic experiences from dreams a few days after I woke up. Now, it *could have* been a hallucination, but I'll just—"

"What happened?" I ask, then realizing that I've cut Sasha's thought off completely with a thirst for knowledge. "I'm sorry, I didn't mean to …"

"It's fine," Sasha reassures. "During my coma, I heard a few discussions between either doctors or scientists about what they'd do if I were to die. Some of them thought I would, and I remember them talking about taking my DNA; then I remember the process of them actually doing it."

"And what would they do with your DNA?" Beau asks.

"They talked about taking it to a lab and going through with a 'procedure'," Sasha replies. "I remember them repeating 'the procedure' a lot."

"Did they ever clarify what the procedure was?"

"The procedure …" Sasha mutters, thinking to herself. "Oh." She pauses, collecting her words. "One of them talked about putting the DNA in some lab capsule and copying it. Taking the DNA, copying it, and something about my brain."

"What?" I ask.

"I remembered more before the mental hospital," Sasha says. "But I've been trying to preserve my memory of it all. This is the most I can give you right now."

"Why would they want to copy your DNA?" Beau asks. "Not insulting you."

"No, I didn't think it was supposed to be an insult," Sasha replies. "I don't know why, actually."

"That's not how morgues work."

"Well, that's not what doctors do with a body after death," I chime in. "Unless you consent to donate organs for studies. You didn't say that they could use your bodies for science, right?"

"I never remember them talking about that."

"So the *only* discussion that they had about what would happen to you if you were to die was that discussion?" I ask further.

"Yeah, from what I can remember," Sasha says.

"I need more confirmation" I blurt harshly, completely without thinking, making the entire series of questions seem like only pawns for interrogation. The situation suddenly sends a wave of confusion over me, and it's then that I notice my knee bouncing in nervousness.

A look of shock crosses Sasha's face.

"I'm sorry, I didn't mean to come off so strong," I apologize.

"It's not your fault, don't worry," I say. "I don't know why I'm so worked up about this."

One thing I noticed about Sasha when I met her was her round facial features. I first noticed the expressions that she'd have and how these expressions would play out on her face; her face and its expressions as well as her general appearance in what she'd wear seemed almost innocent to me. Now, her messy appearance has caused me to think otherwise; her baggy, unkempt clothing and that same messy appearance have told me she's experienced many hardships and emotions. But, even in this, I still see a sort of innocence or gentleness within her; it's almost as though she matured too quickly due to experiences. It's almost as though Sasha wasn't ready for what awaited her in her life.

My curiosity digs a pit deep in my stomach.

Was I slightly insensitive in wanting to know more about what Sasha had gone through, almost portraying myself as an interrogator? Her experiences cannot be nice to reflect on and speak about, can they? Therefore, why would I keep on asking? Why do I *want* her to talk about all the shit she's gone through to me?

Why do I want to know so terribly?

I'm unsure whether I'm the only one feeling this way. Beau seems to have the same curiosity, but it's almost as though I'm craving something that I can't fully receive.

Knowledge.

It's knowledge that I crave, and it's knowledge that I can't fully receive.

I look over at Beau, watching him create small talk with Sasha, trying to comfort her. But, as I observe him more, I see dread in his eyes. Truly, I think he's simply trying to push through the situation despite his questioning and concerns. I don't think he's entirely positive about how to go about asking Sasha questions or discussing topics concerning her, either.

I see Ottie, sitting in almost complete silence, isolating herself mentally whilst trying to interpret everything around her. I see her attempting to make connections she cannot fully understand yet. Every so often, she'll stop zoning out and will try to ground herself back into reality, nearly asking Sasha a question or bringing up a topic. Then, it appears to fade from her mind. She's still stuck on the events of this morning, and for that, I don't blame her.

I see Sasha, anxiously bouncing her knee whilst sitting at the bench, similar to how I do. I watch as she attempts to calm herself down after unveiling information she never assumed she would grow confident enough to bring to surface in her mind again. I watch as she tries to comfort herself and contemplate how to approach Beau, somewhat attempting to help her in order to alleviate the situation. I feel horrible for her.

But what am *I* truly feeling?

I can't see myself. I can't observe myself. I can't even rationalize the emotions I'm experiencing—I can't even begin to categorize or create a label for them. I can't seem to set aside what would make sense for me to feel versus what I'm truly feeling. I can't fully understand myself or my emotions.

I feel as though my questions—my unanswered, debilitating questions—have suddenly become *important*. The notebook page that I haven't touched in what now appears to be forever; I feel as though that has become externally—not just internally—important.

I wonder if I could figure things out if given the chance.

I think I could help myself figure things out.

I think I'm going to try to figure things out.

I want to help Sasha.

I want to help Ottie.

I want to help Beau.

I want to help myself.

And I don't think that any of the people listed above are okay.

In the townhouse, Janice smokes a cigarette on the balcony. As we walk in, she conceals it for a moment as if we hadn't noticed and walks inside, smelling of tobacco. Looking at her face, I notice deep, purple eye bags hanging under her eyes and a general face of great exhaustion. She works a fulfilling data science job from home as Beau tells me, but has been on leave ever since she's taken me in and I believe will remain on leave for the next two-or-so days.

"Kaeda!" Janice says, greeting me. "How was school?"

She's slurring her words slightly, an incentive to let me know that she's had too much alcohol, but I nod in response: a way of saying "it was good" as a lie in order for her to not bother me. After this, I figure I'd clarify instead of being rude.

"It was good," I say. "I'm tired, though. I think I'll go upstairs and finish my assignments."

I go upstairs with the purpose of sleeping. Beau goes into his room, and Ottie follows me without a word. She seems completely disconnected from reality, no different from this morning or during lunch. She zones out at practically everything crossing her path, completely in thought and possibly thinking of a dream; a dream resurfacing a confusing, painful memory.

These actions of silence and deep thought are unlike how Ottie's personality was first presented to me and what I had experienced primarily in my dreams, but they are similar to what I do in reaction to these painful situations. They remind me of who Ottie is to me: my sister. It's those same similarities in how we think and how we respond to certain things that remind me of how we are related and bring to surface the memories that were once only hinted at in my dreams. It's those same similarities that mute the thoughts and questions that decrease any sanity in my brain.

The similarities between Ottie and I and how I notice them increase my sense of self-identity and clarity, if there is any sense of clarity.

Truthfully, I don't know if there is.

I fall asleep.

I wake up.

The chill of the scene—wherever I am—crawls through the air and up my skin. A short gust of wind, my senses adapt to the scene and my vision grows brighter.

The Bynum house.

I didn't want to come back here; I didn't. I didn't want to relive that—that *time*. That *memory*.

That *death*.

But, as I glimpse around the area, I notice that there is no sign of Michelle here—attached to an IV and laying on a death bed or not. My surroundings are as desolate as I remember them; they consist of a seemingly empty house with empty shelves and empty chairs. Aside from me; I lay on the couch with a blanket over me—most likely to rid myself of the house's low temperatures. It's dead in the night; I must have fallen asleep here—here on this couch. But the scene; the scene is strikingly similar to one my mind has played for me during my sleep before.

I wait for the faint noises of arguing between Frank and Michelle from down the hallway and into the master bedroom, but they do not come.

What is of this desolate scene that is significant, or am I here for the sake of not forgetting who I was as a Bynum?

A brief gust of wind washes over me once again. It must have a source—I leave the couch and check for any open windows nearby. There's one near the kitchen; I'll go close that.

As I move closer to the window, however, a piece of notebook paper that appears to have words written on it softly flies into the house with the gusts of wind blowing through the window.

I pick up the paper and read its contents.

It has some.

Kaeda Bynum??/??/34

I'm waiting for a sign here. Genuinely, I am. I know that I'm not superstitious, but this altered reality that I'm living in is giving me no hope for a rational, logical world. I've begun creating connections that I would find nonsensical. I've lost grasp

I've seen this before. There was less to the page last time—there were less words and—

A sharp pain pierces my stomach. I stare at the paper with an expression that I cannot see, but I'm aware of it nonetheless: a confusion. Slight arch to the eyebrows, slight frown of the face; mostly bleak, yes, but confused. Intrigued.

"I'm waiting for a sign here. Genuinely, I am. I know that I'm not superstitious, but this altered reality that I'm living in is giving me no hope for a rational, logical world. I've begun creating connections that I would find nonsensical. I've lost grasp"

??/??/34

Clutching my stomach, I put the paper down on the kitchen counter in front of me.

"I'm waiting for a sign here. Genuinely, I am. I know that I'm not superstitious, but this altered reality that I'm living in is giving me no hope for a rational, logical world. I've begun creating connections that I would find nonsensical. I've lost grasp"

??/??/34

"I'm waiting for a sign here. Genuinely, I am. I know that I'm not superstitious, but this altered reality that I'm living in is giving me no hope for a rational, logical world. I've begun creating connections that I would find nonsensical. I've lost grasp"

"I've lost grasp"

I wake up.

In the blanket of the lower bunk, drool on my cheek and pillow, I wake up. There are sleep lines all over my arms: little pink and red indents on my skin. The fabric of my shirt is light against my body. *Peace.* But also confusion. There's a strong feeling of detachment from the world—I can't tell what day it is.

I can hear the raindrops against the window; they create a light sound. The faint light from the townhouse hallway shines through the tiny crack of the door—that and the deep lighting from the window are the only things illuminating this place. It's dark. I can't hear anything happening from downstairs—the raindrops are like white noise.

What time is it?

I turn to my side and glance at the alarm clock, still adjusting my eyes.

8:23 PM.

I fell asleep around 3 to 4 from what I can remember, only getting home a moment ago.

I can't seem to take time into full consideration as of now; it *feels* like another day—a feeling that is strikingly transcendent of reality.

I push the blankets off of myself and stand up, grabbing my glasses and putting my hair up so that it looks somewhat contained. I walk downstairs with sore legs and to the living room, where Beau sits outside on the balcony with Ottie. I assume Janice is in her bedroom. Before walking out onto the balcony to join my sister and Beau, I grab a glass of water.

The rain makes for a calming sight outside. Ottie glances over at me as I meet them, her face expressing subtle relief that I'm here and awake. Beau gives me a nod as a greeting.

"You were *out*," He tells me as I sit down on a balcony chair, thankfully protected by an awning. "Out like a light."

"Looked comfortable, though," Ottie adds. "We were just talking about Sasha."

"Sasha Walker?" I wonder.

"Yeah, the girl at lunch," Beau answers. "She was admitted to a mental institution. What do you think went wrong?"

I shake my head. "I mean, I don't exactly know," I tell Beau. "She seems hesitant to respond to questions. Very cautious in how she responds, but not cautious enough to avoid the question entirely."

Beau nods. "And you think that this might be because ..."

"Mental institutions typically silence you," I finish. "Doesn't tell us what exactly went wrong, but I think that experience was the primary cause of how she responded. Either that or she was just told to not say anything."

"You're right," says Ottie.

"She's used to staying silent is what I think," I continue. "Because staying silent is what they taught her to do. And when you're taught to stay silent and you're suddenly brought into an environment where you have the freedom to express your thoughts, you become hesitant because of how they had treated you before."

I see the wheels turning in Beau's head, and he glances back toward the view. "Damn," He says. "Have you ever been in a situation similar to that?"

"I don't think so," I reply. "Or, I don't know. But it makes sense. You know what I mean?"

Beau tilts his head for a second. "Huh," he pauses. "I understand. Sometimes, I'll feel like I have a weird amount of knowledge for things that I don't even, well—"

Cutting off Beau, we all hear Janice's voice from the kitchen, asking Beau to assist with something concerning dinner. He grabs his energy drink and hurries inside. Sitting, Ottie turns to me.

"I missed those connections that you used to make, Kaeda," Ottie tells me. "They're darker now, yet still intelligent; though that may just be because of the fact that we've grown up. Still, I really do wonder what happened in the past couple of years that you've been gone. Almost kind of wish that I could have witnessed it: seeing you grow up and stuff."

I nod. "Yeah, I understand," I tell her. "It's been painful—not being able to remember much from my childhood."

"That makes sense. I hope that's a shared view of things," Ottie continues. "I really do. I don't know, maybe someday you'll be able to fully remember what it was like being a kid with me. Sometimes I feel like I haven't parted or grown from those memories of being kids. I'm not sure if I like that fact or not."

I look back toward the rainy view of the neighborhood and nod at her comment. Ottie, with a slight look of disappointment, stands up from her chair and walks inside. Was I lacking in a response?

"I should probably go back inside now," she comments. "I'll see whatever Beau's doing and stuff."

I nod again. Time and time again, I think of how I've disappointed Ottie with my lack of communication or knowledge toward her, but I know that I can't fix this easily—especially still recovering from the state of a long nap. I can't simply bring back what I've—for the most part—forgotten. I can't fix the past if I barely know what the "past" is.

I've lost grasp.

I grab my water and walk back inside. It's only nine now, yet exhaustion still plagues me.

Upon finishing my water, I change into clothes that are slightly more comfortable to sleep in, lay on the lower bunk, and fall asleep.

Seven

Wednesday, November 12, 2036, ?:?? AM.

I wake up.

There's a quiet yet very noticeable sound of a house's air conditioning and a chilling sensation on my skin.

I open my eyes and my senses adapt to the scene, where I'm met with visions of a bedroom similar to ones I've seen before yet clearly different. The interior of the room is different—emptier, now—the walls of the room are a different color; the style is of general difference. Fewer pictures accompany the walls of this bedroom. For the pictures that are there, there are different images: one of a family that is of a different size than the last family pictures I can remember finding in a bedroom out of all of the different ones I've visited. I know where I am; I know who is with me. A foster home bedroom and Ottie.

The noise of the air conditioning is not the only faint sound I notice; as the scene becomes clearer and the pictures on the wall become less of a blur, I notice a vague crying noise and a familiar one at that. Its source is a twin bed only a dresser length apart from my own, with a younger Ottie mostly wrapped in floral-patterned childish bedsheets. She cries into the sheets, gasping for air in an attempt to collect herself and sniffling with each sob. Near her bed at the other side of the bedroom is a child-size body mirror that I can vaguely see myself in—I'm as young as she is, to no surprise. We both wear similar pajamas; the room is incredibly dark aside from the illumination of street lamps peering through the window blinds. Fully adjusting to the scene, I hear not only the sobs of young Ottie but a mumbling of words that becomes clearer to me as I listen in.

"What have they done," young Ottie first mumbles, sniffling. "What have they done?"

The urge to investigate overwhelms me, then a sense of great hesitation.

"What have they done to her?" she cries. "What ... what have they done to my Kaeda?"

My feet hit the cold carpet floor of the bedroom and ignite a slight shiver with the action.

"My sister ..." Ottie continues, "What happened to her?"

I find myself walking over to her bed and developing a strong sense of concern. With each step, the scene becomes less clear and sensical to me, and the noises of Ottie become more evident and audible.

"I miss you, Kaeda," mumbles Ottie. "What have they done, making you feel this way?"

I come as close to the bed as possible; my vision of the scene has never been more extreme. With a strong feeling of dizziness, the refractions of light through the window blinds become warped, the floral pattern of Ottie's bedsheets becomes less clear, and the sounds of the air conditioning alter from incredibly loud to incredibly quiet. *Panic*—I cannot make sense of my surroundings.

Two things remain clear within my view, however: Ottie and I.

I look into the child-size body mirror of the bedroom nearest to Ottie's bed as I had briefly done before, then to notice a sick difference with myself.

A sick being.

A pale face of much confusion. Blood coming from my nostril. A sick being, a confused being, someone who is both myself and not.

Both myself and not.

My knees begin to tremble at the sight—nothing is clear anymore. *A sick being.*

And the scene changes.

Beneath my feet and against my body sit a familiar movement or series of movements that I can directly pinpoint: those of a train. Surrounding me are the faint sounds of one, too. As my vision begins to develop, I notice the emptiness of the moving train and the time of day: early in the morning, when the sky is a deep blue and almost everyone sleeps. The advertisement signs—typically minimalistic yet captivating, or corporate for lack of a better term—are either blank or unintelligible, yet still illuminated. The scene is similar to those I've seen or experienced before—each train ride feels like its own recurrence.

The scene could be interpreted as peaceful, though I still find myself feeling sick. As I sit on one of the many window seats of the subway train's cars, I look outside for a brief moment and notice my reflection, to which I almost feel nauseous. The image of a youthful version of me with a confused, horrified, and somehow simultaneously blank, pale face with a bloody nose crosses my mind. But, as nausea fades, I see myself: Kaeda Bynum Saito.

A version of myself that I can remember directly before I went to bed; wearing an oversized white San Francisco t-shirt, gray pants, and white socks as pajamas. The urge to both sob and hurl is gone as I recognize who I am and what I am not: *sick.*

At least I hope.

The train comes to a stop at an unnamed nearby train station, where a girl in baggy clothing with her hair tied messily waits on a bench. She keeps her head up, staring at the sky, hoping with eyes whose bags emphasize them that search the clouds for some inspiration. I notice the girl almost immediately as the train makes its halt.

The girl is Sasha Walker, and she looks no different from how I had last seen her.

As Sasha boards the subway, she greets me similar to how she does in class each day, carrying nothing with her. Walking to sit next to me at my spot, however, I notice both hospital bracelets on her wrists. The subway doors close, the train leaves the station, and Sasha starts to speak to me.

"I want to understand you," says Sasha. "I do. You seem similar to me in how you think and act, yet so strikingly different."

I don't respond, though I do notice that Sasha is looking for me to do so. I want to, but am left without words to say—the statement confuses yet intrigues me at the same time.

"Why is that?" Sasha follows up. "Why do we feel similar?"

I don't respond again. It causes a minor headache as I know that my lack of response is contradictory to my desire to speak to Sasha, who leans back in the subway passenger seat.

"I think you ask questions similar to my own," continues Sasha. "You're eager to know—it's easy to tell. Is this true?"

Looking out the window and at the moving early morning landscapes, I muster up a nod, just now noticing that I am still subconsciously shaken by the previous sequence of events before the train.

"I'll have you know that my life since my time in a coma has not at all been easy."

I nod again.

"But I think you need to sit with the questions you ask, although they seem to make your not-easy life harder."

I nod again, but there's a pause in Sasha's responsiveness. She wants the statement to seep into my mind. Or, is that her, *but my own subconsciousness who wishes for that?*

The train comes to another stop, where Sasha waves me a "goodbye" and leaves as she claims she has places to be, which is weird considering the time of day. I don't think about it; it's not supposed to make sense.

I wake up to a disturbance of some kind, with no energy left in my body to lean over and check the alarm for the time of day. I'm still unaware of whether I'm dreaming, though I hear footsteps at a growing distance from me at the end of the bedroom and see an unalarming familiar figure with them. The bedroom door appears more cracked open than usual, and a faint light turns on from downstairs, creating an almost minuscule yet considerable amount of illumination into the bedroom. The sound of rainfall is loudest to me as I lay in the lower bunk bed of the incredibly dark bedroom, but becomes quieter and quieter as I fall back asleep.

I wake up again.

5:43 AM, the digital alarm clock beside me on a nightstand reads as I gain the energy to move and check the time. The sound of rainfall that I heard in what I believe was consciousness and not a dream is still prevalent, falling against the bedroom window with a noise reminding me of firecrackers, only quieter. The room is chilly and the blanket that lay over me does not deviate from its area's temperature. Looking beyond the lower bunk, I notice that the door is slightly open and the light from downstairs is turned on, something unusual as Ottie prefers sleeping with the bedroom door closed. I kick the cold blanket off of my body and move off of the lower bunk and quietly check above, where Ottie would usually be sleeping. She's not there.

Why is she downstairs this early?

Taking my blanket with me and putting on my glasses that sit on the nightstand, I walk outside of the bedroom and down the stairs quietly. As I reach the bottom, I quietly grab Ottie's attention.

"Ottie?" I say. I hear a hurried movement, then a response.

"Yes?" Ottie answers, responding at a louder volume than I had called her in. I walk toward the living room, where I heard her, and find her sitting on the couch seemingly uncomfortably, almost as if something was hurting her back. As for her appearance, she looks incredibly sleep-deprived with deep eye bags, messy hair, and a drooped face as though she's sick. Still, amidst this, she looks at me with an alert expression and eye contact. The contrast between this makes me feel uneasy and as though she's hiding something; Ottie doesn't seem like a good liar.

I sit on the living room chair next to the couch Ottie sits on. Her eyes follow me in the process.

"What are you doing down here?" I ask her. "It's early."

"Um, nothing in particular, really," she responds, uneasy. "Why do you ask?"

"I noticed you were gone," I answer. "And the door was open, which was unusual."

"How was your dream?" Ottie asks me, diverting my attention from the topic.

"I mean, it's not important right now," I say. "But I just want to know why you're down here so early."

Sitting on the living room chair for long enough, I notice an odor that's similar to Janice's at times, specifically after she's drunk alcohol. Beau mentioned it to me once.

"I mean, not much really," answers Ottie, fidgeting with her hands and bouncing her knee—nervousness.

There's an uncomfortable pause in the conversation.

I decide to speak up and hopefully rid the area of the strong awkwardness that surrounds it. "You don't seem to be sitting comfortably," I say to Ottie, hinting at the possibility of her hiding something, specifically a bottle, behind her back as it looks abnormally arched.

"I don't know why that would be."

"Is there something behind you at all?"

Ottie feels behind her back for something, visibly in thought during the process. She does this for an uncomfortable amount of time, as though she's planning a response. She pulls a half-empty bottle of whiskey from behind her.

"I found this earlier," Ottie tells me. "Janice was drinking. Isn't that sad?"

"Why didn't you show me that when I first came down here?" I ask her.

"I didn't want to incriminate myself when you looked at me," Ottie responds. It's an obvious lie; she makes zero eye contact with me and her hands visibly tremble as she holds the bottle. "Sorry, I should've shown you earlier."

There's an awkward pause in the conversation again. I decide to speak up once more.

"Ottie?" I say to her.

"Yes?"

"Was that bottle truly Janice?"

"Yeah," Ottie responds with a quiver. "Why wouldn't it be?"

Another awkward pause follows the conversation.

"Because you don't just ..." I start, "... you don't just come down here early in the morning and hide a bottle of whiskey behind your back once your sister walks downstairs."

"Huh?"

"That just doesn't really happen," I clarify, recognizing my explanation was awkward.

Ottie pauses. "Kaeda ..."

"Were you drinking, Ottie?" I ask her.

"Kaeda!"

Ottie looks at me, disheartened and sleep-deprived. She still fidgets with her hands, the whisky bottle on the coffee table in front of us. I hold eye contact with her for long enough, unknowing of how I'm presenting my facial expression, and Ottie's eyes start to fill with tears—I hope I wasn't intimidating my sister. Her suppression of truthful emotions and statements breaks, and she sobs. The rest of the world seems quiet as she hangs her head downwards in a state of vulnerability, so incredibly similar to yesterday morning. I leave the sofa chair and sit on the couch, moving close to her to let her know that I'm not shaming her.

"I'm here for you," I tell my sister, attempting to comfort her.

Ottie wraps her arms around me and continues to sob. "I was drinking," she musters out, "I was drinking and I ..."

She sobs harder. With each breath she takes and faint wail in her sob that follows, I hold her tighter.

"It's okay," I tell her quietly, attempting once more to comfort her.

"And I had a bad dream last night," Ottie tells me, sniffling in an attempt to collect herself as she cries.

"About the same thing as yesterday?" I ask softly.

"About everything," Ottie responds. "Your ... your 'death', that time in my life, Sasha's questions, Beau's experiences, your experiences, and, and I don't want to bring this up, but how you can't remember a lot from when—from when we were kids ... everything is so overwhelming and I ..."

She pulls me in closer and sobs into my shoulder, her tears falling onto and through my shirt.

Ottie continues. "And I hate it, but I feel like things are just getting so much worse and it's all so weirdly similar to before and—" she stops to collect herself in her sob, "And I can't take that. After the dream I had I hated everything so much and was so scared and I thought about how Janice is so blinded to every problem when she drinks. And I felt like I needed that, so I came down here, and I started drinking one of her many bottles of whiskey. I hate it so much, Kaeda. I hate feeling this way. I don't know why I thought this would solve anything."

I don't know how to respond just yet and, while that causes me to feel awkward, I understand that if I tried, I'm likely to escalate the negativity of the situation. I wait for Ottie to say the next thing, still embracing her.

"I'm sorry for getting tears on your shirt and bringing up the fact that you can't remember much," she apologizes. "It hurts sometimes, and I thought that maybe you'd like to know all the reasons I was drinking. I don't know."

"It's okay," I tell her. "I'm here for you."

I try my hardest to not be awkward in my ways of comforting.

With the chaos I've been experiencing the last couple of days, I want to reminisce on what life was like before I moved in with Ottie. But I can't. I can try to convince myself that I might've been happier, but I wasn't. I was living with a parent who never talked to me and was primarily alone with the exception of Juno and James. And, even then, I didn't feel like I had proper company. I like to be alone, but I don't like to feel lonely. And, at the time, I was lonely—Michelle and I were both lonely, though we lived together.

As Ottie begins to walk upstairs to the bedroom briefly thereafter, I say something to her.

"I wish I could remember all that you can of when we were kids."

Her head turns towards me, and she halts her steps on the stairs.

"... I just wish that I had the same recollection as you do," I clarify after a pause. "I don't know."

Ottie walks down the stairs and back into the living room, sitting at my couch. I look at her with a slightly confused expression, tilting my head somewhat—unaware of what her motives are. Then, I quickly realize them.

She hugs me.

I rest my head on my sister's shoulder, her arms wrapped around me in a hug. She says nothing yet everything simultaneously. She hugs me—she lets me know that it's okay.

It's okay to feel—it's okay to feel as someone who rarely expresses their feelings.

It's okay.

Just then, I notice the tears on my cheek that travel to the shoulder fabric of Ottie's t-shirt.

"It's okay," she says to me quietly, gently rubbing the back of my t-shirt. "It's okay."

I repeat the words to myself.

It's okay. It's okay.

I spend the next hour eating a quick breakfast meal and preparing for school, as the mornings have been since Monday. I wear an outfit that doesn't deviate largely from the others I've worn for the past two days to Redworth: a gray San Francisco sweatshirt, black sweatpants, and white sneakers. The morning is quiet as Ottie moves through the day in an uncomfortable silence after the incident with her and the whiskey bottle, Beau groggily gets ready whilst seeming detached from reality, and I don't make any comments. None of us, from what I know, have any resentment towards each other, no, but the silence is inevitable when you feel exhausted already each morning due to some vivid dream or uncomfortable thought sequence and have nothing else to say; each morning is similar.

As we take the bus to school, I notice Ottie micro-sleeping on the seat next to mine, completely worn-out although it's only 7 AM. I don't imagine she received any proper sleep last night, in and out of a dream; I know how that feels: debilitating. I think the whole sleep deprivation idea is new for Ottie after events of the past resurfaced; this is a logical line of reasoning behind her recent vivid dreams—I don't feel as though there is any logical line of reasoning for mine.

The first few periods of school are as usual: I sit and observe, completing all my work during the class so that I don't need to do it later. Fourth period with Sasha is quiet since we have an independent project we work on that disallows talking and only promotes work, though I can tell that she has many thoughts on her mind. Her knee bounces, she glances over at me a few times in an attempt to start a conversation but remembers that she cannot effectively do that, and she drinks a can of coffee which only enhances these actions. As we walk to lunch to meet with Ottie and Beau, she makes comments about the school's atmosphere and people, mentioning that she feels like an outsider, especially after her time being hospitalized. She also mentions that she has a lot to say today during lunch. The grass of the school's campus is misty and wet after this morning, along with the outdoor table benches, in which we wipe off the raindrops with napkins.

As we sit at the table and begin eating our trays of food, I ask Sasha a question concerning her t-shirt reading "Klamath", a national forest in a very northern part of California.

"Did you live up north?" I ask Sasha. "I noticed your shirt."

She nods. "With my dad," Sasha answers. "I've always lived with just him. I miss the north, but he got a job down here and we moved."

I nod, and Sasha continues.

"I kind of wish that I was still living up north," Sasha says. "Ever since I came down here to the Bay Area, I've just felt like everything has been weird. Our house was cabin-like; it was very cozy."

"Where was your mom?" Beau asks.

"Oh, she died when I was four," Sasha responds. "It's okay, though—I don't remember a lot from that time other than it being very hard on my dad. Since that incident, I've noticed my dad changing over time."

"How?"

"He's become very involved in anatomical studies," Sasha answers. "He's not too academically inclined, but I remember him gaining a large amount of interest in anatomy and science."

"That's interesting," I comment.

"Yeah, I kinda thought so," Sasha says. "But since then, it's been all he knows and all I really know of him. He works in researching human biology now at a lab."

"How'd your mom die?" I ask.

"I remember it being a car crash," Sasha says. "A very sudden accident is what my dad tells me."

"I'm so sorry," I say.

"It's okay, it's been a while."

"I would expect some sort of disease if your dad started studying anatomy because of her death," Ottie chimes in.

"I understand that," Sasha says. "I don't know, he never elaborated much on her death and much on her at all since I was so little when it happened. It's been me and him over the years where I've truly developed and remembered everything, so things went with little explanation."

I nod in understanding.

"I had a dream last night," begins Sasha. "I used to have an absurd amount of them in the ICU—vivid ones. It was a long dream," Sasha continues. "Took place in the mental hospital that I was in—actually, Kaeda, I remember you being there. It had to do with the coma and everything that happened. I don't remember a lot, I just knew that it was weird."

My eyes light up, not in excitement, but in intrigue.

A coma.

What if that caused me to not remember as much?

I don't believe in superstitions.

But what if Sasha's dream indicates something she knows that I don't?

"Sasha," I call her, stopping her in the middle of her ramble, "was I in a coma?"

"I don't fully remember," Sasha responds. "You were kind of just a part of the dream."

"But I wasn't in a coma?" I ask. My knee bounces and my mind runs with thoughts; a coma would be highly explanatory of my lack of remembrance of my past. A coma, where my memory of my childhood was impaired. A coma, where the vivid dreams that I might have had, similar to Sasha's, did not leave; a coma would explain so much. But there's no telling whether I was in one, and Michelle never mentioned it. I would've remembered my recovery, right? I would've known if I was in a coma, right?

"I don't know," Sasha says. The words are heartbreaking, and a horrible feeling of stupidity for even relying on them in the first place swells within me. How would she have any knowledge of what happened to me? We haven't known each other prior to Redworth.

I stay quiet. Sasha's lack of remembrance for what happened in her dream isn't her fault. It's natural, and I don't blame her.

"I hated coma dreams," Sasha starts again. "I hated being in a coma. In the ICU, I remember hearing these inconsistent yet intensely annoying beeping sounds; they made me feel so hopeless. I felt so hopeless for those entire two weeks where I was out."

"What's a coma dream that you remember?" Beau asks. "Curious."

"After the doctors talked about my DNA, I remember dreaming about the whole thing," Sasha answers. "I dreamed about them researching it. With vivid dreams, you can almost feel everything, and so I felt so emerged in the process of them messing around with my DNA. It was weird; I hated it."

"Like a test subject?"

"Yeah," Sasha replies. "I felt a lot like one in my dream."

"Huh."

"Thinking about it now, actually," Sasha continues, "That dream kind of encapsulated a lot of what the entire coma felt like as a whole."

"Oh, that's interesting," Beau comments.

"I wish I could explain the experience to you guys in full," Sasha finishes.

Ottie and Beau leave to get another meal from the lunch line; it was surprisingly good today. I stay behind; Sasha still seems eager to speak about something.

"Can I tell you what got me sent to the mental hospital?" Sasha asks. Her wide blue eyes pierce me as she asks the question. She's incredibly nervous, and she's finally found a way to focus her eyes on one thing. It makes me stressed, but I realize why she's done it and the nervousness decreases.

"Yes," I answer.

"After I heard all about the idea of copying DNA and shit," Sasha starts, "I told my dad about it; it was driving me crazy. He took me to the mental hospital and didn't believe me at all."

"And from there they told you to just silence yourself about it?"

"I mean, I still don't know if it's a real thing," Sasha answers.

"Copying of DNA?" I ask. "That's real."

Sasha pauses, looking at me. "Cloning."

"Cloning?" I ask. "Of humans?"

"Yes," Sasha replies. "Cloning of humans; you take the DNA and clone the human. That's what I thought it was, and that's what my thoughts and dreams during my coma led me to believe."

"And that's what you told your dad," I add.

"Yes."

"And so he called you crazy."

"Yes."

"And he admitted you to the mental hospital."

"Yes."

Sasha goes silent for a few seconds. She stares at the trees of the school campus that surround us, the wind rustling through their orange leaves, bringing a few to the ground in the process. Sasha collects her thoughts, beginning to speak again.

"I was never supposed to tell you this," Sasha continues. "It could just be complete misinformation and I'm just feeding it to you."

"I mean, I don't believe that's what's happening," I say. "It's better that you tell somebody."

"Why wouldn't that be the case, though?" Sasha asks. "I have no real reason to believe in human cloning. I'm sorry for doing this. We barely even know each other, and I'm supposed to be quiet about this because it's part of my recovery. And now I'm just making you think for no reason."

"Sasha."

"Why do you take my word for it?" Sasha asks. "Why don't you call me crazy like everyone else?"

"I simply can't," I answer. "None of us are 'normal'. But that doesn't make us 'crazy'." It's not an in-depth answer at all, and it causes a sense of guilt within me—especially since it is the last word I leave Sasha on before lunch ends—but I reflect on the question. Why don't I call her crazy for this idea of human cloning? Her reasoning behind it consists only of dreams that followed from what she heard in her coma. I should be calling her "crazy", in theory, but even rejecting morals and how she'd feel, I don't feel right doing it. Throughout my life, from what I can remember, I've asked myself millions of questions that more than often resulted from recurring vivid dreams. Some I have received answers, some I have not, but that is besides the question. Sasha is another theorist or person with many questions and ideas, just like the rest of us. In calling her "crazy", I would be calling myself, Beau, and Ottie that, too.

After taking the bus home, where Ottie takes a nap aside from me and Beau listens to music through his headphones in the seat in front of us, the rest of the afternoon is nothing short of uneventful. Beau finishes assignments after mentioning how he didn't have time to complete them in class since he napped for each period, Ottie naps in the top bunk, and I sit around, looking for something to do. For dinner, Janice orders pizza delivery. She apparently began working remotely again today from what Beau told me.

The dinner table is tense—each individual with their own complex problems sitting at a table with little knowledge on how to express their issues, though everyone appears—in one way or another—tired. That is aside from me—my mind is crowded with thoughts at this time and I'm unknowing of how I'll rid myself of them. My brain plays the conversation between Sasha and I during lunch repeatedly, not allowing the mention of "human cloning" to escape my thoughts, or the idea that I may have been in a coma. Both are illogical, yes, and I have truly no line of reasoning to back either of them up completely, but they still occupy my mind. I'm nonsensical in my thoughts because of it—as if thoughts so illogical shouldn't be the very thoughts that are mine. But they are and a feeling of hopelessness resides within me.

I drink a small can of coffee, a confusing decision, but I'm confused, myself; a strong urge to research topics that Sasha discussed during lunch swells up within me. During this time, as I sit on the living room couch, Ottie approaches me in her pajamas with her hair still wet from her shower. It's no one else but us on the first floor as she sits beside me on the couch. The sky is dark, vaguely reminding me of this morning, but I shake the thought before it affects me largely and I ostracize my sister for her actions that resulted from what was essentially a meltdown.

"Kaeda," Ottie starts, "I'm sorry. I've failed you as a sister. I think that you've recognized that already."

"You haven't failed me," I respond. "I promise, you haven't."

I don't know if it's reassuring enough.

"But I have," Ottie continues. "Don't lie to yourself. You only think that I haven't recently because you still can't fully remember what childhood was like and how I was to you. I was so much better. I made you smile all the time. I was a great sister, and now you find me drinking Janice's alcohol early in the morning. I'm sorry."

I look at Ottie's face as her expressions grow with sadness and the pace of her conversation amplifies. She continues as though she's about to break as her eyes fixate on the floor and her eyebrows arch. I have a great love and concern towards my sister, and she talks as though I expect more. She talks as though I hate her.

"No you haven't—" I say, trying to cut her off and prevent her from continuing.

"Yes, I have," Ottie refutes. "I'm sorry that you can't remember everything about me beforehand. It would make me seem like such a better person. I'm sorry."

"Ottie, please stop apologizing."

"But I need to," Ottie says. "Kaeda, you'd be better off with your adopted family right now. I'm sorry to put you through this."

"You've done nothing wrong."

Her words form within me the urge to cry, partially because I'm unable to ingrain the fact that what she's saying is incorrect in her head. Partially because I hate to see her hurt like this. Yes, I remember little from when we were younger, but I still love my sister. I still feel *love*. I know that she doesn't mean any harm. I know that she doesn't want to drink, especially for me to see it happen.

I want to tell her that all that she says is wrong, but externally all that occupies my body is shock at her words. I want to only fix the issue from the outside, and it feels like that alone only amplifies Ottie's feelings of being a failure. Because I seem emotionally inept.

"I was so heartbroken when you were adopted and I wasn't," Ottie says, tears in her eyes. "That was so selfish of me. I should've just wished the best for you. So heartbroken and so caught up in my feelings to the point where the caretakers had to tell me that you had *died* so that I could just shut up. And that happened when I was going through the process of getting adopted by Janice. Because even though I was getting adopted already, I still missed you and wouldn't shut up about how I wish I had you back here."

"You are *far* from selfish, Ottie," I reassure her. "Stop belittling yourself; you don't deserve that."

"You belittle yourself by even talking to me anymore because I'm a horrible sibling putting you through horrible experiences," Ottie responds. She starts crying. Her body visibly becomes less tense, and I do the best thing that I could do at the moment.

I hug her, and tears fall from my eyes.

Her head buried in my shoulder, Ottie sobs uncontrollably. Though it's muffled, I hear her repeating "I'm sorry", repeatedly. I hold her tighter at each "sorry" she musters out as she sobs into my shirt.

"It's okay," I say to her, quietly. "It's okay—you have done nothing wrong."

When I tell her that, she hesitates and quietly says "but—", I tell her that it's okay, and she just starts crying again.

"I love you, Kaeda," Ottie says to me quietly.

"I love you too," I reply, sniffling. "You're a wonderful sister."

Everyone's on their way to fall asleep. Beau and Ottie are both in bed, as well as Janice. I'm the only one out here in the living room, and there's an odd peace to the scene. *Peace*—a peace in the late night solitude.

This lasts for maybe ten minutes. Then I only think about what Sasha had said to me and remember why I'm caffeinated in the first place and have my laptop in front of me.

To *know*.

Because I don't think that what she heard about "DNA copying" is a nonsensical concept, and it's worth at least trying to look into. I don't think Sasha's insane, at least not to the extent that she'd be blatantly misinterpreting what she heard.

"Can you copy someone's DNA?"

That's what I type into the search bar.

"DNA Can Now Accurately Reconstruct a Full Human, Scientists Say."

"How Detectives Are Using DNA Technology To Track Down Suspects Immediately By Their Phone's Face ID."

"Will Androids Read Humans By Their DNA? MechanizedLife Suggests They Could."

"Identity Theft Using DNA Samples Is Now On The Rise, Experts Warn."

"We Know That We Can Clone Animals Using Their DNA—But Can We Improve Our Animals? New DNA Cloning Technologies Now Allow For Skill Enhancement."

"What About Our Humans? New Biological Technologies State That Human Replication Using DNA is Definitely Possible."

Huh.

"What About Our Humans? New Biological Technologies State That Human Replication Using DNA is Definitely Possible."

I click on the headline. A news website writes:

"Animal Replication using DNA is nothing new. Scientific corporations such as Zoology Technologies and Dark-Hued Plateau have replicated animals using their DNA for years, either to prevent animal extinction or for reasons unspecified, but many scientists and curious citizens alike ask about human cloning."

"'It's an idea,' says a scientist at Fissure Laboratories. 'And one not out of scientific reach alike.'"

I read through the article. It discusses the possibility of human cloning but mentions multiple times that it's unethical and how that's the primary concern regarding the idea. I agree.

But I can't shake this stinging pain in my head that only itches at me, asking more. None of these articles help me better understand Sasha's situation and *why* the doctors talked about cloning her DNA.

I tell myself that it was only to help them understand her coma, but that makes zero sense. You don't clone someone's DNA for a sample in order to understand a coma.

I tell myself that they only were attempting to find a genetic cause of her coma. *But why clone someone's DNA sample in order to do that?*

I tell myself that I'm too worried about the issues of someone else.

I tell myself that this aching feeling is my own problem and that it's my fault.

I tell myself that it doesn't matter.

I tell myself that ignoring Sasha's issues feels right. It doesn't. The aching feeling gets worse. My stomach only hurts now, and I know it's due to nervousness. My mind feels like a ticking clock. There's no surrounding sound of one right now, but I can still hear it in my ears somehow. A consistent tick. Just itching—and itching at me.

I close the laptop and tell myself that there isn't anything I can do to stop this feeling. But I know that there is, and that's an answer to my questions. And I tell myself that I'll never receive that.

I want to silence my thoughts sometimes.

I picture my thoughts as a running bioluminescent river deep in the night, in the middle of some forest. But the river is harsh, and the sound of it crashing upon rock to rock isn't at all peaceful. If you were to be swept into the river, you'd drown. You'd drown in bioluminescence.

It makes no sense, but I resonate with the picture. And I think that drinking coffee this late was a mistake, because the river is running dangerously fast, and the bioluminescence starts to resemble chaos rather than beauty. Knowing that I have none else to do, I open the laptop again, and I search "human cloning" in the search bar. Nothing really specific—I can't clearly think in specifics right now. Everything's too blurry. The river is too quick.

"Human Cloning—A Possibility? Scientists Discuss New Technology to Make Human Cloning a Safe Option."

I click on the article. It reads:

"Scientists at Neurogenix Laboratories and Bioscience Innovations claim that the cloning of humans could possibly be a safe option in the near future. 'It's an idea to not push aside,' says an executive at Neurogenix Laboratories. 'Successful animal clones and the developing technology behind them seem to make human cloning not deemed impossible or unsafe anymore.' According to a scientist at Bioscience Innovations, 'Human cloning is a very pretentious idea, but nonetheless, it's starting to look possible with new biological technology. The only actual issue faced with cloning is how ethical it seems.' The scientist further discusses how, if cloning is safe, that issue of the idea being unethical could be disproved."

I read the rest of the article. They just tread on and on about how human cloning could be "ethical" or "safe", and, I can't fully explain it, but a feeling boils up inside of me when I read those words. I think the article is bullshit. I think human cloning creates too much uncertainty about the health of a person in order for it to be safe or ethical.

However, I'm open to other opinions, so I look for more articles.

I open up my phone to a text from James. James from my old school—Juno's brother. We were good friends; I remember. But the notification I received is nothing that I had expected.

"Hey Kaeda, I wanted to tell you this sooner, but I felt like I couldn't. The last two days have been so painful for me."

"On November 10, Juno died. She committed, and I still don't understand why she would do it. I remember her having emotional problems around the start of this month but I'm still confused. I meant to tell you this sooner. I'm still in a lot of grief and I hope you're doing well with your sister now."

"I just thought I'd tell you"

"I'm sorry"

"It's been very difficult for me"

My eyes stare blankly at the text messages until I read them over again. They skim over the text messages and my heart rate increases vigorously. The pulse of my heart quickens and my vision gains a blurriness I can't shake. Reality warps beneath my eyes; the emptiness of the townhouse I'm in closes in on me. And I don't know how to respond to James or what he's said.

My throat closes up and the river of my mind hits a waterfall that I'm rafting down. James continues to type and I can't even fully register the anticipation of waiting for what he has to say, because I don't want to hear anymore. The blurriness of my vision only encapsulates the blurriness of my own thoughts; I've seen this recently, and I never wanted to see it again. *I've seen death.* And the lifelessness of what I had seen only projects onto what Juno would look like in that situation, making my thoughts blurrier by the second. They're warped and quick.

My physical self can't keep up.

I can't formulate a response.

I put down the phone.

And the blurriness of my vision becomes due to tears. The river isn't just a vision anymore—it surfaces. It becomes a reality. I'm swept away in the river's dangerous currents, crying. And I can't even begin to explain how crying again makes me feel.

Last time, death was expected. I cried, but it was expected. It was a silent cry. Moreover, just a short mourning. But now, it's a feeling best described as shock. I can't deny the experience; I know it's really happened.

And I know that I'll never see Juno again. That the last time I went to school before living with Ottie was the last time I would ever see her and that was the last time she would ever see me.

I wasn't in the same room with her as she died as I was with Michelle. This experience is far from that one, as well as how my experience is nowhere near that of Juno's family. It's just a shock. I'm silently crying, that's all it is. Silence and mourning. I wish the best for Juno's family as the thoughtful, creative face that they had in their life is gone.

I don't understand it either, but it's not my territory to understand. And so I eventually reply to James, expressing my grief. And the caffeine has appeared to have worn off by now. I pick up my laptop blankly and walk back to my room. I don't understand, and I don't think I need to. I just walk back to my room, my eyes dry from the tears I had shed. The sky is crying with Juno's family and I as it rains outside, barely any light passing through the townhouse windows.

I put my laptop away and lay there on my bed, hair dry and in my pajamas. Although I still have slight jitters from the caffeine, mentally, I'm exhausted.

And, eventually, that sends me to sleep.

Part 3

Eight

I wake up.

Moving through the gaps between my clothing and my skin, a cool breeze passes me gently. I cannot determine yet whether I should feel peace or fear as my vision adapts to the scene and I'm met with a view of a familiar train station: Millbrae Station, the station at which I'd arrive whilst taking the train home from GoldenPine each day. There is no daylight here; only the endless pathway of street lamps—both distant in the parking lots and by my side on the walkway—illuminate the dark scene. The station is unnervingly yet reasonably empty and there isn't a still train to either side of me. The screen designed to indicate the arrivals and departures of trains at the station is blank; a sense of chill trickles down my spine like raindrops against a window.

I think the scene would be best described as liminal. The setting is so incredibly desolate; I ask myself multiple times if I'm supposed to be waiting on a train, then to be quickly reminded that no trains are scheduled to arrive here. My surroundings are eerie and dark, yet bring a weird peace. The pathways of streetlamps cause intrigue. I'm intrigued by the loneliness. I'm intrigued by the absence of people. I would go as far as to say that I like the station as it is right now, even though staying here any longer may debilitate my mind.

Turning to my left, I briefly notice a person sitting on a bench in the distance, waiting on a train. I'm shaken for a moment in brief panic; my surroundings slightly warp beneath my eyes as if I've fallen dizzy. I can't make out who the person is at first until my eyes focus entirely, and the person appears to have dark brown, long braided hair and darker skin. She reads a book while wearing glasses, dressed in jeans and a sweater. I realize who the person is: Juno, my friend from GoldenPine. The girl with whom I'd occasionally ride the train home to study with. The one who *died*.

She glances over at me, and I hear a familiar voice faintly call my name.

"Kaeda?"

I walk over to the bench she sits at, where she puts her book away and awaits me. I sit next to her, and the vision of her eyes—those filled with wonder and curiosity—almost feels refreshing.

It must have been so off-putting for James to see those eyes without life.

Juno has always been so full of personality; the darkness of the scene coupled with Juno aside from me causes a distinct, odd fear: a fear that she'll become void of life any second now—that she'll die in front of me. *And her eyes will not fully shut.*

I quickly muster words out of my system in order to avoid this vision.

"You're alive," I say to her.

"What?" Juno questions. Her expression of apparent wonder turns to an expression of evident concern and mistrust, and my stomach begins to ache as though I've made a gravely terrible decision. "Why wouldn't I be?" she asks further.

"No, it's nothing," I respond, and Juno stays silent, eyes fixated at the floor. A subtle look of betrayal plagues her face and all of its components, arching her eyebrows in melancholy and frowning slightly. There's an awkward pause—Juno doesn't make the effort to say anything to me, understandably, and I glimpse around the desolate, silent station that I've been familiar with for as long as I can remember; seeing it so blank and stripped of its life like this feels almost like looking at something naked.

Then, the unthinkable happens: it snows. Slowly at first, but the snow picks up its pace as its fall persists. Juno remains fixated at the floor, silent in either thought, disappointment, or both.

"It's snowing," I say to her, surprised. "Juno, look."

"I know," she answers.

I subtly knit my eyebrows at her in confusion. "This is the San Mateo area," I remind her. "It never snows here."

"I get that," Juno says, unphased. I want to ask her why she isn't reacting to it, but I hold off and decide not to.

"It doesn't make any sense," I say instead.

"It doesn't have to make sense, Kaeda," Juno says, looking at me. "Nothing here does."

Nothing here does.

After all, she's right—I'm only dreaming. I fixate my eyes toward the dark gray night sky full of snow as the flakes fall on my nose; the moment is beautifully peaceful, yet distinctly off-putting—nothing makes sense.

"I'm sorry," Juno says after a moment.

"For what?" I ask.

Juno stays silent. I wait a few seconds, then realize what she apologized for—her suicide. Initially, I'm unsure of how I'll answer.

"It's okay," I reassure her to the best of my abilities, but it comes out a little awkward. The snow, falling as fast as it is, has covered a lot of the train station walkway.

I want to stay here for a while.

6:52 AM

A painfully bright light shines directly into my eyes as I wake from my dream and lay on my bed, my body in pain and exhaustion—I don't think I received enough sleep last night. Ottie taps my shoulder, fully dressed and ready to leave the house, calling my name: "Kaeda, Kaeda, you've been sleeping all this time". "Kaeda, you need to wake up". "Kaeda, you need to get ready, we're going to be late".

Somehow, the words don't affect me much, and I find myself focusing only on the physical exhaustion within me. As I move out of bed, a wave of extreme dizziness strikes me.

After dressing for school as quickly as possible and rushing downstairs, I find Beau and Ottie finishing up their breakfast as I grab a protein bar and a bottle of water from the pantry. With surprise, Ottie watches me hurry. "You don't need to worry *that* much," she tells me, "the bus arrives at 7:30 and sits there for a solid ten minutes."

"Oh."

I sit and eat the protein bar accompanied by a banana, still unable to shake the dizzy sensation. In a hurried situation and anxious state, I somehow wish that it could be a morning that is perceived normal to me yet abnormal to others: a morning where I wake at 5 AM and am only alone with my thoughts, reflecting on the dream I recently had, as painful as this may be. And I wish that I could sit in my mind and just lay there in silence. And ever since I moved in with Ottie, I've never felt more in touch with my feelings and my dreams yet so, *so* far away from them. And sometimes I find it easy to ask myself if I'm in a more positive or a more negative state of mind than I was before, detached from my thoughts that I both identify with and despise simultaneously. And sometimes I find the feeling ridiculous—I'm here now with my sister and someone to communicate with about my dreams. *Why would I feel worse?* And other times I find the feeling to be reasonable—I can't shake the thought that I've failed as a sister with my lack of remembrance for Ottie and the childhood memories that have so much influence on her and are meant to have as great of an influence on me.

Maybe it's the reconciliation of my past. Maybe it's the change in situation—the fact that I'm facing situations and events I haven't faced before. Meeting Sasha and hearing about her past. Ottie telling me about how she heard from her caretakers that I had died. Beau's dreams and his expression of them; Janice's mysterious issues and ignorance of her son. Juno's suicide. And I wonder where I fit in that list and if I make Ottie, Sasha, or Beau question if they're in a more positive or a more negative state of mind than they were before they started talking to me.

These thoughts are cold and miserable; they cause me to feel a writhing pain within my mind. The river freezes up and the bioluminescent life die as I can't even healthily respond to the questions concerning how people feel about me, my past, my dreams, and anything else that ends up falling into that clump—even if I was unable to do so before Michelle's death.

Thinking too much only makes me feel dizzier as Ottie, Beau, and I leave the townhouse and board the school bus. On the way there, Sasha texts me, telling me she won't be at school today as she feels sick, and I let our lunch group know. Leaving the bus and walking into the school, the first few periods of classes are identical to how they always are, and the only difference with fourth period is that Sasha is not in class. As the bell rings to dismiss students to lunch, I find Ottie sitting outside at the outdoor lunch table as usual as Beau needed to stay after class during lunch for a test retake. Surrounding where Ottie and I sit, I find peace and then prominent feelings of thoughtfulness from today's weather. The orange hues of the trees in combination with the gray, cloudy, 63-degree weather create a confusing feeling—like I'm missing something. Or like I'm waiting for something new: an event, an idea, that is a long way away—long enough to the point where I wonder whether it will ever arrive. The weather is brisk and lonely yet beautiful at the same time. It's question-provoking and unusual, like the dream I had.

"I like fall," Ottie mentions. "I consider spring my favorite season, but fall comes second—I love the atmosphere."

"I agree," I say.

"Fall reminds me of you, Kaeda," Ottie tells me, glimpsing at me. "It always has, for some reason."

"Maybe its the silence?" I suggest.

"I've always found fall to be warmly intelligent—like you," Ottie continues. "Maybe the silence, too."

I smile at my sister.

The weather of the season causes a distinct and interesting feeling—like a transitional period that is so beautiful yet so *bleak*. And I guess fall *does* remind me of myself and what I yearn for, in its silent and desolate beauty: I yearn for a sense of *certainty* in myself and my ideas. I yearn for something *lasting*—something that makes *sense*. I yearn for lines of reasoning and knowledge—that yearning has become distinctly stronger ever since I've moved in with Ottie. And although the unknown is so intriguing, pondering the unknown has recently deeply wounded me—it's caused a down-spiral of my thoughts and panic within my mind.

And the river only gains more bioluminescence by day, making it intriguing and beautiful, yes, but also more toxic–more harmful and more dangerous, similar to how I perceive my own mind. That is how I approach my own thoughts—they are interesting and vast, they are wonderful and unique, but, at the same time, they hurt me. Something beautiful—some intriguing, brilliant question or idea–turns into debilitating misery. They become more dangerous the more you dwell on them.

I think of myself and ask if my mind is really worth loving anymore. I think of Ottie's issues and a sense of somewhat helplessness attacks me. I think of Beau's issues and it's as though I'm not alone, but Beau's a mess, so what does that mean for me?

I think about the concerns and questions of Sasha and wonder if reality is how I used to perceive it. And I think about Juno and what she's done, and I ask myself if I was ever good enough and why I couldn't ever notice her dire need for a healthy mentality.

I think of everything and everything causes me to feel blank—unable to find a solution or conclusion to my thoughts and questions. Silently drained and full of wonder, knowing that my wonder will never receive an answer—blank. Drained. Exhausted, exasperated—the river's bioluminescent blues present feelings of only melancholy and discomfort now. It's pitch black and the blues are just signs of danger: signs of toxicity.

"Kaeda," Ottie says, quietly. I twist my head towards her, enhancing my lightheadedness. I blink my eyes a few times in an attempt to rid myself of the sensation.

"Yes?"

"You looked zoned out," she clarifies. "You okay?"

"Yeah, just dizzy," I respond. Ottie nods, then hands me her bottle full of iced water to possibly help me. I shake my head, and a conflicting feeling of déjà vu looms over me. I can't entirely make out what the scenario was, but I do know that it's relating to a younger version of Ottie and me. I try to hold on to the feeling to look into it more, but it only dissipates.

"Are you tired?" Ottie asks. I nod.

"From what? How long did you stay up?"

"For a while," I respond, "It was because of an unpleasant situation involving an old friend."

"What happened?"

I sigh. "A friend named Juno," I start, "she died a few days ago to suicide. Her brother told me last night."

"Oh, my," Ottie says, "That's horrible."

I nod. "Yeah—it's been weird for me."

"I'm so sorry," Ottie continues.

"It's okay," I say, "I'm not sure if there's anything I could've done."

"I understand," Ottie says. I see her zone out for a moment and visibly try not to choke up. She takes a sip of her water and breathes deeply, erasing the thought; suppressing the emotion. And I find understanding in that.

"Do you, um ..." Ottie starts, "... are you keeping in touch with Sasha?"

I nod a yes.

"Has she said anything different?"

I shake my head no, even if it's a lie. I'm too drained to add another problem onto the plate, feeding the questions that I ask myself. I'm too exhausted mentally to notice something else right now. Even if it's important, I only want to rest.

"Oh," Ottie responds, "Okay."

The conversation is extremely dry, and it's not Ottie's fault, it's my own. I'm giving one-worded responses if I give a verbal response at all. I'm lying and not leading on questions that should probably be answered. I'm being dishonest, and it's all because I'm convinced that it would be more difficult to fess up and repeat something I've said numerous times. The thing is, I haven't; I've only repeated things to myself. I'm warping my own perception of things, destroying my own memory, and I'm fine with it.

Numbness. It might just be that I'm physically tired and light-headed, but I'm terribly numb to any real, external thing I'd discuss right now. Beau gets back from the test retake, and I start to eat my lunch, even if the textures make me feel nauseous only because I have a low appetite right now.

I'm complaining too much.

I'm thinking about things too deeply.

These issues are insignificant; I could push through them. I'd be fine if I only tried. Why am I so dizzy?

I'm sick. Sick physically and sick of my thoughts.

The rest of the school day consists of me feeling too dizzy to concentrate in each of my classes, though I power through them and finish my schoolwork. Beau, Ottie, and I all take the school bus home as usual. I plop onto the couch with a stronger feeling of lightheadedness than before, and Ottie sits next to me, watching TV as I lay helplessly. Beau's gone to his room to finish homework and Janice's in her room at her home desk finishing work. I close my eyes and only focus on the sounds of the TV for a few minutes, immersing myself in an environment of lower stimulus to try and drown out the physical discomfort of my head.

The show seems to approach a death scene from what I listen in on. Mentions of regret, sounds of suspense, and melancholy, ambient atmospheric tracks lead me to that somewhat conclusion. Ottie turns off the TV and leans back on the sofa, taking a deep breath.

I open my eyes and look over at her.

"I don't like death," she says after a moment, almost seeming to choke up. "I don't like the thought of someone just ... *going*. Just *gone*. Everything they've lived for, everyone they ..."

She sniffles for a moment.

"Everyone they *knew*," she starts up again, "Just kinda ... *left*. Left to fend for themselves and wallow in their misery."

I knit my eyebrows at her in concern, sitting up.

"I'm sorry for turning off the TV," Ottie apologizes, about to cry. "I just can't deal with things about ..."

Although she still struggles to talk, I lean in and hug Ottie. She starts to sob into my shoulder, and my vision becomes overwhelmingly blurry without the reason being dizziness.

"I ... I think you know why I don't like death," Ottie musters out in a sob.

"I do," I answer with a subtle sniffle.

"I'm sorry for holding onto this," Ottie apologizes. "It must be so scary for you to hear what they told me. I don't ... I can't understand why they'd ever ..."

"It's okay," I reassure her. "Don't apologize."

"I can't help it," Ottie cries.

I nod. "You're okay," I say, patting my sister's back gently.

And I think I remember what my role was as a sister when Ottie and I were younger: I provided comfort and a sense of stability even if, at the time, I didn't feel sufficient comfort or stability myself. Now, I don't remember *how* I felt, but that's how it feels now. A silent comforter.

"You've always been a great sister," Ottie tells me, parting from my shoulder. "I don't know if you remember that about yourself, but I want to let you know that I really missed you when you were gone. Especially when I thought you were gone permanently."

"Thank you," I say in response.

"It's no problem."

The middle of the day has never felt so similar to the end of one. I want to tell Ottie all about what Sasha told me. I want to tell her what I've been researching, but I find it insignificant. Now, I don't know if she'd think the same way, but, then again, I'm too tired—too drained of any energy or coherent thought to talk again.

Ottie leaves the living room to play on her laptop, and so I stay here, laying on the couch with a blanket over me. The cloudiness of the outdoors calms me, and I only become more tired by the second.

I'm so tired,

So exhausted,

So *drained.*

I fall asleep.

As I open my eyes, an overwhelming feeling of nostalgia hits me.

A child's bed with a patterned blue blanket with roses and soft green bedding, uncomfortably close to another child's bed with a vibrant colored blanket with polka dots and pink bedding. The room looks like a childish dorm room yet somewhat homier, compact with two wooden closets. Clothing, books, and inexperienced drawings with colored pencils clutter the floor and furniture. It's light outside. I can't be any older than twelve here.

A young Ottie walks in, about age ten. At first, the image of her face seems to be distorted. She holds a book in one hand and a bottle of orange juice in the other, seemingly happy as her face develops. That's when I realize where we are—a foster home.

"Kaeda!" Ottie calls. "I think I overheard Mrs. Thimes talking about adopting us."

I suddenly watch myself in the third person.

"Really?" A younger version of myself responds. "No way."

"Yes way!" Ottie says. "Maybe she will, and then, I don't know, we'll have a family? I don't know, Kaeda—what do you think of Mrs. Thimes?"

"She's ... nice," my younger self answers. "But too uptight."

"Uptight?" Ottie asks. "What does that mean?"

"Too organized and 'perfect' about everything," My younger self clarifies.

"Oh," Ottie says. "Well, I guess you're right, but I just wish that we had parents."

"We did," my younger self says. "And then they left."

"Sometimes I still wonder *why*," Ottie asks. "Why *did* they leave?"

"Because they didn't want us," my younger self answers. "They couldn't handle us."

Ottie tilts her head in confusion. "Then why'd they eat the seedling from the doctors?"

"The *seedling*?"

"Mrs. Thimes' kid told me that, when parents want to make a baby, they eat a seedling from the doctors," Ottie tells. "And then the baby grows and pops out."

"That's ridiculous," my younger self says.

"Well that's what Mrs. Thimes told me," Ottie continues. "She also told me that you were named after our mom's last name: Kaeda. And that my name isn't at all Japanese, so maybe one of our parents was part French, or something."

"I think Ottilie's a German name."

"Part German, or something."

"We don't look German at all."

"Yeah, you're right," Ottie responds. "Well, maybe our parents just thought the name was pretty."

Ottie shrugs and walks out the door, still holding her book and orange juice. The scene switches to the first person.

I study all of the drawings on the floor. One is signed by Ottie, who wrote her name in big bubble letters and colorful crayons. The drawing is of the two of us in a big house in what looks to be a magical forest. Surprisingly, the purple and pink trees she drew are drawn well, and the house has a sufficient amount of detail, even if the penmanship is messy.

The drawings that I've done are signed by me in smaller, messier handwriting with a pencil. My drawings seem of things I physically remember, the one I focus on is of a house's living room and fireplace. I colored the details of the drawing in colored pencil, but it's unfinished and still looks like a messy sketch completed by a 10-year-old.

The scene fades before my eyes to the sound of Beau calling my name faintly.

6:28 PM

I wake up.

Beau peers over me as I lay with dry eyes and messy hair, holding the blanket on the couch. It's much darker outside, almost appearing to be nighttime. I can smell the delivered food from the dining table near the kitchen. I need to wash my face—my skin feels uncomfortably dry after my long nap.

"Oh, good morning!" Beau's mom, Janice, says to me nervously. I mumble an unintelligible response and walk to the bathroom to situate myself. The cold tap water I splash over my face forces me to feel somewhat awake, but my environment is still a blur, even with my glasses. I blink rapidly in the mirror while I stare at myself. A feeling of dizziness still lingers after sleeping, but I walk over to the dinner table and push myself through it. We're eating pizza today.

I can tell that Ottie wants to say something to me as she eats her food, I just can't tell what it is. She looks over at me multiple times and hesitates to talk, bouncing her leg in anxiety. Beau silently eats his food, zoning out multiple times and looking to be drained overall. He looks like he had napped recently, too.

After we finish eating, I sit back on the couch and wrap myself up in the blanket I had slept with. Once everyone leaves, Ottie sits down next to me, not turning on the TV. She still looks nervous while bouncing her leg.

"Kaeda," she starts, "Are you sure that you didn't hear anything new from Sasha?"

And now is the time when I'll have to make the decision of whether I tell Ottie about what I've been researching. I don't want to feed into her concerns or worries—I especially don't want to see her drink again.

But I want to tell her because I'm not sure if I'll be able to comfortably go about my day knowing I've lied to Ottie many times.

"It wasn't anything particularly new from Sasha," I start, "but, rather, something new I've seen."

"Really?" Ottie responds. "Which is?"

"You remember what Sasha had said about the doctors copying her DNA?" I ask.

"Yes."

"It's a large possibility that the whole idea of human DNA copying in labs is real," I say. "I don't know why they would've done it to Sasha or what significance it holds, but there are a lot of articles about the idea, and–"

"They relate to cloning, right?" Ottie asks.

I look at her. "Yes, how did you—"

"Beau told me, and I started looking into it myself," Ottie answers. "And I don't know what to think. I don't know if Sasha was supposed to be some 'subject', or if she's just hearing things. I don't know if it's us who's looking too into it—I don't know if the whole thing is just a fake, and I don't know if it's even important and whether we're doing the right thing."

"I don't think Sasha was hearing things," I tell Ottie with a weird amount of confidence.

"But we don't *know* that," Ottie responds. "It could very, *very* well be fake."

"No, but I just don't think—"

"You only don't think that because you probably don't want it," Ottie says. "You'd hate to see everything you had pursued to be *pointless*. You fixate on big ideas and problems and lose yourself when they become small because you like the search for answers. You like the knowledge and the unknown *even if* it eats you alive." She breathes in. "I don't ... I don't know what goes on that we don't know about. I don't know a lot about Sasha, or what happened in her coma. I don't know about the doctors and what they were trying to say. I just feel like your moving here was supposed to be a breath of fresh air for me, or something that feels like the past, but I'm beginning to realize that it's not. And that you need help. You need something big in your life to just make you *relax*."

She looks at me again, tears in her eyes, going silent for a few seconds. Her teary eyes almost stare at me in disbelief or disappointment, either in herself or in me. And I can't make out which one it is yet.

"You're a really great sister, Kaeda," Ottie continues. "I'm sorry, I just ... I wish problems weren't so big and didn't happen so often, maybe."

Multiple responses run through my head, but I can't seem to pick out which one is okay to use, or, rather, which one I agree with more on an emotional level. But, over the course of a few seconds, I don't ...

I don't want to respond.

I want to sit here and think, even if it brings tears to my eyes. I want to think about this piercing feeling that I'm experiencing and whether it's Ottie's fault or mine. I want to sit and watch my surroundings sit in silence with me. I want to reflect on my own questions and the answers that I'm pursuing. I think I'd like to sit here; I think I'd like to think for a moment.

Even if it's bringing tears to my eyes.

Ottie scoots in closer to me on the couch with concern written all over her face, her eyes glazed with tears as she asks if I'm okay with remorse, choking up after each word. She cries for me, over and over, with worry and regret, but everything around me is blurry and insignificant. I sit still as tears run down my cheek, persisting, trying to make me move. I don't hate Ottie at this moment or what she said—I wonder if I hate *myself*. And she's only pointing out that hatred and questioning to me. The piercing feeling—over and over. But I don't hate her for making that piercing feeling appear—I don't hate her at all. I hate myself because what she said is so painfully true, and it pierces me.

I think I want to take a break from researching all of this mess; I want to sit here and take a break. Ottie sits with me for the next couple of minutes, obsessively asking questions, emotionally exhausted and intense. The conversation, summed up, goes:

"Did I make you feel horrible?" She asks.

"No," I reply, still a little choked up.

"I'm sorry."

"But you didn't make me feel ..."

"I don't know what else to say," she finishes.

She's as emotionally and socially inept as I am.

Ottie eventually goes to take a shower, followed by her heading to bed. I take a shower after she does, dress in my pajamas, and *plan* on going to bed, but for the fifteen minutes I'm there, I don't budge. The long nap I had taken earlier screwed up how tired I should feel right now and I can't fall asleep anymore, so I walk over to the living room and listen to music for the next couple of minutes through the headphones of my laptop, finishing schoolwork that I didn't complete over the weekend. Even if school feels so unimportant right now, I'm passing time and allowing myself to feel accomplished in *something*. To feel *achieved*, at least.

11:58 PM

Finally, exhaustion swells up within me. I take out the headphones, close the laptop, and prepare to walk over to the bedroom until I get a phone call from Juno's contact.

I pick up the phone, and it's not her family or siblings—*it's her*.

Nine

Friday, November 14, 2036, 12:00 AM

I hear Juno's voice through the speaker of my phone, greeting me in words that my shocked mind doesn't entirely register. I don't notice it at first, but my hands are shaking uncontrollably as I grip the phone with a force enough to hold it steady amidst the harsh trembles of them. Nothing has changed about how she speaks—she still has the same voice she had spoken to me with before: a voice full of wonder and curiosity—the voice that I remember prior to her depression. Now, however, there's a greater sense of innocence—an innocence that was not nearly as present, if at all present, as it is now—hearing Juno speak to me with no recall of what happened. With no recall of what her family told me.

Juno, speaking to me, *with no recall of how I was told that she died*.

"Hello?" Juno says to me over the phone. "Kaeda, are you there?"

I try to muster up words, but they come out in a nervous stutter. "I ... I'm here."

"It's been quite a while since we've talked," Juno says, "I've just been up late and wanted to see how you were doing."

"I'm ..." I start with a distinct and awkward stutter, "I'm doing okay. I'm doing fine. Uh ... I uh, I wanted to ask what you've been doing for the past few days?"

"Oh, not much, really," Juno responds. "Whatever's typical. I don't recall a lot, that's the thing. I'm kind of forgetful.""You are?" I ask, without remembrance of her being very forgetful from when she and I attended GoldenPine.

"Yeah," Juno says. "I am."

"Has—" I begin, collecting my words. "Has your brother said anything recently?"

"James?" Juno asks. "No, not really. He's been fine. Why do you ask?"

"He hasn't said anything to you?" I question again.

"No, he's been fine, Kaeda," Juno answers again, repeating herself. "Is everything okay?"

No, not at all.

I want to tell her. I wish I could. I wish she knew what I was told so she could clarify everything and help me understand what the hell is going on, but I can't just tell someone that I was told that they *died*.

I can't respond to what she's saying, either. My voice hesitates to speak, yet I'm interrupted by my own mind constantly. Juno over the speaker, talking to me normally, as though she does not know about what happened and what I had been told. And she doesn't have any idea—she has zero clue, at least it seems that way.

It's terribly confusing.

But *why* would I be lied to about someone's suicide? *Why* would Juno's brother, if anyone, try to tell me that Juno had killed herself? And why would he tell me with so much—what seemed to be genuine—*feeling*?

I can only ask myself "why" over and over, painfully searching for answers, but that's the problem—I can only ask *myself*. I can't say any of this to Juno for fear that it would make her lose her mind. She talks to me as if nothing ever happened.

She talks to me as if it's all okay. She talks to me as if I've lost my mind, and I know she doesn't mean that, though that's how I interpret it.

"What ... what were you asking?" I ask Juno, forgetful of what she had originally asked me, wound up in my thoughts. And I know I seem even more mentally unwell—even more delusional—causing Juno to question me completely. I wish I could tell her, I really do, but a burning feeling inside of me just knows that I *can't*. A burning feeling inside of me just knows how shitty I'd feel for it—for making someone question their own existence. Making them question the fact that they are alive—as if that was a mistake. Maybe I'd really cause her to kill herself.

"I just asked if you were okay," Juno responds. "And I think I might already have a response to that."

"I'm, um ..." I start, stuttering. I find myself licking my lips in between words, but focusing on the nervous traits I'm seeming to have right now only increases my nervousness. I don't know what to say. I don't know where to start.

"I'm fine," I say in a complete lie.

"Are you sure?" Juno asks. "Did something happen at home?"

"No—no, nothing happened," I respond. "I've been okay."

"Really?" Juno persists. I wait to answer and open up the messages app on my phone whilst simultaneously on a call with Juno, trying to make it appear I haven't gone radio silent and mumbling complete gibberish. I then open the message history between James and me, trying to either text him or simply see what he had told me about Juno's death, making sure I'm not delusional. But, to my surprise, I find that the texts have been completely wiped. The message history between us has completely *vanished*, no trace of what I had said or what he had told me. All of that: *gone*.

Staring at the blank message tab, It's as though it's me who's lost it. That, somehow, although it felt authentic, I had hallucinated the entire event. Everything that James had said about Juno: hallucinated. Everything that I had said to Ottie and Beau: lies. Everything that I had so blindly believed about Juno's death: delusion.

I don't know where the texts went. I don't know if James had purposefully deleted them and is playing a giant trick on me, but I don't see how that is possible for anyone to do, especially someone like him. That's completely unreasonable. I just ...

I've just lost my mind.

That's the problem here, *isn't it*? I've just lost it. Somehow, all of this was a facade, even if I had checked the messages multiple times. That must be what happened.

I hallucinated the whole thing.

But the many times that I tell myself that the event being a hallucination or dream is the case, I don't feel right. There exists a yearning, itching feeling inside of me that I can't pull out, yelling muffled yells that tell me that there's still *more*. I don't know if I can call that feeling logic or not, because I'm not sure whether the conclusion that I had hallucinated Juno's suicide is logical or not. I don't know how to label the feeling. I don't know what's right and wrong; I don't know if I should say anything to Juno; I don't know if I should stay silent and allow her to think I'm delusional as I scare her accidentally without even saying anything about her suicide. The suicide that I had made up in my head. The suicide that was *fake*.

"Kaeda?" Juno calls for me over the phone. She must have been calling my name multiple times over the call because of how loud and concerned she sounded in saying my name; I must've been tuning out what she has been saying subconsciously for however long it's been since she last asked me a question. And I think that's the case, because there's a weird ringing in my ears following hearing her over the speaker.

"Y–Yes?" I stutter back.

"What's wrong with you?" Juno asks. "Is everything okay? I'm concerned."

"I think I just misinterpreted something," I answer.

"Misinterpreted?" Juno asks. "Misinterpreted what?"

"Something I heard," I answer.

"Oh," Juno replies, "And what was that?"

And now is the decision where I'll either tell Juno that I had been told that she had died or go completely dry. But within me exists a feeling—a feeling of aching familiarity. This event is strikingly similar to one I've experienced before.

Ottie.

My sister, faced with the same dilemma. The same decision on whether I should tell someone close to me I had been told that they died.

How could a situation be so *similar?*

Why do people lie to other people about someone they love dying? That's uncommon, or so I thought.

No, but there's no way that's the case.

But what is it that Juno and I have done that causes someone we're close to to be told that we died? Was it all spread misinformation?

But no … not from her own brother. Not from James—not from the student I remember having a distinct interest in philosophy—not from the brother who was so incredibly concerned for his sister in her depression that he would unintentionally annoy her by begging the continuous question: "what's wrong?". *Not from James.*

I decide to ask myself these questions later. And I also decide to tell Juno that I was told she died.

"I—I was told you were dead," I admit after multiple hesitations.

"*Dead?*" Juno asks, completely shocked by the tone of her voice. "What? By who?"

"Someone at our school," I answer. "Anonymous account that I know is from our school."

It's not entirely incorrect, but it's definitely not truthful.

"Oh, God," Juno starts, "That's horrible. Why would they ever lie about something so serious?"

"I have no idea," I respond. It's as though a burden has been lifted off of my back, but, as it's being lifted, I realize it's only a considerably insignificant part of the weight. There's still a lingering heaviness weighing me down—the burden of not telling Juno the full truth about her supposed "death".

"And that's why you were so nervous?" Juno questions.

"Just confused," I say.

"Why would you believe someone from our school?" Juno asks. "Genuinely, just wondering why–"

"I don't know," I respond, cutting her off. I just then realize that my way of answering her questions is only making things worse. I just want to leave this call, yet I want to stay because of the fact that—maybe—it's drawing me closer to answers. These conflicting feelings—this absolute nightmare of a dilemma—feels like I've been pulled into the undertow of the bioluminescent river that is my mind. Taken under and pulled away without mercy, drowning in the toxic waters—unable to do anything about any of it. Mentally, I'm tortured.

"I'm exhausted," I finally tell Juno. "I've been lacking sleep for the past few days. I ... I really need to go to bed."

"You don't seem okay, Kaeda," Juno persists.

"I'm exhausted right now."

"Okay, well ..." Juno hesitates, "... I hope you feel better. Sleep well."

I hang up the call.

12:16 AM.

12:16 AM. What the digital clock aside from the television screen in the townhouse living room reads as I stare blankly at it, the electronic smartphone "hang-up" sound ringing through my ears. My senses are blurred. My mind is blank yet not—a distinct numbness resides within me, yet my mind is still full of many questions and thoughts.

As I sit in a silent numbness—a solitude without peace—I begin noticing the intricate details of my surroundings and physical self. My quick heart rate, my bouncing knee, my sick stomach, my dizziness—I can't help these feelings and actions. I can't help the way I'm reacting to this confusing situation, and I can't determine whether I should text James. I don't know *why* or *how* the texts were cleared; I don't know if my own mind is tricking me; I don't know if I should be completely honest with Juno—I don't know the cause of this mess. This disaster that I can't help but allow to get to me, eating me up from the inside out, seeping itself into my brain, and causing me to ask so many questions that seem nearly impossible to answer.

If I could only make peace with myself.

I would be so satisfied if I could only make peace with myself, but that appears impossible now.

I've fallen into a pit of complete confusion, and I don't see myself getting out any time soon. I don't know what to tell Ottie; I don't know what to tell Beau; I don't know what to tell James—I don't know what to tell Juno. I don't know what to tell Sasha. I don't know how to deal with this—I don't know what to tell myself to do.

I could tell Ottie everything I had heard, but would that only confuse her more about what the caretakers told her? I'm beginning to question the entire situation over again, asking myself if the caretakers *really* told her that I died with bad intentions. Maybe they thought I did, somehow, someway. But I don't know. I was never there to experience it.

I could tell Juno exactly what James told me and what I've seen, but that would only escalate any problems she may have. That would only cause conflict and confusion. I don't even want to elaborate on what I think could happen if I had told Juno everything, partially because I'm not sure, and partially because I don't think the outcome would be bright in the least.

I could tell James, confronting him. I could tell him my dilemma, ask him questions—all that I could think of concerning the situation. But there's so much uncertainty surrounding him and what he told me. Did he *really* tell me that? *What* was the situation, *why* are the texts cleared, and *how* is Juno alive right now?

I could tell Sasha, but that might only advance her questions.

I could tell Beau, but that might only advance his questions.

And I think I've decided who I'll tell next, because what I need is a search continuation. I need it to make *enough* sense; I need *some form* of certainty or knowledge surrounding this topic in my life.

I need to feel okay, but it's almost as though the only way that I could do that would be to escape from my problems—from my questions and the issues surrounding me. But I'm entirely unable to do that—to escape from these burning thoughts and wonders in my mind would be completely nonsensical.

The bouncing in my leg has stopped. The dizziness still lingers, but it begins resembling tiredness. I'm worn out from the questions I've asked in the past period where Juno and I were calling—her talking to me in complete normality as I hesitated to speak and acted like an idiot. I'm drained of questions, unable to ask any more. I'm weak from the heavy burden on my back that I've begun to let pull me down. I'm still swept into the undertow of the blue neon river, but I've resisted struggling now. I've only let myself move with the water, even with the damage it does to my body.

I bring everything back to the bedroom to find Ottie sleeping soundly in her top bunk; her innocence and lack of knowledge toward the topics that roam my mind, those that I had just briefly discussed with Juno, through my perspective, is heavily nostalgic. This nostalgia for this dynamic—this dynamic with one innocent, energetic twin sister and one painfully thoughtful one—causes me to wonder what must have happened when we were children for that dynamic to even be present. As I continue to watch Ottie, a realization crosses my mind: this townhouse is littered with questions as the people who sleep in it live with unsatisfied minds. They live in curiosity and uncertainty, questioning their past, their future, and their present. Their dreams—whether they may ignore them, the workings of their minds—everything that revolves around a group of questions each individual has that seem to have been built up over time. This townhouse and the people living inside of it are full of questions about their lives—some coping through substance use and others coping through investigation concerning those questions—and I find that to be both beautiful and deteriorating.

I lay down on my bed. I can hear the vibrations of my phone on the nightstand next to me, but I ignore them. I let them run until they stop, unknowing of what they are, yes, but weirdly unbothered. In this mess of a situation, I find peace in ignoring it all. I understand that ignorance will never last and that—knowing how I am—I'll get over it and return to the issue at hand, but it's as though there's no other option for me but to escape in this present time. I choose to leave the situation for this period. I choose to leave the situation alone for the night as I understand that I am unable to deal with it.

It brings me momentary peace if I avoid the thought enough, and it's as though I am too tired to avoid doing just that.

As I lay in my bed and my eyes grow heavy, it begins to rain outside—hard enough to hear the raindrops hit the window and for that noise to become something to lull you to sleep: a white noise. I find myself only focusing on the sounds of the rain. The peace of the scene—even if that peace is only falsely believed by my own tired self, and even if that belief is only short term. What matters is how it sends me into a state of subconsciousness as my questions silence and my thinking decelerates—I am not part of reality anymore.

I fall asleep.

Friday, November 14, 2036, ??:?? AM

A cool breeze passes over me, and a faint aroma of dew follows. Around me are sounds of communication from different distances and, as my eyes adjust to the scene, I notice that one of those sources comes from two very familiar people. Those of whom sit across from me at a very familiar round green picnic table—the one at GoldenPine that Juno, James, and I would frequently sit at during lunch hours. The sight of the GoldenPine courtyard and its students—both my lunch group and the groups of others in the distance communicating in such different ways—brings me an unusual amount of nostalgia for a dream. Typically, a nostalgic dream would involve my childhood. This one, however, looks as if it could be from a little over a week ago, so it's considerably odd that I have such great longing for a time so recent. I ask myself *why* and find myself quickly receiving an answer: At this time, the struggles that I thought were so great were ones primarily of my own mind that did not directly involve other people. Now, my monumental struggles involve the questioning of my own sense of reality and whether it is valid because of a significant event directly involving another person. Therefore I have nostalgia for such a recent time: I miss the simplicity of it, even if there was no genuine simplicity to begin with.

I notice Juno's body language as we sit at the table and James tells me about a group of students from one of his classes. Juno keeps her head down with a melancholy expression, scrolling through her phone and sighing frequently. She scoots away from her brother as he speaks more about the group of students, forming a barrier between herself and him. Not only is it her body language, though—through the lenses of her glasses is a clear vision of her deep eye bags. I remember this moment; this scene is a memory.

Monday, November 3, 2036, 11:21 AM

"Juno?" James calls for his sister after finishing his topic, glancing over at her. He lowers his speaking volume and Juno groggily brings her view toward her brother. "Are you doing okay?"

Juno nods slowly with a blank expression. It's clear that this is a lie, and James notices it immediately.

"Really?"

Juno nods again, turning away from her brother.

"You just seem very down."

"Shut up, James," Juno mumbles. "You don't help anything."

James' facial expression changes quickly from a gentle concern to shock. He looks down at the floor and away from Juno.

"Wow," he says, "Thanks."

Juno looks over at James with a quick change in her facial expression as well: annoyed to greatly concerned.

"Oh, no," says Juno. "I'm sorry—"

"You can't treat people like this, Juno," James says, cutting his sister off. "I don't know what's been going on. Are you nervous about Will?"

"Will has nothing to do with this," Juno responds. "Please, leave me alone."

"I'm just trying to help you," James reassures his sister.

"Go, please."

James appears to pull out his phone, messaging a friend to ask about a backup lunch plan. As he receives a response, he tells Juno that he's going to find a friend who's at a philosophy club meeting and eat there instead. Juno responds with a quiet "okay", and James leaves while Juno carries the same melancholy body language and blank, exhausted expression.

The dream fades, and I wake up.

6:56 AM

Ottie taps my shoulder repeatedly, saying my name just as she did yesterday morning when I slept in. What I can see of her is blurry before I put my glasses on, and she appears to look dressed and ready, but I've only just woken up. I'm going to be late.

I still have a lingering dizziness, the same one I had yesterday. My stomach hurts and, as I continue moving throughout the morning, I notice that it's aching in nervousness. I'm stress sick, but not sick enough to miss school. I eat a somewhat substantial amount of food, and we leave.

The school bus is quiet today. The fog is so chilling yet relaxing—a looming dread resides within it, but still convinces me that it brings peace. Trees, streetlamps, and bus stops vaguely show themselves in the thick fog, vague enough to where you can't tell what else is lying ahead. You can only see the broad, tall structures. Everything else is unknown to you.

I hate the unknown. I hate it so much. That's terribly weird for me to come to terms with—I used to be so incredibly intrigued by all that was unknown to me; there was a blank canvas where I could learn and understand a myriad of topics.

But, now, I think of not knowing and it only reminds me of the complex, life-changing topics that I don't understand and am hesitant to believe I ever will. I think of it and it reminds me of Juno—why I received the texts I did—why she's alive right now. I think of it and I hear this cluster of sounds and see this cluster of visuals, tormenting me because *I can't piece them together*.

I hate the unknown and the eerie feeling it gives me, even if I can't seem to stop myself from exploring it—and exploring it repeatedly. What I do—the lack of self-control I have—only hurts me. I'm so thirsty for understanding that I seem to lose my sense of what it actually means to understand.

I don't like to talk to myself in my head like this, trailing on and on with an idea or criticism of myself and avoiding fixing it. Yet I love it. I love making these connections and realizations that seem to allow me to understand more about my mind every time that they're made.

We get off the bus, and it's slightly chilly. I want to talk to Ottie or Beau, but I don't want to risk their sanity. One of them—if not both—would become caught up in the mystery of Juno's mortality. The mystery of what I was told. And I have a feeling that person would be Ottie, connecting these experiences back to her own, not letting go of the idea that something is gravely wrong—even though that observation is correct.

Eventually, I will have to tell her and embrace the consequences that come with it. She might lose her mind, she might flail around with ideas and questions; her trauma might be resurfaced and she may question everything she's ever believed. Telling her now seems tempting, and it's not because I want to see her lose herself, but rather I'm curious as to what she might think of. How we could work together and create new possibilities. It might be beneficial to tell Ottie, even if I might lose my mind, too.

The classes in the first half of the day are unimportant to me now. Come lunch, I sit with everyone again. I wait to tell anyone about Juno out of uncertainty about the situation and not knowing if it's the right time, but I also ask myself if any time is the "right time" to talk about something so detrimental and confusing. Sasha plops her bag down on the ground and sits against it. She looks tired, as do I.

Lunch is an internal battle. I look over at Sasha, Ottie, and Beau, and I wonder if I say anything to them. I don't know how visibly nervous I am, but I can feel my heart rate increase any time I consider admitting to them what happened last night. My hands are shaky, and then I realize that my nervousness is, most definitely, visible.

"You okay, Kaeda?" Sasha asks.

"Oh, fine," I respond, jolting my head over to her.

"Really?" Sasha insists.

"Yes, fine," I answer. It's a complete lie, but I'm not sure how possible it is to tell the truth right now. I find myself staring into space with my thoughts and the voices of Ottie, Sasha, and Beau becoming only a blur to me. My thoughts become like a piece of music—they drown everything else out—but a piece of music that doesn't relax me: a piece that is *confusing*, with *dissonance*, and that piece is the questions that I ask myself about Juno. *Why* she's alive, *why* I was lied to, and *what* the entire situation means. And I could talk about it with everyone around me and they could try to devise something, but I don't feel like I can yet. My stomach aches with a pain that engulfs me, nervously asking *questions*.

Everything seems to melt away into a pool of confusion; I'm lightheaded and unable to think or speak. I can't even tell if the surrounding people notice because, in my eyes, they have all turned to blur although I wear my glasses. I can't even notice what expressions I make, what I'm doing, how I feel—whether I'm saying anything.

And then I realize, at that moment, that I'm on the verge of tears.

The event shocks me back into reality.

"Kaeda?" Ottie says, with strong and distinct concern in her tone of voice and facial expression. She sits next to me and arches her eyebrows at my face. "What's wrong?"

"It's, um ..." I start. My mouth is dry, and I'm not sure if I can go on.

"You look like you carry some kind of guilt," Beau comments.

"It's not ..." I respond, "It's not that. I promise."

"Well, then what's wrong?" he asks.

"It's, uh," I start, "It's Juno."

Sasha looks at Ottie and Beau, asking who Juno is. They tell her that she was a friend of mine who died a few days back. They tell her that I must just be taking it difficultly, and I want to say something, but it starts off with incoherent stutters.

"She's, um ..." I say, licking my lips in nervousness. My stomach pain increases with each word.

"She's alive," I tell them.

"*What*?" Beau asks. "Was it a failed attempt?"

"No, she's alive," I say. "She called me last night. It was her voice, acting like nothing happened. A day after I had been told that she was dead. Dead for a few days."

"Holy shit," Sasha says.

"Do you think that they just lied when they told you about her death?" Beau asks, bouncing his leg in nervousness yet looking at me with intrigue.

"I don't see how her brother could lie about something so serious," I respond. "That was *never* like him. He was always morally and ethically correct—he was knowledgeable of philosophy and seemed to be a large voice of reason in our little group of three."

Beau and Sasha rapidly ask me questions about Juno, about her brother, and about what I was told. I answer incoherently and only in stutters, unable to tell if the burden of the situation is becoming less or becoming more with everything I say to them. Their voices turn to blurs in my head again, but one thing I do notice is how Ottie says nothing. She stares at the ground in stunned silence, almost like how I believe I did a few minutes ago. And, immediately, I figure out why.

She experienced a terrifyingly similar situation.

I can't reach out to her now—that conversation would need to be private and especially not in school. I can't just resurface these critical situations with other people around, unknowing of her sensitivity to this. But, in retrospect, I can't help but feel like that is exactly what I just did.

The expression on Ottie's face is an expression that I don't believe I've seen on her before—a blank, nervous, fearful expression—an expression that says: "I don't know what just happened, I don't know what is about to happen, and I don't know how to change it". Unknowing, confusion, fear, yet something of dissociation. *Uneasiness.* More than one word is needed to describe the emotion that she feels right now.

And, seeing that, I regret saying anything right now. Because now I have two people interrogating me as their curiosity devours them inside and one person who feels like her traumatic past experiences have just resurfaced. *I wish I had said nothing.*

I'm reluctant to answer a single question for the rest of lunch.

The last few periods of the day go by, and the bus ride home is quiet, even if some people wish it wasn't. Beau looks at me from time to time on the bus, appearing reluctant to ask anything because of my responses earlier, yet eager for knowledge. Ottie sleeps on the bus, saying barely anything to me, though looking like she would like to.

Once we enter the townhouse, Beau walks upstairs to his bedroom whilst Janice stays locked in her computer. Ottie and I are the only people sitting in the living room, and I notice exactly when she feels ready to have a conversation with me.

"Kaeda," she starts, sitting next to me on the couch. "What *exactly* happened with Juno?"

"I was told by her twin brother on Saturday night that she died from suicide a few days prior, and that he awaited telling me because of how his family has been dealing with it," I answer. "Then, last night, I received a call from Juno. She talked to me and seemed to be genuinely at peace and happy, but I got so worried and anxious—I stuttered for almost every word—which made her feel off. She seemed to have no knowledge or reconciliation of anything that happened." I breathe in. "It was almost as if nothing had happened at all. Especially ... *especially* when I checked my message history with James; the texts were wiped. I forgot to mention any of that at lunch."

"They were *wiped*?" Ottie repeats in surprise.

"Yes, wiped completely," I answer. "Any trace of what he told me about the situation was gone."

"I ... I don't understand how that could've happened," Ottie comments in distress. "The other person can't wipe your message history. You have to wipe it yourself. Did you do that while you were, maybe, super tired? Or something?"

"Not from what I remember," I answer. "And I remember a lot about when James told me that Juno died."

I see Ottie portraying the same emotion that I had seen during lunch from her, yet now she seems panicked. She seems frantically trying to find a solution to the problem: her eyes shooting around the room, her hands slightly shaking, and her struggling to talk. She licks her lips in nervousness, and, gradually, I notice more of myself in the emotions of this person.

"Kaeda, do you understand how *insane* this is?" Ottie sputters to me while finally locking eyes, speaking louder than she had before. ''This is a person who just *died*. You were told that they died, and, suddenly, they're alive. And no trace of their death exists anymore."

She inhales shakily.

"Do you know what that sounds like?"

Kaeda, do you see a recurrence here?

I instantly respond.

"Yes, I do," I tell her. "It's the same situation where you were told by the caretakers that I was dead."

Ottie arches her eyebrows in a weird ambition. "*Exactly.*"

I'm pulled into a situation that now forces me to think differently, yet I'm not sure what I'm thinking anymore. But I sure as hell don't perceive things the same way as I used to.

I'm forced into a mess that I don't think I can solve. I don't know what will come out of it; I don't know what's true and what's false; I don't know if the mess of a situation is all for nothing or means everything. I don't know what to tell Juno, Ottie, Beau, Sasha, or myself. I'm losing it. I don't know if Sasha's problems are related or unrelated to the mess with Juno, nor do I know if any of these questions and problems are worth my time. But, yet, I still feel like I'd lose a purpose if they weren't, though it's as though I'm losing myself by constantly trying to find answers.

It hurts me. I'm weak and drained of any energy to solve anything anymore.

And then I receive a call from Juno.

"Holy shit," Ottie blurts. "Uh—um ... pick—pick it up."

I pick up the call.

"Juno?" I say.

"Hi Kaeda," she replies. "How are you after everything? Are you doing okay?"

"I don't know," I tell her.

"Oh," Juno says. "Well, I'm sorry. I don't know how I'm feeling either—I had a bad dream after I went to sleep last night. I think it was because of the call, but it was very ... mentally disturbing."

"Oh?" I respond. "How so?"

A bad dream.

"I saw myself differently in the dream," Juno says. "I was angry. I saw an emotion within myself that I hadn't seen before: I was angry and sad at *something*, though unsure of *what*."

"Angry and sad?" I ask. "How?"

"There were these vivid images that I was living through of me just being *mad* at myself," Juno says. "*Mad* at myself for *something*. Like I had done something terribly wrong that was causing me to feel horrible emotions. I hate to think about it now—it was horrible."

"Oh, man."

"I saw these situations of me at school before with you and James—just horrible," She continues. "Just feeling *horrible*. It was this weird feeling of burden; I was both angry and sad because of it. It confuses me because I was never like that with you guys. I was never like that."

"You weren't sad at school recently?" I ask—I know that she was. Both James and I know that she was; we saw it firsthand: her distress.

And she's claiming that she wasn't.

"No, I don't remember ever being that sad around you guys at school," Juno replies.

I gather my words and prepare to give her confrontation without it being either too passive or too blunt.

"Juno, you talked about it with both James and me earlier this month," I tell her, trying not to sound aggressive. "... I'm sorry, but that's what I remember."

"Do ... do you think that I just blocked it out?" Juno asks after a few thoughts, with worry in her voice. "I don't understand why you have those memories."

"I just don't understand why you don't," I reply.

"Kaeda, I'm just trying to—"

"How much do you remember from earlier?" I ask her; I'm being too blunt.

"I can't recall a lot, but that's kind of how I've always been," she answers.

"Really?"

"I mean ... I think," Juno says. "I feel like I'm losing it here. I truly don't know what to tell you."

"I'm sorry, Juno," I apologize. "I didn't mean to come off so blunt."

"I feel stressed," Juno says. "I have to go. Goodbye."

The call ends. *Shit, I'm horrible at confrontations.*

"Man, what was that?" Ottie asks. "Was she really that sad before?"

I nod my head. "I feel like I'm losing it here," I mumble to Ottie, repeating Juno's words.

"Why can't she remember it?" Ottie asks again.

"I don't know, but she saw it all happen in a dream," I answer. "Thing is, that dream might've just been a memory of hers."

"She can't block things out that quickly, can she?" Ottie asks.

"I don't know," I answer. "I really don't. It just seems like everything relating to her suicide doesn't exist anymore."

What if I was only delusional?

I mean, what if that suicide didn't happen? Maybe I just ...

No, that's nonsensical. These situations have felt *too* real and have had *too* much reasoning behind them for *too* long for that to even be a possibility. But, even then, it feels like this entire mess is completely nonsensical as well.

The bioluminescent river confuses me—it's hit a point where there are two pathways and I start to wonder which one will the current run faster through; I wonder where the pathways lead. And I start to lose my mind a bit in the process. I need to sleep—I need to somehow get away from this.

Dinner comes and passes. I take a shower after everyone else that is using the same bathroom as I am and truly just stay silent in my thoughts. Looking back on it, I can't recall a lot of what I was thinking from the period between dinner and getting ready to go to sleep. Just numbness. Feeling like I'm on autopilot after a situation that has confused me to such a high intensity.

But, as I get ready to end the day, a few thoughts appear in my head.

They all relate to Sasha and the things that she told me.

I fall asleep.

Ten

Saturday, November 15, 2036, ??:?? AM

I wake up.

A distinct aroma surrounds me as I begin to open my eyes: the aroma of a certain building, a medical building—a hospital. As my vision adapts to the scene, I notice a plain room of minimal, uncomfortable furniture—a room of ineffective rehabilitation. A mental hospital room; I briefly recognize it from a very vague dream I've had before, only about a week ago.

As I look down at my body, I find myself dressed in an uncomfortable hospital gown. The light blue sheets of my twin bed are uncomfortably scratchy and void of any warmth as I sit on them, similar to the hospital gown, whilst the walls of the room are plain white and lack decoration of any sort. Next to me sits a nightstand and a few large open shelves in a corner of the room, but they, too, are empty of character.

My surroundings, beyond the small window of the bedroom, are void of any illumination. Aside from the faint sounds of the air conditioning system running throughout the building, the room is dead silent. The atmosphere of this place is cold; the surroundings of mine are brutally lifeless. Though I doubt that I've ever truly been here before and have no familiar emotion towards this place to reflect on, I hate being here now.

I hate it so incredibly much.

I hate the vividness of this dream in particular: how each detail is clear-cut and inflicts great torture upon my brain. Yes, most of my dreams are very vivid, however, this one and its incredible amount of graphic detail in contrast with its dull surroundings are a source of grave confusion. I don't have time to ask myself why an area so void of life appears so colorful inside of my mind and, even if I *did* have the time, I don't think I'd like to ask myself that at all; dreams with high vividity are typically memories, and I don't want to wonder whether I've been here—especially followed by *why* I've been here.

I leave my cold, hard bed and walk towards the door. As I try to turn the handle, I'm met with something I'm technically unfamiliar with concerning memory but, in a dream, I've witnessed this visual briefly before: a handle that lies against and into the door itself—a handle that is ligature resistant—you cannot hang things on this handle. I turn it in an attempt to leave; I don't want to be here, standing in this lifeless room of torment.

As I walk through the door and out of the room, I don't encounter the rest of the hospital—I'm in *my* room: the room from my old house right outside of San Francisco. It's the same time of day here as it was in the hospital and, even though I expect a wave of comfort to wash over me following my leaving, there is no comfort. Instead, I'm met with something objectively worse: a wave of anxiety. As if something horrible is waiting to happen—as if I've done something terribly wrong that is leading me to expect a horrible punishment of some sort. As if I've said something to alter my reality. As if I've broken the dream and, slowly, *it's turning into a nightmare.*

The feeling nags at me like an upcoming task that I've pushed off—I try to dig a hole for it, but it only continues to resurface and bite back at me. Although I'm unsure what, I know that I've done *something* wrong. *Something* to make me feel this immense amount of nervousness. My stomach hurts, my leg bounces as I sit on my bed, and my surroundings seem somewhat warped ... I can't focus on anything. And yet, although I *know* that this is a dream, I cannot shake the terrifying feeling. It seems so real and far too vivid to only be in my head: a dream of madness. I thought that, maybe, the mental hospital would've been worse than my bedroom, but at this moment, they seem identical. If these places are so different, *why is it that they feel so similar?*

Maybe it's the unintelligible digits on the alarm clock next to me. Maybe it's the liminal time of day, the silence of my room—the mess of my surroundings. Maybe it's the fact that I'm aware that this is a dream, yet struggle to ignore how real it feels. Maybe it's that there's a horrible weakness within me—I'm *weak*.

It's as though I've made some kind of effort that ended up being completely futile and I am now dealing with the consequences. But why is that *nervousness*? *What did I do to receive this?*

I get up from my bed and leave my bedroom, only to find myself leaving my house entirely. The front of my house and the familiar neighborhood in which my house sits lay before my eyes; chilling gusts of wind softly wash over me like waves of a river and pass through the familiar tree leaves—sleek and dimly lit street lamps are my primary source of illumination amidst the barren, pitch-black sky. There is no sound aside from the soft gusts of wind rustling the trees; the area is completely void of life. I've seen this many times before—I've felt this many times before.

Loneliness.

Yes, there is no one around in this neighborhood—I'm alone. But moreover, I'm *lonely.* I'm unable to go to anyone, unable to express any thoughts I have—unable to talk. Within me rests a feeling of terrible seclusion that I wish didn't exist. I wish I could go to someone. I wish that there was *someone here.*

Glancing around the lonely scene, a sign of life accompanies me on the sidewalk beside my mailbox: a notebook page. A notebook page, laying on the sidewalk—I walk over to pick it up.

I expect a certain familiar one that I've seen in my dreams before, but that doesn't appear.

I don't think I've ever seen this page in my dreams before.

Kaeda Bynum, 11/6/36
What made me forget?
- I wish to remember.

    I don't remember when the questions started. But I
    wish to.

What was it like to live before adoption?
- Ottie—what was she like?

    Energetic, creative, kind

Why do I feel this way? Why do I feel so numb?
- ~~My own mother's death doesn't change this fact. Does this make me a bad person?~~

    ~~No, no—you're not a bad person for feeling numb.~~

- Michelle was incredibly depressed because of Frank after their son's death—she considered suicide and made a will in the process.

~~Why am I so obsessed with productivity?~~
- ~~To forget about this page.~~

The notebook page of unanswered questions—I haven't touched this page in a while. It induces within me a combination of feelings: nostalgia, anxiety, and curiosity. Confusion as well, but I think that sources from the fact that each emotion induced by that page is so different from the other—nostalgia being the most confusing.

Why nostalgia?

This page is only from a few days ago.

I think nostalgia exists here for a reason similar to the nostalgia produced by a previous dream scene—the issues at hand within my mind were not as severe as they are now. I was dealing with them individually; there were no problems with the validity of reality. It was only a lack of memory that plagued my mind—it was only issues with silencing my feelings. Everything was *internal*.

Now, the questions I ask myself question *the world*. They question death—they question *life*. They question other people. I am not the only issue at hand anymore as I once believed, and I subconsciously long to return to that period where I was.

That's the apparent feeling of nostalgia: *longing*.

The scene changes.

Sitting on the bed of a mental hospital bedroom once more, dressed in a medical gown of scratchy fabric. From behind, I hear the bedroom door open accompanied by a soft light from its crack and, for a moment, panic swells up within me. The whir of air conditioning throughout the building becomes uncomfortably loud—my legs tremble and my hands sweat. Though, as I turn around, panic leaves my body as I notice who the person opening the door is—the face of a friend: not Juno, but Sasha. She looks at me wearing a hospital gown identical to mine with a facial expression drooping in exhaustion; dark eyebags hang under her eyes—she appears to not have slept in days.

"Come here," Sasha says, "I found something."

I walk towards her from my bed.

"It's a room to answer questions," Sasha tells me. "It answered mine. Here, just look."

I follow her out the door of my room, where we end up in a vast, quiet hallway aligned with what appear to be capsules on each side of the room. They're similar to rehabilitation chambers that you'd see in a sci-fi movie, but more in-line with a hospital-like, bleak atmosphere. The hallway that they surround seems to fit that, as well.

"Walk down," Sasha tells me. I start to, and the vague scene starts developing, yet quickly diminishing as the dream continues.

I wake up.

My heart beats quickly as if it's trying to escape my body. I can tell that my mind is running with thoughts, yet I'm not sure what they are. Against my skin is an uncomfortable dampness as my clothing does not feel completely dry—I've woken up in a cold sweat. As I touch my palms together, they glide against each other in moisture. I can't fathom a physical feeling more silently uncomfortable than this one as I lay in my bed in the early morning in my sweat with a pulse oddly quick and a dizziness that, still, seems to have not faded.

The silence and melancholy of the early morning form an aching feeling that I can't get rid of. There's a knocking at my mind—a distant reminder of something I want to forget. I used to find comfort in the loneliness of this time of day, but right now that comfort seems nearly impossible to find again. My surroundings are unsettling and lack any peace amidst the silence of them.

I don't want to think about the dream; I want to blur out any confusing thoughts and questions that appear in my mind. But it's painfully evident to me that all feelings and experiences will only point back to the thoughts that I'm trying so hard to erase. Maybe it's not the dream itself that I don't want to think about, but how deeply it confuses me; how it presents to me these experiences and questions I can't answer.

I'm terrified of my own mind. I'm terrified of the dream. I'm terrified of Sasha, of Juno, of Ottie, of Beau; of myself. I'm terrified of anything connecting me back to a problem that seems so much bigger than me—the problem of *why* I keep encountering so many puzzling events: Juno's "death", Sasha's coma, Beau's dreams as well as my own, my lack of remembrance for Ottie; the fact that Ottie was told that I died. But I know that, despite my fear, I can't run from these events—they live with me and I would feel incredibly unsatisfied to have never solved them.

Juno being alive after I was explicitly told that she was dead is objectively the largest problem I've had to face. For the sake of solving the issue and knowledge, I wish that I could treat it as such, but, for now, I just feel tired and avoidant of all problems, yet know that I will inevitably have to deal with them until I receive some form of clarity—I can't just push these issues away.

I don't know what my subconscious was trying to tell me through the dream I had just recently; it felt like a giant wave of weird, sick, twisted déjà vu. I have the confusing, debilitating need to forgive myself for something I haven't done. I have the need to stand outside in the empty, liminal hours of the early morning and let my worries flee. There's a heavy burden of nervousness and guilt over *something—something* I'm unable to understand. A horrible pit within my stomach—I'm a failure to myself. For some unknown reason, these feelings strike me as a lot more vivid than most which follow my dreams; signs of a memory—*anything but this, please.*

My phone vibrates on the nightstand directly next to me; I pick it up. It's Juno, with multiple texts.

"I can't seem to think, Kaeda"

"I had another horrible dream"

"It's hurting me"

"Do you ever remember me hating myself? I can't seem to get that thought out of my head, as if it's happened before"

I don't know how to respond to this—if I even go through with responding at all. Not because I resent Juno or don't care to talk to her, but because I simply can't deal with these questions; this recurrent similarity of events.

It's hitting me.

Juno felt such a strong, particularly vivid memory of her feelings that continued to linger after a dream that she had: one that had meant something about her past that she couldn't remember. Dreaming of an event with zero conscious remembrance of it: that's nonsensical—that's insanity. Not only does that make Juno insane, or Beau, that makes me insane, too.

Has this entire journey been complete and utter insanity?

I've taken so many varying paths in the last ten days to where I don't know what is right and wrong anymore—what's true and what isn't. One thing is for sure, though: everything has changed. These 5 AM skies, though still so empty and lonely, aren't what they used to be. Now, in this loneliness of the early morning, I find a great sense of fear and torment rather than peace and thought. I fear my own mind, more than I was before the incident with Michelle. I fear what it can do in this loneliness with all of these newfound problems. Nothing is the same, and I doubt things ever will be. Because, with these additional issues that concern existence and the validity of my own mind itself, I begin wondering if what I'm living is truly reality.

I wish I knew more about my biological parents. I wish I knew more about Ottie, about Beau, about Sasha, about Juno, and about Beau's mom, Janice. I wish I knew more about myself. I wish I knew more about the past and how it has a trend of shaping the future. I wish I knew *more*.

I decide to reply to Juno.

"I remember bits of it, yeah," I text back, with almost an immediate response:

"That's so weird. I can't recall any of that, I swear."

"But you see it in your dreams?" I ask.

"Yeah."

I don't follow up with any other texts in the conversation between Juno and me; I don't feel as though I can. I want to erase it all from my head, but I know that each time I repeat that wish, it's a complete lie. I'm hungry to think, even if it's poisonous.

I don't want to let my mind run more than it already does, but I also want to try to dig for an answer in it. I think letting it run is the only way to find that answer.

I can't focus on physical feelings right now, but I know that my heart rate is much higher than what is healthy. I know that these questions that I ask all of the time have a drastic impact on my health, but it would hurt me to stop. I need to keep searching. *I need—*

"Kaeda?" Ottie says quietly from above. "You okay?"

"I'm fine," I respond with a hoarse voice.

"You're tossing and turning a lot down there," Ottie comments. "Enough to wake me up. Are you stressed?"

"I think a little, yeah," I answer, lying.

"No, it's very clear that you are," Ottie refutes. "What—did you dream about Juno?"

"No," I respond quietly. Ottie comes down from the top bunk with a confused expression on her face.

"What did you dream about, then?" Ottie questions. She has more energy than I expected at this hour.

"A mental hospital and my old house," I reply. "But it didn't even feel like a dream until maybe the end. It felt more like a memory—it was much less confusing and abstract than a dream. And I could remember certain details like I had lived out the experience."

"Well, have you?" Ottie asks me. It was not the response that I was expecting.

"I ... I don't ..."

I stutter in my answer.

"I don't think ...?"

God, the question gets to me; Ottie pierced my mind with the most simple question about the dream I had. I should respond with "no" because I don't remember ever going to a mental hospital, *but that feels wrong*. Because, truly, I'm unsure. I dreamt briefly about this the morning after Michelle went to the hospital, just about a week ago.

If I think about it logically, no, I've never lived out the experience of going to a mental hospital; I can't remember it ever happening. But my life is so void of logic currently with these puzzling situations that I've been wound up in, and I only feel drawn to the possibility that *I might've.*

Juno *for sure* has felt those negative feelings recently that she can't remember. I remember her sulking before I had moved, her melancholy writing and facial expressions, the concern that James had about her depression, and her obsessively negative questions about herself and others. She would dig a pit of negativity and doubt for herself and grow helpless in that pit. I remember it vividly—it supposedly caused her death. But that's all gone and only in her head now, disguising itself as a dream when, really, it's all a memory. So, in this world, logic is dead. I don't understand the inner workings of the experiences I live out anymore if there are even any inner workings to understand, as much as it pains me to consider the possibility of that being the truth.

There's a possibility that Juno and I are experiencing a very similar thing. I hate this possibility, but I will not fall into a stage of denial and try to convince myself that it's completely impossible because, really, it isn't.

"I don't know if I have or haven't," I reply.

"It's not uncommon for you to forget things that happened," Ottie says. "Like how you forgot quite a bit about me. You knew I existed, you knew that we knew each other, but you didn't remember our experiences like a normal person would've."

"What makes me *not* normal, then?" I ask.

"The fact that you don't remember a lot."

"Well, what causes me not to?" I ask again.

"I don't know, Kaeda," Ottie answers. "That's for you to find out."

"Could it have been a concussion?" I question, my voice picking up a pace. "Do I have some sort of neurological problem?"

"Calm down," Ottie says.

"If I do, why hasn't anybody told me about it?" I continue to ask rapidly. "When did this all happen?"

My phone chimes with a message notification from Beau, reading "Please quiet down". I didn't notice it, but I've been asking these questions at a high volume.

"Kaeda, I don't know," Ottie states. "I'm sorry that I don't have any idea about what screwed you up like this."

Ottie looks at me with arched eyebrows. The dark blue hues of the sky align with her eyes. Her hair is a mess, yet she seems more awake than she is during the day. I don't know how I'm looking at her or what expression I'm giving, but I find myself restless. I'm worn out and exhausted, even though the day has only just started.

Ottie's arched expression fades. She looks into my eyes with concern and sadness, and I've noticed that this is a recurring pattern. She lashes out at somebody out of stress; she keeps the emotion for a few seconds, and she breaks. It's a recurring pattern in her as it is in me.

"I'm sorry, Kaeda," she tells me, looking down at her sheets with guilt and anxiety. "I do this too much."

"It's okay," I reassure her.

"I just don't have the answers to all of your questions," Ottie says.

"Nobody does," I tell her.

"No, don't think about it like that ..."

"But it seems to be true," I continue. "This experience, in and of itself, seems more like a dream than like reality. This is so obscure, Ottie—I can't just expect that my questions will someday become answered."

"I don't know what to say to you," says Ottie.

"I don't think you can really say anything."

"But, no, I have to play a part in this—I was told that you were dead just as you were told that Juno was. And both of those things are lies," Ottie tells me. "There must be some sort of connection."

"But is it just time to *give up* on finding that?" I ask.

Ottie shakes her head at me. "No, it's never time to—"

Though I couldn't hear the footsteps beforehand, I notice Beau entering the bedroom, exhausted.

"The topic intrigued me. I heard most of it," Beau starts. "What did you dream about last night, Kaeda?"

"I dreamed of being in a mental hospital," I say. "And it felt just like how a memory would."

"There you go," Beau says. "That's a memory, then. I've had the same thing for a while now. And I've kind of just decided that something's wrong with me—I can't remember the experiences that feel just like memories. I've kind of just decided that they are memories."

"But how can you know for sure?"

"I don't, but it makes more sense for them to be real than to be fake, right?" Beau suggests. "If they feel so real and happen so often, what would make them *not*?"

"So you think that you knew Ida before," I conclude.

"Briefly, yeah," Beau says. "I think I knew her somehow. Maybe not too well, but well enough to think about her and remember her face."

"But you don't remember her, that's the thing."

"No, but my subconscious does," Beau says. "I can suppress a memory as much as I'd like, but my subconscious always makes the connection. So I *do* think that I knew her somehow."

"Yeah, but being admitted to a mental hospital seems like it would be so much bigger than that," I say. "I couldn't suppress it that easily."

"I don't have all the answers to your questions either, Kaeda," Beau says. "This is just the conclusion I've come to for myself. I don't know if I'll ever see Ida again, but I know we had some sort of connection before I moved to California."

"You won't be able to know everything," Ottie tells me.

I don't respond. I'm aware of what Ottie tells me, obviously, but this is something that I *yearn* for. It feels so important and seems like it could change the trajectory of everything: how I view myself, the topics I study ...

I don't know where to go from here. I think I'll talk to Sasha and continue talking to Juno about this, but I'm not sure how far it'll go; I don't know if I'll ever be sure. That can eat me up inside all it wants, but I'm uncertain how possible "knowing" truly is anymore.

Accepting a harsh reality is something that I know I've never been good at, no matter how much I've seemed to forget about myself.

The morning passes on. Beau and Janice leave for synagogue around 8 AM as Ottie and I get ready, have a quick breakfast, and eventually go out for lunch to a local deli Beau's familiar with as Sasha and Beau join us. Beau's mom, Janice, returns home after synagogue.

The ride on the city bus that we take to the deli where we'll meet Sasha for lunch is as bleak as that of a school bus. Certain times of day only feel like passing periods, and I think that feeling may be mutual across Beau, Ottie, and I. Everyone stays locked inside of their own mind like strangers on a bus, although we all know each other; even Ottie. I think I'm ruining her.

This person who she once knew became dead to her, and not in that she hates me—because I know she doesn't—but in that she thought I was gone forever. She accepted that reality and moved on, just to find out that I was alive and going to live with her. That was a high of excitement for her, yet insane amounts of confusion; why would she have been told that I died for so long just to be told that I'm actually *alive*? And, on top of that, once I *do* live with her, I can barely remember who we were as kids.

Maybe I really did die—maybe I really am dead in her mind; her version of me has vanished. The kid she knew—the one that I barely can remember—has vanished. Now *I'm* here, and I don't do what I used to. I'm not childlike anymore. I think too much and let the thoughts eat me up inside. I'm hooked on too many problems in this reality. In her mind, I'm really just *dead*.

We arrive at the deli. It's owned by a Jewish family that Beau is familiar with, hence why he brought us here. The windows into the deli are plastered with different posters advertising the food and the origin of the business. An old "Open" sign flickers its lights at the door, and the required modern technology used creates a contrast with the vintage furniture, photos, and signs I see. It's oddly comforting to walk into a place trying to adapt to advanced systems yet still keeping the same old feeling.

I order and sit at a table with Ottie where we meet Sasha, and Ottie reclines into a dark brown, leather armchair. She wears an uneasy expression across her face, looking down at her shoes and not speaking. Beau picks up the food and sits down with us, reading a photo book of San Francisco that must be at least fifteen years old. I stare at the egg and cheese bagel in front of me and hesitate to eat. I have a weirdly low appetite currently, but I eat the bagel.

"Kaeda, I need to talk to you about something in private," Sasha tells me as Beau leaves to order a soda and Ottie walks to the bathroom. "It's really important."

"Really important?"

"It's about everything these past few days," she clarifies. "We can walk outside and I'll tell you, just let Beau know you'll be gone for a moment."

Sasha and I sit at a garden table right outside of the deli. With the weather conditions, there is nobody within earshot of us.

"There might be a solution to your Juno question," she starts.

"What do you think that my 'Juno question' is?" I ask.

"I think you're asking why she's alive when you were told that she died," Sasha answers. "And told by her own brother, too. No one would ever do that, especially when you guys are all close."

"What do you think the 'solution' is?"

"Well, I don't think that … what's his name … James could've been entirely wrong," Sasha says.

"What?" I ask. "What do you mean by that? Juno's alive."

"No, but—" Sasha pauses. "How much of what I told you I heard about during my coma have you been looking into?"

I go silent—I can't attempt to lie when I'm not good at lying.

"Kaeda ..."

"I've been overwhelmed," I tell her. "I'm sorry, I really am. It's just that this has been eating me alive every time I research it, and with everything else, that's only destroyed me."

"But, come on ..."

"Still, please tell me what you think the solution is," I say.

"I just think that Juno could've been cloned, that's all," Sasha replies. "I thought maybe you would've been as avid about this topic as I have been."

That's a solid theory.

"How'd you come up with that?" I ask without hesitation.

"The deeper you dig into stories and articles, the more you find out about what 'cloning' could really be," Sasha says. "What I heard about during my coma. I was close to death that week, you know. I made the connection when I read more and more. People have similar experiences to what you've heard with James and Juno. And especially if Juno can't remember things from the past."

"Sasha?" I ask.

"Yes?"

"What did you hear about 'things from the past'?"

"I mean, just like side effects of stuff. If cloning *is* real, and Juno *is* a clone, she could very well have problems with memory," Sasha explains. "Now, I don't know if cloning is a thing, but with the technology and motivations that our world has, these questions could not be insane ones."

"What were the stories that you heard?" I continue to ask. "About people having similar experiences?"

"Oh, just people remembering a mention of a death, but then that person being alive," Sasha says. "Like what you heard about Juno. If what we're hearing is a real thing, cloning could really just be a human revival, you know."

"How valid are these stories?"

"I mean, one was a news channel," Sasha responds. "I'm surprised it didn't get the attention I thought it would. They never aired it, and my dad always watches the news. He would've probably said something."

"So are the stories really true?"

"Kaeda, even if they weren't, you *know* that they could very well be," Sasha tells me. "You're living in one. You've seen one up close." *She's right.*

It's scary how insane I've started to perceive myself. It's as though my lack of picking up on that automatically only proves to me how detached I think of myself and the problems that I face from reality. It's as if I'm living in a dream.

"These problems are huge, Sasha," I say. She nods her head in agreement.

"They are much bigger than us."

"How would we even know if cloning is real?" I ask. "I can't just go on thinking that Juno's a clone of her dead self with no confirmation."

"I don't know if we will ever know."

"But I can't just go on *not knowing*?" I continue. "This is serious. I don't want to ask myself more and more questions."

"We can't just drown in this—"

"If it is, what does that mean for Juno?" I persist. "How would she go on with life, knowing she's something that was never supposed to happen?"

"I don't have the answers to your questions," Sasha says. "I'm sorry. Why is this bothering you so much?"

"How *isn't* it bothering you?" I ask, fidgeting with my hands. "If this is a thing, you could've ended up like her. And that's horrifying. Right?"

"Calm down," Sasha tells me. "We don't even know if cloning is real. That's still a question that bugs me, but I don't think that these weird unexplainable experiences are really that unexplainable."

I know why it's bothering me; if it was real, there's such a high chance that I'm just like Juno.

A clone.

That is why I can't stop asking Sasha all of these annoying questions that don't have answers. How would I go about living, knowing I'm not technically supposed to be doing so?

Many things could be miscommunications. After all, Ottie's caretakers telling her that I died could've entirely been a lie, made up as a tactic to shut Ottie up about wishing the Bynums adopted her along with me. Causing her to believe that I simply don't exist. That could very well be what happened, but, with this possibility that Sasha brings up of these experiences being due to human cloning, I can't help but ask myself if I'm really supposed to live.

I don't know how to continue the conversation with Sasha. I *know* that I have questions, but I don't know *what* they even are. I don't know how to properly address this topic of cloning; I don't know if this topic will ever be properly addressed, and therefore I'm not sure that I will ever find an answer as to what it was that Sasha's doctors had been referring to when talking about the possibility of cloning her using DNA during a coma. Even if cloning was a human revival and Juno was a clone, how would we tell her? How would we even be sure?

How can I even be sure that what I'm stressing about is a real problem?

Ottie and Beau decide that they'd like to visit an aquarium with me, considering that there's not much to do today. I agree with the decision, though, despite that, the city bus ride back home is desolate—at least for me.

Ottie and Beau seem more enthusiastic, in somewhat of a state of bliss somehow after all that's happened—they hadn't heard what I did during lunch. I decide to wait on telling them, and they, fortunately, forget to ask during the bus ride. I don't think I could discuss cloning in a space such as this.

The bus stops, and the three of us get off; Ottie already reserved for us free tickets online. Throughout the surrounding speakers, a quiet ambiance plays. There's a group of children with what appears to be a teacher chaperone walking throughout the aquarium chatting, a couple quietly talking to each other about the exhibits, and a few other people viewing the area in comfortable silence. The lights are blue and soft as an atmospheric detail. I didn't know what Ottie had in mind while deciding to go here, but it's almost as though this was the comfort and peace that I wasn't aware I needed. It's too bad that I'll have to tell Beau and Ottie about Sasha's theory in such a beautiful place like this.

"We have to see the otters," Ottie says.

"Why?" Beau asks.

"Because that is practically my name," Ottie responds.

"Right, right."

Throughout my time walking around the place, the blue lights dim with each exhibit. We stop at a dark, jellyfish-centered area. They swim in empty blue waters with their fluorescent skin. They seem so mindless yet so interesting.

I figure I'll tell Ottie here while Beau focuses on another smaller window of jellyfish.

"What Sasha told me today was interesting," I start. The blue reflections against Ottie's glasses can't help but remind me of what each morning seems to be: a painful yet interesting conversation with my sister to remind me further that I'm not who I once was.

"What did she tell you?" Ottie asks. "She seemed awfully secretive about it."

"She told me about something she thinks cloning may be," I respond. "The cloning that she heard about during her coma: one that would supposedly relate to what could've happened to her."

Ottie looks at me, puzzled. "And what's that?"

"The possibility that cloning is just human revival," I answer. "Like what happened to Juno when I was told that she died—just to realize that she's alive."

"So her brother would've been right, then?"

"Yeah, exactly," I say. "He would've been right about the whole thing, and then she would've been revived as a clone of herself. That's basically the theory."

"And how'd she come up with that?" Ottie asks.

"Because she found out that I'm not the only person with a story about someone I know having 'died' and then suddenly being alive," I respond.

"Yeah, well no shit," Ottie says. "I've had the same experience with you."

"Well, I'm not entirely sure about whether that was a fault of the caretakers or not."

"Nobody would have ever said something like that just to make me shut up," Ottie says. "That's sick. They were never that sick."

"Sasha also found articles about possible human cloning being for the purpose of revival," I continue. "There was something relating to this on a news network, but they never really aired it—"

"Do you think that if this is real, you're a victim, Kaeda?" Ottie asks me, cutting off my sentence. I look back at her and back away from the window.

"I ..."

I stutter in response; *why would she ask me that?*

"I truly don't know," I answer.

I hate my answer to the core.

"I'm sorry that I'm not the same person I was," I apologize.

"It's okay," Ottie consoles me. "That's not really your fault. I have my own questions about everything, but I don't know if they'll ever be answered, either. Just like yours. They're too complex."

"It's good knowing I'm not alone," I say.

"You never are," Ottie tells me. "This mess affects all of us. It affects Beau, even if he may not talk about it."

"How does he deal with things?" I ask.

"Denial, I think," Ottie replies. "He used to talk to you a lot about dreams and everything that you ask yourself about, but he doesn't as much anymore. He feels like it's only occupying your time and mind, and we all know that you're a mess."

"Yeah, you could say that," I say.

"He kind of just tries to accept this weird present time," Ottie says. "It's gotten to the point where he's kind of in a loop of feelings—I think that's how to put it. He varies from day to day."

We continue walking throughout the exhibit.

"Do you think cloning is real?" Ottie asks me.

"I don't know," I say. "But I do think that there are too many experiences that don't seem like coincidences anymore to indicate that something is definitely wrong."

"We just have to find out why they happen," Ottie says.

"Exactly."

Ottie falls asleep on my shoulder during the bus ride home. I think that my communication with her, even in this mess, is helping her feel reminded of when we were only kids in foster care, only having each other.

Ottie is a pleasant sister to have.

"How was the aquarium?" Janice asks, smelling of cigarettes. "I heard you all got free tickets."

Ottie nods. "Yeah, that was the case."

"That's great," Janice says. "I have a date with a coworker named Charles tomorrow from morning to evening. We're going to have brunch, watch a movie ..."

"Nice," I say bleakly.

"Kaeda, have you ever been on a date?" Janice asks.

"No, never," I answer.

Janice looks at me weirdly. "Hm."

Dinner is another serving of takeout considering that Janice, from the looks of it, doesn't feel at all well enough to cook something for all of us. Sometimes I question how long she'll live with the frailness of her body and the substances she's consistently using.

"I think I'm gonna go to bed earlier tonight," Beau says with a serving of sushi in his mouth. "I don't feel the greatest physically."

Concluding dinner, I walk out to the balcony and take a seat on one chair, checking any messages from Juno. She's only sent me one, simply asking if we could call later. Beau approaches me, opening the door to the balcony, and sitting in a chair near me.

"What did Sasha talk to you about today?" he asks.

"A theory about cloning," I respond. "It's really interesting, but scares me at the same time."

"Oh, that," Beau says. "What did she theorize?"

"That human cloning, if it's real, could just be a human revival," I say. "And not in a beneficial way; in the way that dead people are cloned and technically brought to life after their death."

"Hell, how did she come up with that?" Beau asks.

"Juno," I respond. "Juno and several other experiences just like the ones I've had. Where you're told someone's dead, but, suddenly, they're alive. And you can't refer to old experiences, because they somehow disappear."

"Oh, god."

"Yeah."

I can't help but ache in the pain that my stomach is bringing me because of this conversation. Beau was never told that Ottie thought I died—he never knew because Ottie never talked about it. She was too scared and in too much pain to do so. I'm using Juno's experience as a way to discuss this theory that Sasha has brought up with me, but I'm not using my own. Because I can't.

Because Sasha does not know and neither does Beau. And neither does Juno nor James. Only Ottie and I know, but, if everyone else were to, they would immediately think that I'm in the same boat as Juno. And I hate thinking about how I would feel if they categorized me in that way, no matter whether it's true. I can't shake the feeling that I'm only another subject of study.

I want to tell Sasha and Beau, but I don't feel like I can.

"How would we ever know if cloning is real?" Beau asks. "We don't have the insight that scientists and doctors do. We only base our opinions off of what we've seen, and what we've seen could swing in multiple directions."

"I just don't understand how someone's own brother, who I *know* that they're close to, would lie to a close friend of theirs about their own sister's suicide," I say. "There's no way that could've happened with someone like James. And the deleted messages. And Juno's memory loss."

"That is weird."

"It's very weird," I say. "I don't think it's some practical joke, I think it's an authentic experience."

"So you think that cloning is real?" Beau asks.

"I think ..."

I pause for a second.

"I don't know."

Beau looks at me. "If I'm being honest," he starts, "it sounds like you do."

"Like I think cloning is real?"

"Yes, I think you do," Beau says. "What you're saying is *practically* telling me that you do."

Do I think that cloning is real?

It's as though I've lost touch with myself so much to the point where I can't seem to answer that question. I don't know where my beliefs lie. I really don't know how to–

I get a call from Juno.

"Hello?" I start.

"Hi, I saw you read my message," Juno says. "Something interesting happened today."

"What?"

"Déjà vu, multiple times," Juno answers. "And it all relates back to the dream that I had, with the horrible feelings you tell me I had before you moved."

"I promise you, I saw it firsthand."

"No, I believe you," Juno reassures me. "I do. James says something similar, but he doesn't seem to know a lot. He just says that he remembers me being really depressed before you moved. For a while, actually."

"Yeah, that was the case," I say.

"But I just don't understand how I forgot about it all," Juno continues. "How could I forget about such a vivid, significant time in my life? Did I have a concussion?"

"I truly don't know."

"I don't really expect you to, I just don't understand myself anymore," Juno says in return. "I'm sorry for confusing you, Kaeda. Did you ever find out who told you the lie that I died? The person from our school?"

Shit. I *just* remember lying to her about that.

"... No, I haven't found them," I say hesitantly.

"Oh man," Juno says with a sulky voice. "I just don't know why anyone would cause you so much confusion. I hope you find that person—I already hate their guts. I really hope they didn't lie to anyone else."

"Yeah, me too," I say.

"Yeah ... well, I kinda just thought that I'd let you know about how I'm feeling," Juno says. "It was nice talking to you. I hope this isn't too much on your mind."

"It's not, don't worry," I lie.

"That's good," Juno says. "See you."

The call ends.

"This whole thing is confusing me to a point of no return," Beau says. "So Juno had memory loss?"

"What, you heard the audio?" I ask.

Beau nods. "I know I have some memory loss myself, but I don't think it's due to something so drastic."

"You have memory loss?"

"Well, yeah," Beau says. "How would I have forgotten Ida for so long? Janice says I concussed."

"Why does everyone have a concussion?" I ask.

"Pfft, I don't know."

"I don't think that Juno had a concussion," I say.

"I don't know what I think," Beau says. "I have to take a shower and head to bed. I'm not feeling very well."

"Goodnight," I say.

"Night."

I take a longer shower tonight. I need to clear my own head of its annoying, confusing thoughts and questions. I don't know how to feel about Juno, or the possibilities that Sasha talks about. I feel bad for not contributing as much to research on this topic as Sasha is, but, at the same time, I feel like these interactions with Juno are enough.

I still don't know if I should tell Sasha about the other experience I've had with someone supposedly "dying" but actually alive: the very experience that relates to me; the very experience where I am the one who "died". The thing that Beau said to me, asking me if I think that cloning is real—I still don't know how to answer it. Because I can't be so sure anymore. I'm not even sure of myself.

I don't want these feelings or questions to turn into a loop—I do want an answer, eventually. Although I'm not sure what I think of cloning, looking within myself, I feel more drawn to what Beau concluded about me. I clearly ask all of these questions and don't believe that these events are only coincidences, so there must be something wrong. And with these articles and stories that Sasha revealed to me, as well as my own experience, I think that cloning *could* be real.

I finally fall asleep.

Eleven

I wake up.

Opening my eyes feels dreadful now—especially knowing that I'm doing it inside of my mind, where I only anticipate chaos.

But I must open them, anyway. Blinding, bright white lights pierce through my eyes; the sound of buzzing fluorescent lighting and the quiet whir of air conditioning systems surround my ears. I hear a very faint chatter of people and the hurried footsteps of doctors from afar—now I know where I am. I'm in a hospital, specifically the room of a hospital as I begin to look around and notice familiar sheer, white curtains: the ones I saw back in San Francisco; the ones I saw with Michelle. I'm not laying down—I'm sitting at the side of a hospital bed with her next to me—the mother of mine who died almost a week ago. She still looks at me with her tired, desolate brown eyes, but it's still somewhat refreshing to see her alive. No doctors are in the room—it's only her and me.

"Kaeda," she starts. "Kaeda, you ... you're ..."

"What?" I ask softly.

"You're in a lot of pain," my mom continues. "I'm sorry to have to put you through this."

Pain?

"I mean, I wasn't the one to ..." she pauses, "... I just feel as though I could've maybe prevented it all from happening. With Cace and Frank—that whole situation."

I understand she may feel responsible for Cace's death in a sense, but why would this be *my* pain? Is it that she feels responsible for putting me into a family that had not recovered? I try to ask her a question, though, out of my mouth, I hear no words.

What does she mean?

"The death of my son," Michelle continues, as if she was answering my unspoken, vague inquiry. "And the arguments between Frank and I afterward. I'm sorry you had to see that; I'm sorry that you had to find Cace."

Find Cace?

"Alive," she answers another inaudible question. "I'm sorry that you had to find him like that; his death and then his revival. It's wrong—it's unethical that it happened. I'm sorry that you had to find out."

Cace lived?

The amount of running questions throughout my mind is too much to ask Michelle—she keeps talking over my attempt to ask her anything.

"And I'm sorry about what it did to you," she continues. "It led you down a path that only caused pain for you and me. I'm only starting to find things out now, which really, really sucks; it serves no purpose—meaningless. I'm going to die soon."

"Please don't go," I muster out.

"It's all up to you now," Michelle asserts. "Just don't put me through what they put Cace through: what they put all of these people through. I hope that you can maybe start finding things out, too."

Finding things out?

"Your subconscious is screaming at you, Kaeda," my mom tells me finally, fire in her blank, dark eyes. "I can hear it."

The scene fades out aggressively, with details of the room warping and crashing into one another. I want to respond. I want to stay in the room and keep on talking, even if I can't understand it all. Just now, I'm seeing my mom gain life, but I know that there's nothing I can do. I know that this will all end and that, right now, all I can feel is hopelessness. There's nowhere I can go but wherever my thoughts take me, and they're too unpredictable to allow me to feel safe in them.

I wake up in the same bedroom I had fallen asleep in, yet there's an uncanny, unsettling sense residing in this room. The presence of Ottie has faded as the sounds of her sleeping are gone—the scene is too quiet. The view from the window is close to pitch black and the digital clock is completely turned off. Here, nothing feels authentic—the bedroom is void of life. It's the eerie, unreal version of a place that I'm familiar with. But I do notice something: scattered papers all over my bed—all over the lower bunk. Pages ripped from a notebook that act as almost a blanket to me. I sit up to sort through them all, but they appear to be completely blank.

Except for one that I find, hidden under stacks upon stacks of blank pages. There's somewhat large writing on it, but the words appear to have been written by me. In my handwriting, the page reads:

"It's all in your mind now,
you just have to dig deep enough to find it."
Huh?

I stare at the paper in weird disbelief at what I see, but I don't feel angry; I only feel uncomfortably targeted—I long to escape this. I wish something here could disprove whatever my own mind is trying to tell me. The words that my mom had said just a moment ago continue to ring throughout my ears even though I'm unable to hear in this place: "Your subconscious is screaming at you, Kaeda, I can hear it."

This one page invokes that same feeling, but I have to remember that this is only a dream. I could forget it all; these words that evoke such powerful feelings in me could essentially not matter as soon as I wake up. This *is* my subconscious, and whatever I'm hearing in these places is what is yelling at me.

I want more time to register these thoughts. I can only hope that I'll keep them in the morning. Because Juno, her dreams, her subconscious—

The scene changes again, and I find myself recalling my surroundings. They're nostalgic, dating back to around three years ago—when I was just fourteen.

I'm back in my house in San Francisco, seated at the kitchen island. It's dark outside, but I can hear the cars passing throughout the neighborhood and towards the city—it's not an empty hour of the night.

As I further gain my senses, I begin to hear faint yet aggressive chattering down the hallway. I quickly realize whose argument this is: Michelle and Frank's, or my mom and dad's, as I'd call them at the time. The volume of their voices increases just like how it had increased before when I encountered this in a dream. This scene is a memory—it's far too recurrent for it to not be.

"Why would you ever consider that?" says Michelle. "It's wrong and I won't agree to it."

"Why? Why wouldn't you?" asks Frank. "How ... how sudden his death was. It's the right thing to do. Do you even love our son?"

"Of course I do!" Michelle yells back. "And that's why I think that this isn't right! It's so complicated. Everything about cloning is so ... it's so wrong and I can't ..."

"Maybe you think it's complicated because you're too ignorant to understand it," Frank says, louder. "Because I sure as hell find it okay."

There's a pause in the conversation, and I hear faint sniffling from my mother.

"... Cace left for a reason," Michelle states. "Whatever that reason was, it was his will. This is completely wrong and he never would have wanted it, especially with all of its side effects."

"Like what?" Frank refutes. "Memory loss? Why would he want to think about those suicidal thoughts he had before he died?"

The phrases and words that were once muffled when I first had this dream are now uncovered completely.

"You want too much for our child," Michelle says. "And I know that sounds like a horrible thing to say, but what if he left because of how stressed out he was? What if this is just another …"

"You'll never understand!" Frank yells, seeming to have slammed a surface in frustration. "He was so *smart*. So driven; such a wonderful son." He sounds like he's tearing up. "And you don't get it at all. Shit, you weren't even involved."

"You know how horrible my issues are!" my mother cries. "Don't tell me that I wasn't there, or that I didn't love Cace. I loved him, and that's why I feel like this would just be another …"

The scene fades into another one that seems to take place in a similar environment. As my vision develops, I realize that the environment is not only similar—it is identical; that environment being my old house in San Francisco. Here, I find myself sitting at my old bedroom's desk, staring out of the window in front of me as I peek through the blinds. Looking around my bedroom, I realize that it's pitch black—only the light from the outdoors allows me to see anything, and that is not much light at all. It's the middle of the night, and I'm visually fixated, for some reason, on my house's driveway. That is until I see the interior lights of what I remember Frank's car turn on and I'm met with a striking visual: Frank and Cace sitting inside the car.

If I'm living here, then wouldn't that mean that Cace is supposed to be dead?

Frank would have gone through with his idea, then. *He must have cloned Cace.*

I see Frank check the trunk quickly where I then receive a quick glimpse of what was inside of it—several suitcases. He must be trying to escape. *He must be trying to escape with a clone of Cace.*

An overwhelming urge to leave my room and notify Michelle swells up within my mind—an urge that begins devouring my thoughts. Amid this, however, a striking pain enters my stomach:

Don't do that.

Why?

Don't tell Michelle.

I want to tell Michelle. I hate this idea of 'cloning'; I want to let her know her son was—

The dream ends.

6:02 AM

Holy shit.

Beside my bed and against the nightstand is my backpack—my backpack containing a non-academic notebook. I open to a random page, avoiding the page of unanswered questions, take a pen from Ottie's nightstand, and immediately start writing.

"I'm sorry that you had to find Cace"

"Start finding things out, too"

"Memory loss"

"Cloning"

"Side effects"

"Before he died"

"It's only in your mind now"

"Dig deep enough to find it"

"Your subconscious is screaming at you,"

"I can hear it."

These phrases stare into my eyes like a summarization of my subconscious struggles—similar to how the one written paper that was in a dreamlike version of this bedroom did. They pierce me like a sharpened, glistening, long spear. On this notebook page of phrases, I feel my innermost questions answered, yet the answers are extremely vague and unsatisfying. I feel as if I'm staring at a poem—I feel like I'm staring at a twisted, puzzling poem. I feel like I'm staring into a mirror—*I feel like I'm staring at myself.*

It's now, this quiet hour, where I begin to feel encapsulated by my own questions. The ones that go unanswered continuously, the ones that hurt me, the ones that cause confusion among so many people including myself. I feel like my own identity could only best be described by the questions that I ask. I think I am the research that I do—I think I am the ideas I have, despite how they make me feel. In this thought, I ask myself one more question:

Do you think that cloning is real?

I answer it:

Yes.

The scene is overwhelmingly silent and tranquil, even if my mind is nothing of the sort. I have to remind myself that this earth keeps turning, even if unethical practices happen in secret, like the cloning of humans that Michelle most definitely was referring to in her dream. There are too many encounters with those who were dead now living and forgetful of the past in order for there to be no scientific explanation. There are too many articles, too many speculations ... nobody to study them properly.

Therefore, the news articles on cloning possibilities and "revival" stories are never aired. They're never aired because God forbid this issue becomes publicized—the institution cloning these people you hear about would be exposed and therefore destroyed. Lives brought here without knowledge of their death and what caused them to die ruined, eyes opened, protests in the streets.

How will I ever tell Juno about what I think, and how will I ever know for a fact that it's real?

It's not common for me to believe in something unconfirmed completely, but I can't seem to let this idea go. I can't find a way of erasing this from my mind, even if I'd like to.

Ottie's tossing and turning tell me that she's woken up somewhat, so I move from my bed and stand on my tiptoes to tap her on the shoulder.

"Ottie?"

"What is it, Kaeda ..." she groans.

"I had a crazy dream," I tell her. "I have a paper with quotes from it that I wrote directly after I woke up. Here, I can give you the context."

"Man, you're like my caffeine," Ottie says. "Which is really weird because I used to be the hyper one here."

"I'm serious," I say to Ottie in a quieter voice.

Ottie nods slowly in cooperation as I hand her the paper full of quotes. "Who's Cace?" she asks after skimming over them.

"The son of my adopted parents' who they essentially replaced me with," I explain. "He died, and, for a second time, I lived out hearing an argument between my mom and dad. Only this time did they mention cloning him."

"So who said 'I'm sorry that you had to find Cace'?" Ottie asks.

"My mom when she was at the hospital," I answer. "Right before her death. She also said the thing about subconsciousness."

"And the 'they would wipe memories'?" Ottie follows.

"From my mom when she and my dad were arguing about cloning Cace," I say. I take the paper back to write a brief explanation for each quote and who it's from, handing it back to Ottie once I'm done.

"Man, I don't know what to tell you," Ottie comments. She hands me back the paper, looking at me. "We're living in an interesting time, Kaeda. Do you think that cloning is real?"

"Yes," I answer.

"Do you think that Juno's a clone?" asks Ottie.

I hesitate to respond. "... I ..."

"Or, you: do you think that you're a clone?"

"Why would you ask me that?" I question with a greater tone of defensiveness than I anticipated.

"Well, because I was told that you died," Ottie explains. "But you're alive. And you also have memory problems."

"But what if I had a concussion?" I ask.

"What if Juno did?"

"Juno didn't have a—"

"I don't think you're a clone, Kaeda," Ottie clarifies, cutting me off. "I'm only asking you what you think you are. You think cloning is real, so—"

"Do you?" I ask. Ottie looks at me, confused. "Do you think that cloning is real?" I repeat.

"I don't know," answers Ottie. "I really don't."

Still, I can't seem to put the topic down; I can't seem to shut myself up. I don't like to theorize and feel alone in the theories that crowd my mind. But I can't seem to stop it—I can't seem to calm myself down. I don't think I *should* though; I think I should keep on thinking and asking myself questions; I think that's what makes me who I am. I feel so alone in this annoyance that having unanswered and unconfirmed ideas and questions about the world brings me; somehow, everyone around me seems to let it go so easily. While I feel Sasha is in a similar boat to me, there are still not enough people to try to get an idea through. I don't have a definitive group that feels as passionately about answering these questions as me; I feel *alone*.

I feel alone and misunderstood, and the silence of early morning only emphasizes that feeling.

The rest of the morning is nothing interesting, except for how Beau is refraining from going out with Sasha, Ottie, and me for lunch today because he feels sick. Janice's supposed to leave for her "date" with a coworker soon, and Ottie explains to me her skepticism of the lab at which Janice works as a data scientist because of the fact that Janice makes "bank" yet only works from home, never discusses her laboratory job, and it's impossible to find her current career on her online career-based website profile, where she lists her previous jobs, her university and high school, and even the fact that she is currently employed. Both Ottie and I recognize that we can't say anything regarding cloning in a very public area, like the city bus that takes us to the deli we ate at for lunch yesterday, so we stay virtually silent throughout the ride.

Arriving at the stop, we walk shortly to the deli, meeting Sasha there.

"Did you tell Ottie about everything?" Sasha asks me. I answer "yes" and order food for everyone at the front counter.

Ottie and Sasha first talk about people from school and things I don't find too interesting, but my mind seems to ache with the thought of not having told Sasha what had actually happened to me. Sasha and Beau, both. Both completely unaware of the fact that Ottie had been told I died; completely suspicious of the possibility that the whole idea of "cloning" is strongly related to human revival. Everything with Juno and everything Sasha's found through different articles: those events seem to line up with their suspicions about cloning.

Looking back on my dream, it doesn't feel like one; it feels like a memory. Like a distant, warped, isolated memory. The difference between reflecting on your dreams and reflecting on your memories is that, at least for me, you *know* when one is only random information stored in your brain dumped into a series of confusing scenes; none of it makes sense. The dream I had, though, had clarity. *Clear* dialogue, *clear* scenes, *clear* connections—and I feel like I've been in that situation before. *That* is how someone perceives a *memory*. Not a dream.

But what if I'm being illogical—what if I'm looking too deeply into this? What if cloning isn't truly—

"Kaeda, you okay?" Ottie asks me. It was then that I realize that I had been zoning out, not answering anyone else's questions or responding to what they may have said. I nod my head. "Yeah," I answer. "Yeah, I'm fine."

The thought is haunting. The melody of these thoughts is a dread that I can't eliminate yet can't get enough of; as depressing as questioning all you've done is, I can't seem to stop and don't know what would happen to me if I were to. It's here in my mind where all of the greatest connections occur, it's here where the most captivating questions are asked—I'm unable to conceptualize who I'd be if the questions and thoughts that torment my mind yet fulfill it didn't exist or had no reason to.

There's a dissonance inside of my head that I can't seem to let go of. Everything builds up yet crashes at the same time, and somehow it's beautiful yet so mad. I'm forming these thoughts that I find so incredible, yet I'm asking these questions that I find so deteriorating. The bioluminescent river of my mind is so beautiful, yet it's so destructive. But, like the questions and thoughts, I can't eliminate one and expect the other to stay there. I can't have a beautiful, captivating river without its dangerous neon blues. I can't have great thoughts and wonderful perceptions without the haunting questions that follow them.

There is always a haunting underside to the beautiful surface; at least in my experience.

"Kaeda?" Sasha calls. My eyes shoot back to the scene—I feel like I had made a silent promise to not zone out again that I find inevitable to break. She asks the question.

"Do you think that cloning is real?"

I nod and finally feel somewhat brought out of the endless space of my mind.

"Yes."

"And what led you here?"

"I think it was Juno," I say. "And everything we heard about. What they talked about while you were in your coma ..."

I pause. "I just wonder *how* it works," I continue. "They've done this with animals, yeah, but ... but I hate how I don't have explicit certainty. I need to *see* it."

"You have enough proof, though."

"Yeah, but I still—"

I stop mid-sentence. My mind goes to Juno and the pure emotion that James expressed to me following her death, Juno's lack of remembrance of her memories right before her suicide, the fact that the texts were wiped out ...

I don't want to keep on asking myself questions. I truly don't. I hate what it does to me, gutting me from the inside and leaving me trapped inside of my head, ruining my sleep and seeping into my dreams. I hate asking questions. I hate it, but it's also what I've started to identify myself as: someone with many wonders, spiraling down some Fibonacci sequence inside of my own head. Wonders and questions unanswered. I wish I would stop, but I don't think I ever will.

"Kaeda, you *do* have enough proof to think cloning is real," Sasha tells me in an attempt to get me out of my head.

"But what if it isn't?" I follow with.

"You haven't come so far in this mess just for you to question it all again," Sasha says. "You need some sort of confirmation."

"I never have confirmation."

"What, are there any other things you've heard of other than Juno?" Sasha asks. "Ones that help give you an idea about cloning?"

I think about Juno again. What James had told me. How Juno acted, unknowing of her own memories. Her dreams, her weird experiences—but, most of all, I start to think of *myself.*

I don't want to call myself a victim of cloning, because I'm not sure if I am. I don't like superstitions or supernatural ideas; I don't; but I don't think cloning is either of the sort.

I have weird dreams, too. And lack of memories about Ottie, all of that. I had a dream about my mom's son and how he was apparently cloned and, yes, while it felt like a memory, I'm still not sure if that was just my mind filling in blanks with the topic I've been thinking about the most.

I don't want to tell Sasha about the fact that Ottie was told I died and that I remember little from my past, mainly because I'm not sure if I trust her enough. I can't be sure that she will not obsess over this and treat me as less, like a subject with insignificant feelings and ideas. Like someone to study and only to study. Yet, she's a subject herself, with her coma stories.

"Not really," I lie. Ottie looks over at me in confusion, as if I had done something wrong; I did, but I don't think I'm at all ready to fess up about–

"That's not true," Ottie refutes. "We have more experience with cloning suspicions."

I guess she had other ideas.

"Like what?" Sasha asks. I don't at all know what to say at this moment. I don't know if Ottie's going to suggest that I start talking about it or if she'll talk about something completely different: something she heard about that I didn't. But, no, that wouldn't make sense at all. I don't speak up. I don't say anything. Ottie, please say something.

Ottie, why won't you say—

"My caretakers told me Kaeda died," Ottie finally spurts out after a long inhale. The way she says it unintentionally brings back a long-ago memory: a childish moment between Ottie and me where one person would tell on the other. For a quick moment, that nostalgia seems to calm me down. Suddenly, I'm tense again.

"They told me this about a year after she was adopted," Ottie continues. "Obviously, she wasn't dead, so when I heard that she was coming to stay with me, I immediately figured that they had lied to me to get me to shut up about wanting to go with her and her new parents. But that always seemed a bit unlikely."

"That doesn't work, though," Sasha says. "She doesn't have this memory loss that Juno has."

Ottie looks at me. Something about her ambitious facial expression tells me that she doesn't want to lie about this—any aspect of it.

"I wouldn't say that," Ottie says. "She barely remembered the experiences we'd have as kids or the time spent at her new house before her parents split up. She tells me that."

"I might've concussed a year or so ago," I say with uncertainty. It's all I can get out of my system in this uncomfortable conversation.

"But you have no actual evidence to tell yourself that's true," Ottie says. "The only way we can advance in these questions is by coming to terms with the possibility that we might be directly related to them."

Shit.

Those words hit me like a train. I *know* she's right in what she's saying. It's what I wanted to tell myself, but could never surface that idea out of my head; it seemed impossible. I didn't want to be a subject in this mess; I *don't* want to be a subject in this mess, but if it helps, it helps. And I know I want to—and have always wanted to—help in putting together this mess of a situation.

I sit in a weird, almost painful silence throughout the rest of lunch. Neither Ottie nor Sasha drop the topic of cloning, and now the entire situation with Juno doesn't feel nearly as personal as I had at first considered it. I'm afraid that now, talking to her about these confusing experiences she's encountering and the mystery of her memory loss contains even more lies. Am I wrong for feeling that way: for wishing that I was more of an individualist in this entire mystery and keeping my own ideas closed off to myself?

I think I am. I wish I could tell Juno about the reality of the situation and make her wonder if she's a victim, but I'm afraid of sending her down that infamous mental spiral she so strongly had, strong enough to kill her.

I hate asking questions.

I hate uncertainty.

I hate it.

There's a knot in my stomach that won't disappear and, hell, it makes passing time so much worse. Even when I'm not thinking of cloning and clones and everything surrounding that brutally obscure yet terrifyingly down-to-earth topic, my body still finds a way to remind me of it. And that's the nervousness: the bouncing of my leg, the fact that my stomach is hurting, the dizziness and sensitivity to my surroundings that I feel. I give in and think of it anyway, even if it hurts. At least that pain gives me a more coherent explanation of why I'm physically feeling horrible.

The more I think about this mystery, though, the more the pieces seeming to come together hurts. I should be happy that these questions I so long asked are finally being somewhat answered and that a pattern is associated with it, but I'm not. It hurts me. It tears me apart, asking myself whether I am a clone and sick like Juno is.

I don't recall saying a word on the city bus ride home. I don't recall saying anything to Ottie, nor do I recall her saying anything to me. I wonder if she hates me now, for some reason. I wonder if she can't control that. That is if she does. I might not know for a while.

I hate asking questions.

I hate uncertainty.

I hate it.

I open the door to the townhouse, and I don't see Janice, unsurprisingly. Though I do see Beau on the couch, only he looks visibly terrified. Not at Ottie and I's arrival, no, but something entirely different. He bounces his leg uncontrollably. His eyes dart around the room.

Finally, he speaks.

"I hope Janice doesn't get back for a while," he greets us nervously, with a hoarse voice from his sickness. Ottie nods.

"Yeah, she can be overbearing," Ottie adds.

"No, you don't know," Beau says. "You don't know what happened."

What happened?

My look of confusion seems to be noticed by Beau. As I approach him closer, I notice the redness in his eyes, either from sickness or from crying. The sniffling between each word he says doesn't help, either.

"I found … a lot," Beau says, leading Ottie and me to Janice's bedroom upstairs. "I don't know where to start."

"What do you mean?" Ottie asks. Beau hesitates to answer as he grabs a closed cardboard box hidden in Janice's closet. He opens it.

"Arizona," Beau says, briefly. As Ottie and I peer into the opened box, we found a plethora of things. Photos, an old phone, a hospital bracelet … the box seems endless as Ottie and I struggle to search the items. Except, the search stops once one photo flips over its blank side.

It's a photo of Beau with a girl of Indian descent, with short, black hair and somewhat of an intelligent demeanor.

It's Ida.

The girl next to Beau in the photo is Ida.

I look over at Beau and find him visibly choking up as he looks at the photo.

"I found those," Beau struggles to say. He picks up yet another photo from the box, again with him and Ida in some garden. They look happy, like a couple; like how he had described their seemingly fictional relationship in his dreams. Except, it was never fiction.

"I knew I knew her somehow," Beau comments. "But there's so much. How could I have forgotten her like this? Why … why would Janice hide these?" He continues choking up, struggling not to cry.

"This is insane," Ottie says, shaking her head. She picks up the hospital bracelet from the box with Beau's name on it, then holds it up. "Do you remember this?"

"I don't think so," Beau answers. "I don't remember a lot of these photos. Did I go into a coma? Was that the bracelet?"

"I mean, you could've …" Ottie responds. The two continue talking, searching through the box. I search too, but I primarily focus on the one photo I had picked up at first of Beau and Ida. Thoughts race through my head on Beau's lack of remembrance towards any of this—the fact that these largely important items and memories were all hidden …

I don't want to assume things.

I don't want to ask more questions.

Is Beau sick, too?

Stop asking questions.

Please.

You know your mind can't take it.

I can't stop myself, but I can't say anything aloud. The thoughts can only race through my head and overtake everything else.

The entire scene becomes blurry now as Beau holds the different photos and his hospital bracelet, teary-eyed. I hear him ask himself if he had gone into a coma multiple times.

Or concussed.

Or ...

Those are the only options. I can't know for sure if he's made the one connection I so often like to make about what feels like everyone. I can't tell if it's just me and my warped perception of things; I don't feel like I can go to anyone or do anything important to confirm this idea of cloning. This terrible, unethical, idea of reviving people from the dead just for them to only feel *sick*.

I don't want to bring up cloning at all with Beau's situation; I'm afraid it will only make things worse. I don't want him to both mourn over the lack of remembrance of his lover and beautiful experiences in his life as well as the possibility that he could've been cloned. *Would he believe me?* I don't know. *Would I believe myself?*

I don't know, either.

"I have to ask Janice about this," Beau says, tears in his eyes. "Why would she hide all of this from me? God, I can't—"

His dialogue stops. The sound of the air conditioning within the room increases in volume. The light from the outside seems brighter in my vision. My head hurts. My stomach aches. My knee bounces uncontrollably.

Beau breaks.

Tears stream down his face, which he instantly hides in his hands.

"I'm sorry," Beau mutters with a mouth full of saliva and tears. "Sorry, I don't know why I'm crying—"

"No, it's okay," Ottie reassures him. I can tell she's nervous in her shaky breaths and the fact that her eyes shoot around the scene, rushing to put away the photos. "It's okay, it's okay."

"I shouldn't be crying about this," Beau musters out. "Just ... just put all this shit away, I can handle this myself."

He leaves the room, wiping the rushing tears off of his face.

"Beau ..." I say, at last, attempting to be somewhat of a help in this situation. I don't know how to comfort him, but, in a way, I feel his pain. An entire situation, or series of situations in your past, is close to unrecognizable to you. Knowledge has been stowed away; knowledge about your own life and experiences has, for so long, been kept away from you.

Juno seems to experience this.

No, stop it.

Ottie turns to me. "This is horrible," she says, closing the box and subtly shaking her head. "I'm going to put this in Beau's storage—not Janice's."

"Are you going to confront her about it with him?"

"Maybe," Ottie says. "But this is disgusting. This is unethical."

"What, the fact that she hid all this?" I ask.

"Yeah, that, but," Ottie starts. "But I think he may be like Juno."

She thinks ...

I look at Ottie with my eyebrows in a knot, hesitating to respond. "In that ..."

"You know what I mean, Kaeda," Ottie answers.

I know exactly what she refers to.

She thinks that Beau is a clone. And, on top of that, she thinks that Juno's a clone, too.

I don't know what to do from here. Genuinely, I can't fathom it. Not at all was I expecting Ottie to come to me with these beliefs of hers as she hasn't explicitly told me anything about what she thinks; anything until this point.

I wonder if she'll tell Beau about my "death". I wonder if *I* should tell Beau. I wonder what goes through Ottie's head that causes her to speak up to me about this—speaking up so blatantly. I wonder how she perceives the entire situation. I wonder what other words she wishes she could say. I wonder how she feels.

My sister's becoming a mystery to me, and I think it's my fault.

I think this lack of remembrance I suddenly came to her with after she had built up so much hope in me, hope that I would be the person who I used to be, has silently destroyed her. Personality-wise, I wasn't drastically different. It's just the personal experience that has seemingly faded from my mind of our past that makes Ottie feel this way. As though she's unable to come to me with her thoughts or ideas, afraid that I wouldn't interpret them like I used to. Afraid that my mind would only stray to one idea and one idea only: cloning.

What's painful though, is, I don't think she's wrong. This idea—these questions that I ask myself—have been eating me up inside.

And, in that, I almost feel bad about perceiving Beau's situation as something produced by cloning. I feel as though I'm giving into this perception of me that Ottie has. But confronting him ... also feels necessary.

I think I'm beginning to hate this journey.

I think I'm beginning to hate myself.

"I know exactly what you mean," I respond to Ottie. I leave the room and, upon doing so, I'm met with a distant vibration from the living room coffee table, right where my phone is. As though I'm receiving a call.

And I am. It's from Juno—she's calling me.

The text of her name plastered across my phone screen doesn't help in the skeptical feelings I can't deny towards Beau's finding of his old memories. Old memories, kept from him, forgotten by him, and appearing in his dreams.

"Your subconscious is screaming at you, Kaeda, I can hear it."

That is what this reminds me of.

I pick up the phone.

"Kaeda?" Juno starts somewhat anxiously. "You there?"

"Mhm," I respond.

"Sorry for calling you out of the blue," Juno apologizes. "I wanted to let you know about how I've been feeling lately since I know it concerns you."

"Mhm."

"... Well, I've felt the need to sleep a lot more," Juno continues. "I've felt exhausted just doing mundane things. School is bringing me down, too—I can't remember half the shit from just a few weeks ago or around that time."

"What?" I ask her.

Unable to remember recent experiences.

"Yeah, my teachers have been upset with me for poor performance," Juno further explains. "But it almost feels out of my control. And the exhaustion doesn't help, either."

"Do you take a lot of naps?"

"Well, yeah," Juno answers, "The exhaustion becomes unbearable if I don't. And I dream a lot; I dream in almost every single one of the naps I take."

"What do you dream about?"

"Oh, each dream is depressing," responds Juno. "They're like the ones I told you about the other day. Dreams where I'm just, essentially, angry. I'm just angry and sad at everything in each one."

"Do they ever include any potential memories?" I ask.

"I think they do," Juno says. "Each moment feels almost like how a memory would. It's reminiscent, not very confusing or weird. Why do you ask?"

Oh.

"I ... just wanted to know," I tell her, awkwardly. It doesn't sound very convincing, and there's a weird pause in our conversation.

"Kaeda, what's been putting you off lately?" Juno asks. "Other than the incident with someone telling you I died. Or, is that what this is?"

I don't know how to lie my way out of this.

"It's that, yeah," I answer honestly. "You ..."

I stutter in an attempt to continue my answer. I don't want to give away everything about my suspicions; that would only scare Juno. *But, do I need to?*

"You don't remember many recent events," I say. "And you have a lot of dreams, and they include things that feel like memories ..."

I don't receive a response.

"I just don't understand what happened," I clarify. "I don't understand what went wrong, in a sense."

I feel rude.

"You don't think I died, do you?" Juno asks me.

"What?" I ask. "What do you mean?"

"You don't think I actually could've died," Juno continues. "Obviously I didn't. I mean, I wouldn't be here if I did."

"I don't think you died, Juno," I say

"... Good," Juno finishes. There's another pause in the conversation.

"I don't really know what happened, either," Juno says. "But I didn't die. Technology isn't *that* advanced yet."

"Yeah, you're right," I answer.

"... I have to go now," Juno says. "I may call you later, though. See you "

"See you."

The call ends.

I don't know what to think.

I felt as though I was gaining a nice, comfortable confidence in my thoughts on cloning. Or, at least starting to gain one. But does it *really* make sense?

Shut up, Kaeda. You're drilling bullshit into your head again.

But, really, is this all a lie that I'm so desperately attempting to believe?

No—think of Sasha's experience. One that mentioned cloning up-front.

Was she only dreaming?

Why would the doctors take it to heart in how they did if she was only dreaming?

I need a break.

No, you don't need a break. You need to face things upfront and deal with them if you want to get anywhere. You need to force yourself to become comfortable with the uncomfortable problems you face in order to ever overcome them. Then, you won't need a break; then, the hardest problems become mundane tasks to you.

Will you let Juno's lack of knowledge about this entire thing stump your own suspicions?

No.

Thank you.

Janice arrived home soon enough in time for dinner, but Beau fell asleep. Ottie let me know that he cried himself to sleep and hasn't woken up since, but Janice won't wipe the smile off of her face from her date. And she chooses, unexplainably, to tell me about it.

"You wouldn't believe how amazing he is," Janice says. She winks at me, and, if I wasn't as detached from the conversation, I would visibly show queasiness to her. "In *all* ways. I hope you find a date sometime soon. You're smart from what I hear, right?"

"I don't think I care to find anyone right now," I mutter.

"Oh, come on," Janice continues. "I didn't live out my teen years enough. I wanted to go into science, and even though I still work in science, I sometimes wish I hadn't. I found my ex-husband through science, though. He worked for the same lab corporation at the time. I still work there, but he quit his job and divorced in Arizona when the corporation branched out in their interests."

"What lab corp?" I ask.

"Oh, it's not too well-known."

"Just the name?" I ask.

"... The corporation has multiple names per department," Janice hesitates in a way similar to how I was over-call, as though she's lying. Maybe, unknowingly, my tone had changed from mundane and monotone to interrogative. She knows I'm begging for an answer, which makes her uncomfortable, and she hopefully doesn't know why.

Anything about a "lab" is only causing me anxiety and a strong, undeniable desire to know the ins and outs of the lab's details right now. *Secretive and has something to do with humans.*

"His name was Alexander," Janice responds. "Rosenberg. He was Jewish like Beau and I, but he would never talk to me enough for me to really enjoy being in that marriage. So he did exactly what I wanted him to do and left. He works for some other corporation now—he disapproved of my work at the lab, for some reason. I don't think he liked women."

As Janice continues her dialogue, I get up from the kitchen chair and begin to hurriedly walk to the room. Janice musters out a "Where are you going?" after detaching from her reminiscent mind-set, to which I say that I "need to finish homework". That's a lie, though; I finished all my homework Friday.

Upon entering the room, I grab my laptop from my bag and instantly open it up, repeating the name to myself quietly. Beau still sleeps.

He's probably dreaming of Ida right now, and that dream might just be a memory that has been stowed away from him.

I type in "Alexander Rosenberg San Jose California scientist" in the search bar. I find him on a career-related site as well as his history of working at the laboratory, which I did not find when Ottie and I searched for Janice's profile and her career history.

"Worked at Neurogenix Laboratories Department of Neurotechnology 2021–2034."

I type the name of the laboratory into the search bar.

One article appears:

"'The possibilities science is creating are unimaginable,' Former Scientist of Neurogenix Laboratories Writes.':"

And another:

"Neurogenix Laboratories Appears to Hint at 'Possibilities in Cloning' With New Neurotechnology Invention in their Department of Neurotechnology and Department of Transhumanism."

And another:

"'How Secretive are Neurogenix Laboratories?' Northern California Residents Answer Questions About Science's Up-and-Coming Neurotechnology and Transhumanism Laboratory."

And I don't scroll any further before clicking on the second article from a science discovery news website, directly mentioning cloning.

"The cloning of animals is an idea widely spoken of in this day and age and acted upon for research, but the cloning of human organs such as the brain, or even entire humans, is a newer concept in our scientific world. However, a Californian laboratory known as "Neurogenix Laboratories of Neurotechnology" seems to aim their studies towards human cloning despite criticism of the idea that names it 'unethical'."

I continue reading. The article discusses different neuro-technological advances in Neurogenix, but slowly strays away from the topic of human cloning as if it somehow became unimportant. I type something into the search bar again.

"Neurogenix human cloning"

I don't see any articles regarding the lab except for the one I had previously clicked on, only discussions of whether it is ethical in both articles and discussion posts. The articles don't mention Neurogenix, but a few discussion posts do.

"If human cloning were a thing, which lab would be the one to really spark it?" A discussion post title writes.

"Neurogenix. They're a fairly new laboratory somewhere around Northern California known for being secretive, apparently," A comment reads. "They work to invent neurotechnology devices, but their new inventions have definitely related to human cloning in their new device that is supposed to 'capture memories'. There's not enough information on their studies to really tell, though."

"Oh, Neurogenix seems to have a lot of suspicions right now," A reply to the comment reads. "A few things on them directly mention human cloning. But the company's *huge*. It would be hard for someone to try to do much investigation."

"I live in Northern California," Another reply reads, "And Neurogenix is a topic that no one really knows how to talk about."

"I tried getting an internship with Neurogenix a year or so ago when I lived in the bay area," a reply reads. "Someone told me they did those at some point in time. One of their employees got really upset at me for asking."

I spend the rest of my time deep-diving for information on this place, and I only find what I had expected. Vague concerns and suspicions about the place and what they aim to do or even may be doing. I go back into my history, though, and find the links of people telling their stories of having people they're close to reported to have "died", then to only be alive later on. I read through them again, and none of them mention a laboratory. They took a handful of the posts down.

A few of the users, from what I can remember, were from Northern California and had it mentioned in their profile.

The posts from those users are gone now.

Should I make an account?

Should *I* post something?

If I made one, it'd be anonymous. I would give away the area that I live in, though, because I really do wonder if that has anything to do with this issue. The fact that the posts about human cloning and their experiences with "dead" friends from the users with their location set to Northern California are the ones that have been taken down, and the fact that Neurogenix is *in* Northern California ...

I just want to know if there's a correlation.

I create an account under the randomly generated username "foggedglasses6302". Under the "weird experiences" page of the website, I write my discussion post, just like the others.

"I was told my friend died by their own brother, just for them to be alive and unknowing of their own memories," writes the title.

"Just 6 days ago, my close friend committed and their brother (who I'm close with as well) told me about it two days later over text, with a lot of pure emotion in what he said to me about how he was responding to their death, etc. The next night after their brother told me, I received a call from my close friend who I had been told committed where they talked to me as normal—nothing auto-generated, and the texts that their brother had sent me were wiped. We had a conversation where I kept on stuttering over the pure shock that they had even called me, and ever since they have been telling me about how they've been having "vivid dreams" about events and feelings that are actually past experiences that they've had but can't remember. For example, I remember my friend feeling intense feelings of sadness and anger whenever I'd talk to them a week or so before their death, but now they have no memory of it. These are the feelings that constantly appear in their vivid dreams, from what they tell me.

"I'm not sure what this is, but it's an experience of mine that has been bugging me for as long as I can remember after hearing about it."

I submit the post and, after reading it over, I realize something:

I haven't talked to Juno's brother in a long time, let alone about this.

I close the laptop and stow it away completely. Instantly, I pull out my phone and call James. It takes a bit, but he picks up.

"Kaeda?" James starts. "What's up?"

I try to calm myself down to reach James' demeanor.

"I was just wondering how you and Juno have been doing," I tell him.

"Oh, Juno's been off," James says. "I've been okay."

Oh.

Does he have no recollection of this, either?

I stutter in an attempt to respond. "That's interesting," I muster out. "Hey, uh, did you ever send me any messages about Juno in the past few days?"

James audibly struggles to respond. "It's really weird you ask me that, because that's been a recurring dream of mine," James responds. "But from our chat history, no."

"My phone must've been glitching out then," I say. "Because about four days ago, I remember you sending me messages about her."

"D—Do you remember what they were about?" James asks, still audibly nervous. Now I can't respond.

But I want to. I don't want to keep lying. Though it doesn't sound like it directly relates to this, what Ottie had told me earlier seems to ring at me right now.

"The only way we can advance in these questions is by coming to terms with the possibility that we might be directly related to them."

That.

I need to toughen up in order to get anything done.

"They were about Juno ... and I'm sorry for this," I respond, "dying."

"Committing?" James says under his breath.

"Y—Yeah," I respond, stuttering awkwardly in nervousness. "I'm really sorry, that's just what I remember—"

"You're kidding me right now," James says, cutting me off.

"I'm so sorry, James," I apologize.

"No, it's fine—that's exactly what I see in my dreams," James tells me.

"Really?" I ask.

"Yes," James says. "You're crazy, Kaeda. But *why*? *Why* do I dream about that, and why did it appear on your phone once?"

"I don't know," I somewhat lie to him. "But what do you mean by Juno being 'off' lately?"

"Oh, she's been sleeping a *lot*," James says. "And she won't talk to us much. She's been down. Are you sure you weren't seeing things with the messages?"

"Well, I don't know," I respond. "But that's interesting."

"It's insane," James says. "I don't want to tell Juno about the dreams I had, especially when she's feeling like this. That thought scares me."

"It appears in your head a lot, though," I say. "With the dreams and such."

"I will not lie to you," James says.

"Oh my god," I mutter. "I'm sorry, this is just really insane."

"No, I know," James says.

"I ... I need to go now," I stutter.

"Bye, Kaeda," James says.

"Goodbye," I finish.

It will be impossible to sleep tonight with the sheer amount of thoughts running through my head. The fact that James hadn't actually remembered the event of texting me and the pain of finding Juno, but indefinitely has dreams about both of those events—that sticks out like a sore thumb to me in this whole never-ending series of questions about human cloning and the mind-wiping of it all. It's horrible. It's horrible that I see this firsthand, and even worse when I realize that I have a very low chance of ever stopping this.

Cloning causes confusion. It causes Juno to feel down without explanation and unable to speak about what she sees in her own head because it's obscure yet not and, on top of that, most of it is real.

I'm going to need to be medicated to even fall asleep. Inside my head is a deep desire to tell Sasha, to rant to Ottie, and to ask Beau questions, but I don't think I can get that out of my system right now. I'm too amped up in thought to think properly. It's not a delightful hyper, it's a shaky, mad, intense experience that seems to want to control me.

I go to take a shower. I brush my teeth, take sleep supplements, and knock myself out within minutes.

Goodnight.

Twelve

I wake up.

A familiar chilling sensation trickles down my skin; I'm met with the dark desolation of a hospital bedroom—not Michelle's, no: the mental hospital bedroom I encountered a few times in my subconscious, each encounter more vivid than the other. As I sit on the hard mattress and its cold sheets, I can't help but notice within me a deep sense: a deep sense of overwhelming dread.

I hate this.

I hate every second that I'm here, living inside of my mind as it tortures me. I hate the vivid sounds that surround me in this room that I long to be unfamiliar with, while I realize I must understand that, as much as I wish that was the reality of my dreams, it is not. I hate the soullessness of this mental hospital's bedroom and the severe lack of any rehabilitating decoration. I hate feeling like I've completely lost my mind—like I've gone completely insane in what I dream and think whilst simultaneously being unsure whether that feeling is truthful. Am I insane? I don't know—I don't think I've ever met sanity.

I don't think that a single person in my life who I've had meaningful conversations with has truly been *sane*. I don't think I've ever truly *had* sanity—even as a child; I was still a thinker. And a true thinker is not truly sane.

Amidst my thoughts, however, I'm disturbed by an aspect of my physical surroundings: a powerful gust of wind makes its way into my room, reminding me that the window is open. Somehow, that's allowed in this mental hospital of my mind.

I'll go close that.

But the window doesn't close. The wind becomes harsher with every thought that crosses my mind and the scene only evolves into further madness. The wind, although it only blows through the hospital's small window, steals what it can inside the bedroom turning the place into a madhouse—even if there wasn't much here to begin with. The cold sheets of the mattress entangle with each other and blank notebook pages fly inside the room. Now, I notice that there has evolved a personality or "soul" to the environment: a heartless, destructive one.

As the wind picks up rapidly in its pace, my dreamlike state rushes toward the bedroom door as I manage to open it and escape the madness. I expect to be met with a sort of hospital hallway, although it may be a desolate, never-ending one, but I'm not met with that at all; an extremely harsh gust of wind pushes with great force against me. Instead, now, I'm falling from a building.

A wave of drastic panic crashes onto me, similar to the gusts of wind. Falling from a height I cannot comprehend, I know that this will be my end—this is how I'll die inside of this dream. I can't process the outdoor environment that surrounds me as I rapidly accelerate in the air—all I know is the bleak, pitch darkness of the sky. All that I can focus on is the faint patch of dark grass that waits for me at the end of my fall.

I don't want this to be the end.

I hate falling.

I don't wish to die anymore.

Please, I hate—

I wake up in a room I've known for long, huffing for breath in a cold sweat; my old bedroom from the San Francisco house I lived in with Michelle, my mother, before her death. Looking around, I'm still in the dead of night as I was in the mental hospital; aside from me sits my mother: my mother with a terrible worry plaguing her face. It's nice to see her again, though not like this.

"Are you okay?" she asks me with concern. I don't gather enough energy to respond, or to even process what happened. I remember falling—I remember falling and the passionate *hate* that followed.

"Dad—or Frank—left us," my mother continues, clarifying the situation. "I hope you can at least remember that part out of all that you've forgotten."

All that you've forgotten.

The words strike me like a sword. What she's said in my dreams recently has been greatly significant—I don't want to forget a single word she murmurs whenever I truly wake up.

"Did I die?" I wonder, still huffing for breath. With the question, my mother looks away with a look of great regret.

"You were supposed to," my mother responds, "but they've revived you. What happened is not 'all in your head', trust me."

"So I was never insane?" I follow. "They never needed to send me there?"

"You were only knowledgeable," my mother answers. "That's what they name 'insane' now, though. Don't lose yourself."

"Why do they do this?" I ask her.

"Because they don't view humans as human anymore," she tells me. "Only as subjects of testing. This is what happened to Cace; this is what happened to you. Genuine feelings are dead."

"They would much rather prefer mental anguish over rest," I add.

"Exactly."

I hadn't consciously asked a single one of those questions—only consciously felt the questions leave my mouth.

As I start to stand up from my bed, I notice a notebook page turned over on my nightstand. My mother, Michelle, has disappeared as I try to glimpse back at her before picking up the page and turning it over; my eyes avert back to the nightstand and I take hold of the page, worried it may disappear, too. Turning it over, I read its contents.

It has many.

Kaeda Bynum, ??/06/34

I'm waiting for a sign here. Genuinely, I am. I know that I'm not superstitious, but this altered reality that I'm living in is giving me no hope for a rational, logical world. I've begun creating connections that I would find nonsensical. I've lost grasp of my own self—I've found myself falling into this theory that is cloning. But it's not a theory—I've seen it before. I saw it with Cace; he couldn't have just existed like that, alive after death? I saw it. I need to tell Michelle. I'm going to tell her.

??/15/34

I'm an idiot. I'm a fucking idiot for telling her—I'm an idiot for not letting the idea go. But I couldn't then and I know I can't still. Human cloning is real, Cace is proof.

Michelle knows it. I just wish that she would admit that knowledge instead of sending me to this place. I hate every moment that I'm here—it's so painfully lifeless. I hate every moment that I'm here and cloning crosses my mind.

I hope Michelle takes me back. I know there's some good in her somewhere, I know she regrets what she did. She's dealing with it still.

??/??/34

She won't take me back—it's been forever, or at least has felt like such. Michelle won't leave her depression. I want to leave mine.

I want to escape this. I'm losing myself because of cloning—I'm losing myself because it exists and I told Michelle. I should have never told Michelle. I should have kept it to myself—I should have drowned out the idea entirely—living in bliss. But I can't do that. I can't live in bliss. That's impossible for me and I don't think I can take living anymore

I repeat the words quickly and quietly to myself. *I can't let this disappear.*

Before I can even register them, however, the scene changes, warping into a train station that I know: the one near my home back in San Francisco—the one I would always arrive at after school. I stand there, waiting to board the next train: a train that would bring me to a place I'm unfamiliar with—a train to bring me to a place of escape. Waiting to board a train to get me out of my thoughts. Waiting to *leave*.

I look over to my side, sitting on the station's bench, and find Juno sitting aside from me, her eyes drooping with exhaustion and face displaying grave melancholy. She glimpses at me before waiting to muster up something to say.

"I hope you know you're no different," she says to me, quietly. I tilt my head subtly in confusion.

"What do you mean?" I question.

"You're no different," Juno responds, somewhat annoyed and exasperated by my simple question. "What do you think I mean?"

"What, that I died?" I ask. No response from Juno.

"Did I?" I ask again.

"*Did you*?" Juno asks, her eyes swelling up with tears. "Did you die? Are ... are you dead right now? Are you–"

She breaks into a sob.

"Why—why would they do this to us, Kaeda?" Juno cries, struggling to collect her words. "Do you know how much it hurts me to feel like I ... like I shouldn't even be here? Like I shouldn't even *exist*?"

I move closer to Juno. "I wouldn't say that ..."

"Since when were you optimistic?" Juno asks. "I miss your logical pessimism and my dreamy optimism. I miss James' mixture of the two. I miss feeling okay before everything crashed and burned and ..."

"Remember our old group and everybody's friends that they'd invite?" Juno continues, ending her previous thought. "Remember Oscar and his brother?"

I nod lightly, my eyes averted toward the station platform. "I do."

"I miss feeling okay," Juno cries. She repeats the phrase to herself. "I miss it, I miss it, I miss …"

A train's oncoming headlights and the faint sounds of its movement along the tracks indicate to me that its arrival is near. I look over at Juno with an expression that I can't place; one of sadness and an additional emotion, somewhat unfamiliar, as she looks at me, terrified of what she encounters in her head. I begin to place that additional emotion: a subconscious, undeniable understanding of another person. One that almost brings you to tears—tears in your eyes because you've felt what they feel. Maybe you feel it now as you see them—as you see them in their struggle.

Empathy.

"I'm sorry, I have to go …" Juno tells me, tears in her eyes, as she hurries away from the area, sobbing once more in her exit. I stare ahead as the train arrives, slowly walking toward its entrance. Through my vision passes dull colors of sadness and mad, obscure colors of fear: a horrifying scene of deterioration, as though the train is crashing while I'm inside of its capsules. A quick scene that I can't make out inside of my mind, a quick scene of—

The scene changes.

Frustration. Frustration and annoyance at my brain for disturbing a scene that could've been: a scene that could've meant *something.*

"The scene changes."

I hate it.

A smell and vision of a cool night in the desert seem to surround me as my senses return, and I find myself standing in the middle of an empty road in what looks like Arizona. A blood moon rises high in the dark sky and I notice canyon-like structures in the distance.

I seem to be standing near a mesa—a plateau—and it instantly reminds me of someone.

Beau.

There he is, sitting against a car at the side of the road with someone, crying. He holds his chest as though he's hurt as I come closer, and that "someone" next to him looks like Ida. She rests her head peacefully on his shoulder, breathing in and out in a deep sleep and holding onto his arm.

But he looks mortified.

Why?

"What happened?" I ask him. He looks up at me sorrowfully with pink eyes full of tears, sniffling, appearing with the same expression he had when he found the pictures yesterday—when he found the box of memories. Beau then moves one of his hands away from his chest, where a healed wound in the shape of a medium to small-sized hole lays. It looks like how I'd imagine a gunshot wound to look, with light stretch marks surrounding the abrasion.

"This was never supposed to happen," he says to me, crying. "I'm ... I'm not even skeptical anymore. I'm terrified at what this reality has become."

This reality.

"I'm terrified at what that ... that stupid idea of 'cloning' has done," Beau continues. His tears of sadness and fear turn into anger. "I'm terrified at why Janice hides everything. This is the altered present. The past, the future ..."

"And the altered present," we say in unison, my voice quieter than his. Beau sobs continuously, clutching onto his chest as small amounts of blood begin to appear on his hands. The wound appears to have opened from what I can infer from the blood.

He looks at himself, fearful. "*No ...*"

I slowly take steps back. I can't handle this. I can't handle—

The scene changes.

I'm standing in the middle of a hallway with a liminal, medical appearance to it. *The mental hospital? No, this is something differ-ent.*

As I glance to my side, I notice Ottie standing with me. Suddenly, different details of the area begin to appear, like minimal metal signs against the wall. I look closer, studying the newly developed details.

"_____________ of Neurogenix Laboratory Corporation" reads one.

Neurogenix.

"Why are we here?" I ask, turning to Ottie.

"To reflect on your reality," Ottie answers. "I'm sorry that you're familiar with this place. That must feel horrible."

What?

"I'm sorry for out-casting you, or wondering why you simply can't remember what I can," Ottie says. "I know why, now, and sometimes I feel like I really just prefer *bliss*. I wish I didn't know. I wish you didn't either."

"Was I cloned?" I ask her, but receive no answer.

"I just wish it never happened," says Ottie. "I love you, Kaeda. I love you so much."

She collapses into me with a hug, beginning to sob, though the act fails to rid me of the great physical tension I feel in this place. Still studying the laboratory surroundings, I manage to respond to my sister—quietly and with a slight stutter, but I say the words.

"I love you, too."

The scene melts away, and I have trouble deciding whether I would've liked to have stayed.

My senses gather once more to form a dark yet familiar scene, oddly haunting in its luminosity. The Redworth schoolyard be-neath a dark, clouded sky, void of all people; except for one person: Sasha, sitting at our lunch spot as normal. As I glimpse towards her and meet her face, I notice the slanted position of her eyebrows, her mouth hanging open slightly—the deep, purple eye bags surrounding her round, blue eyes. I notice her tense body language as she sits; I notice the horror that plagues her face.

"Kaeda …" she begins, her hands in a slight tremble against the picnic table. "I wish … I wish we never had to ask these questions in the first place," she says to me. "Come here—sit."

I sit where I normally would: across from her. The coolness of the night chills me; I bounce my knee in what I struggle to tell is either the low temperature or subtle anxiety.

"Our questions: they may deserve answers," Sasha continues, "but I doubt that we'll ever receive them. You can research—" Sasha shivers, "you can research all you'd like, but you will never reach a full conclusion unless you look inside of your mind. Sleep on it. Dream about it."

There's a pause in the shortly lived conversation, and Sasha says one last thing:

"Maybe the dreams are your answers."

5:12 AM

I wake up.

A rush of adrenaline quickly consumes me: an immediate desire and motivation to write all that I heard in the dream down—down on a notebook page; to collect my thoughts. But there's something else.

Some sort of other feeling; some sort of other *drive*. A drive that I notice in my physicality: my hands tremble with what is not excitement or passion of any sort. My hands tremble with fear—a dread that follows this adrenaline. This adrenaline is not of passion or excitement. It's of horror.

I only move my head once to situate myself in my wake before I feel a distinct and plaguing dizziness; my stomach aches sharply as I begin to sit up as if my abdomen was a delicate one that was never meant to move, almost as if I'm not human. As if I was never human.

I stare at my hands in the dark solitude of the early morning. I glimpse at my arms: they're riddled by sleep marks from what I can hardly make out in this lack of illumination. I stare at the digital alarm clock beside me, similar to the one in my old bedroom. I think of my old house and the early mornings I'd spend—the ones that, in retrospect, were worse there. A lot has changed—I think I sleep better when someone else is in the room.

A lot has changed and I cannot shake the thought: I am not who I was, whatever I was, whenever I was. This doesn't happen to everyone: these horrifying images and captivating words that my subconscious spits out at me in my sleep.

This doesn't happen to everyone.

Why does it happen to me?

There are the questions. There are the questions that live with me—the ones that have never left for as long as I can remember, begging to be answered while a great void lay underneath their words on a notebook page. Thinking in this solitude, an urge to cry resides within me, yet a dam inside of my mind that has been built up for years upon years prevents me from letting those tears flow.

And that's the numbness of it all. That's the knowledge that I can't exactly do anything about these questions and the complex feelings and dreams that follow; the knowledge that I must only stow them away so that I can better my research and achieve *answers*.

But aren't the dreams my answers?

I need to wake my mind. The dreams have always been my answers—how illogical yet objectively "logical" I was for believing otherwise.

I grab a familiar, non-academic notebook, and flip to the same piece of paper I wrote in yesterday.

"Sasha: 'Maybe the dreams are your answers'"

"Mental hospital imagery, cold, windy, dull"

What was that other part of it?

Right.

"Falling to my *death*. Waking up in my old room, Michelle next to me, questions asked, but I wasn't actively answering any of them: 'Did I die?'"

That was one.

"Michelle: 'You were supposed to 'What happened to Cace ... this is what happened to you.'"

No, there were more.

"'... they've revived you. It's not all in your head (Michelle)"

Oh, and ...

"But I can't do that. I can't live in bliss. That's impossible for me and I don't think I can take living anymore"

"Train station with Juno, late at night, 'You're no different' she said to me. 'Why would they do this to us, Kaeda?'"

"'... to feel like I ... like I shouldn't even be here? Like I shouldn't even exist?'"

"' I miss feeling okay before everything crashed and burned and ...'"

"*Terrifying* quick scene of the train crashing, etc."

"Beau in Arizona ... hand over his chest with a hole and Ida. 'This was never supposed to happen ... I'm terrified at what reality has become'"

Wow.

Staring at me: a mirror—a mess of my own mind. My subconscious, spit in fragments onto a notebook paper in penmanship similar to that of scribbles and clearly written by a trembling hand. Still, although each detail is a fragment: uncategorized and with terrible handwriting, these dreams don't strike me for a second as random. While they have never struck me as meaningless in any way, there's a melody that they each hold—there's a similarity between each that is much larger than the simple connection that they all formed inside a dream. It's abstract; it's complex and I can't easily describe it. It's entirely obscure. It's esoteric.

And I want to act like I don't know what that similarity is.

I want to act like I don't feel it—like I don't understand what has been written on this paper by my own hands. As if I was writing without any thought at all; as if these words were foreign to me. As if I wasn't looking into a mirror; as if the words didn't scream at me, begging me to make the connection—begging me to answer the questions. *Answer the questions*; there is no void that sits beneath my writing from November 6th anymore.

There is no absence. There is no misunderstanding. There is no doubt—or there isn't supposed to be one. There is no illogicality—no incorrect theories. A theory is alive: a theory I've acknowledged lives in others, but never in me. That theory is alive: it's living in me.

And I want to act like I don't know it.

And I want to act like my fists don't clench and my limbs don't tremble—tremble vigorously against the lower bunk. I want to act like my skin doesn't drip of a cold morning sweat and my eyebrows don't sit in an uncomfortable arch; I want to act like my body is not tense—stiffened tensely like a tightrope. I want to act like I'm not sitting here with tears in my eyes that I don't move my hands to wipe—as I bite my tongue to keep them in and silence their flow, as I stare at the paper and its horrifying language. I want to act like I'm not debilitatingly dizzy as I read the page, my eyes moving rapidly to cause such an extreme feeling. I want to act like there's no terribly loud ringing in my ears; I want to act like I haven't seen this before. I want to act like I'm not crying; I want to act like I'm not angry. I want to act like I didn't die.

I want to act like I'm not a clone.

I want to act like this never happened—like this never happened to *me*.

Is this how I should've truly studied cloning; *by looking into myself instead of looking into others?*

"This was never supposed to happen ... I'm terrified at what reality has become."

"You were supposed to."

"I hope you know you're no different."

"I'm sorry that you're familiar with this place. That must feel horrible."

"I just wish it never happened."

"The only way we can advance in these questions is by coming to terms with the possibility that we might be directly related to them."

"I was told you were dead."

The scene is a blur. The scene is a blur until the harsh ringing of my ears—the roaring noise in a silent room—disappears. Disappears and I hear a familiar voice call my name.

"Kaeda?" Ottie says, waking upon hearing me cry; I'm not silent enough.

Ottie calls again. "What's wrong? Kaeda?"

"I just ..." I manage to say, spit leaking out of my mouth.

"It's okay," Ottie attempts to reassure me. She walks down from the top bunk, sits at my mattress, and hugs me. The tension in my body only slightly releases, but the hug is warm nonetheless; I'm at home. I catch a glimpse of the past and what it's like to have a sibling that is your best friend: someone you cannot live without. But am I really living—living as only an artificial creation?

"What happened?" Ottie asks me in my thoughts. "Bad dream?"

"It's ..." I start to respond, my voice quaking as I attempt to speak the words, "It's not only a dream. Every ... Everything is *bad*."

"No, don't say that ..."

"But it feels true," I respond. The tears stop falling to the extent that they were before. "Everything *feels bad*."

"Like what?" Ottie asks.

"I'm not ..." I start, quaking, "... I'm not supposed to be *here*. I'm not supposed to be *alive*."

"Shut up, Kaeda," Ottie says to me, raising her tone with a quake in her voice—a passionate denial of a true reality. "Shut up ... shut up with that *nonsense*."

"But it's true," I continue. "I died—nobody lied to you. And ... and now I'm here, and I'm not supposed to be."

Ottie begins choking up. "Shut up ... please, don't say those things."

"But I'm just like Juno," I respond. "And Beau's just like me. And, no one ... no one is happy like this."

"But ... but you need to *live*," Ottie tells me with a crack in her voice, beginning to cry. "Please."

"I'm not going to die," I reassure her. "But I fear what is to come with me."

My sister rubs her tearful eyes. "Why?"

"Because enlightenment hurts, as much as you know me and I know myself for chasing it," I say. "This reality hurts ... I wish it never happened."

"But ... things will get better," Ottie says, looking up at me in a hug. "I promise. You'll find justice in this."

"But will I?"

"Yes ... yes, you will," Ottie says, wiping her tears away. "Things will be okay."

I can tell that Ottie doesn't believe those things to the core because she sits in an observable mixture of despair and disbelief throughout the rest of the morning. She doesn't say much, only a slight word where she states that she wishes things were different. And Beau treads on through the morning in complete exhaustion, without a word to Ottie or me—and we don't speak a word to him. Janice doesn't wake until the time where we leave. A silence: a dead silence.

And the bus ride mirrors that same quietness. School is dull—Sasha's out; she said she feels sick. From class period to class period until lunch, I sit at my desk—silent. But I don't complete my schoolwork at either desk, instead, I rest my head without sleeping. I rest my head in *silence*, with the continuous and uncontrollable shaking of my knee accompanied by terrible dizziness and stomach pain. There is nervousness—I observe that. I feel nervous *physically*. But I don't *feel* it.

It doesn't plague any of my thoughts. I play through the events of last night's dream, over and over. I pick out each phrase and repeat it to myself in my head—my head that rests on the school desk. And, at the end of each playthrough of my dream, I repeat the words to myself silently: "I want to act like I'm not a clone".

And that is when I feel something: a brief terror. That's when I become in touch with the physical discomfort of myself—that's when the stomach pain and bouncing of my knee align with my thoughts. I play through the events of last night's dream, over and over.

"This was never supposed to happen ... I'm terrified at what reality has become."

"You were supposed to."

"I hope you know you're no different."

"I'm sorry that you're familiar with this place. That must feel horrible."

"I just wish it never happened."

"The only way we can advance in these questions is by coming to terms with the possibility that we might be directly related to them."

"I was told you were dead."

I arrive at the lunch table, and ask Ottie a question before Beau arrives.

"How did I die?"

Ottie looks at me, at first, confused, but eventually glances to the floor, reflecting on the past. She mumbles to herself words that are incomprehensible to me, with a look of worry on her face.

"They never wanted to tell me directly," she says. "But they hinted at it. They had talked about some 'tragic accident' and that you needed 'help'."

"Mental help?"

"I don't think it was a suicide: your death," Ottie says. "But I never knew exactly. I don't know—they never really told me."

A remembrance of writing from my dream crosses my mind.

"I should have kept it to myself—I should have drowned out the idea entirely—living in bliss. But I can't do that. I can't live in bliss. That's impossible for me and I don't think I can take living anymore"

Lunch is painful—I don't speak a word to anyone. Beau hardly talks whilst Ottie studies for an upcoming test to take her mind off of what contaminates it—similar to what I do. But I can't bring myself to study or finish schoolwork. Just today.

Just today: for just today, I can't bring myself to do anything.

Aside from skipping the last few periods: I can bring myself to do that. Throughout lunch, I silently consider the idea. I would go somewhere—preferably by the city bus, maybe by train. And I know I'd hate myself for doing this at any other time, and that I'll hate myself in the future, but it seems like an okay idea.

I make sure to tell both Ottie and Beau about it and, while they question me, they don't seem to mind once I tell them, with little elaboration, that it's for mental reasons. Rather than walking around outside of campus, I decide to take a train to the outskirts of San Francisco: where I used to live. With these past few days and their events, this is dire; they have increasingly detached me from the bliss that I had experienced during that time. To others, what I experienced is the farthest thing from bliss. Now, to me, it is bliss itself.

I take a bus and arrive at the train station, sitting on one of the platform's minimalist benches and waiting for a train. The station's silence and encouragement of complete and utter individualism reminds me of the blissful time that was only slightly under two weeks ago when the only questions plaguing my mind were the ones that I have the answers to now. And those questions didn't seem entirely real—the bliss was in convincing myself that they had to have been unreachable, though that thought was incredibly discomforting.

They were so obscure—so abstract and complex—they must have been out of reach. *Right?*

The familiar train arrives, and I board. It's somewhat empty, only consisting of people who appear to commute to and from work, most likely on a lunch break. I'm not sure of everyone's backgrounds, but they all seem so devoted to their own mundane actions. Listening to music, reading a book, and even sleeping. That's the individualism of it all.

I miss being one of them, completely devoted to my mundane actions rather than focused on my inhumanity because of my past. The past that, during my blissful moments, I was unaware of. *I was never meant to find out.*

That was the "bliss"—it was only a product of cloning.

Is cloning bad?

Yes—yes, it is—you're convincing yourself the times where you had mentally struggled day-to-day were times of bliss. That is how corrupt you are.

But, I would prefer that over–

It's accepting these things that you cannot do. This is the corruption that comes with finding out. You should talk to Beau, Sasha, Ottie, or Juno ...

But I don't feel like this is their struggle.

You have people to support you. Maybe you should go back home at the next stop and discuss all of this over with them.

I killed myself—I was never happy. Cloning saved me.

How do you *truly know* your death was a suicide, though?

I do "truly know"—I know because I remember the occurrence. I remember falling off of the building that appeared to be the mental hospital I've dreamt of continuously—I remember falling to my *death. I remember falling to my self-inflicted death.* I remember the words on the page:

"But I can't do that. I can't live in bliss. That's impossible for me and I don't think I can take living anymore"

I remember that phrase.

I couldn't take living anymore; I committed—that's how I died.

I was never supposed to find out.

I was never supposed to know.

I was never supposed to meet this reality: this abhorrent reality; this altered present.

A shake of the car jolts through my still body. Immediately, my eyes dart around the area, and I notice that I'm not the only one confused or somewhat panicked. Others are too and, following the shaking, the train cars sway back and forth over the railway as none of them are low to the ground.

I hear something announced over the train's intercom, but I can't make out what it is. What I can hear spirals into muffled, incomprehensible sounds. They're loud, then quiet, then loud again. I'm too dizzy to stay calm and my head begins to ache, simulating some pulsating pain. What I can recognize, though, is that the other people around me are silently panicking as well. Finally, I can make something out over the intercom.

"Please stay calm, everyone, we are just experiencing a malfunction in the train cars and the railway," the voice states with blankness. "It should be fixed soon."

That doesn't solve anyone's panic. The cars continue to sway, increasing in momentum each time. While my senses still feel warped, I can hear a passenger say, "It doesn't *feel* goddamn 'fixed'" from behind me. My leg bounces uncontrollably.

Worry.

My mind runs through images: images of Ottie, Sasha, Beau, Juno, and Michelle. It plays out events unfinished and questions unanswered. My thoughts torment me with the possibility that I could die here and leave them behind.

For the second time, I would die. I would die here.

Should I even be living?

The train cars sway harder. The noises from within them increase in volume and, with that, the processing of them inside of my brain becomes increasingly warped and incorrect. Then, I hear a—

No.

No, please.

Then I hear a crack—

I don't want to go, please.

Then I hear a crack from beneath—

SIMILITUDE

SIMILITUDE

My eyes did not fully shut.

Death is silent and loud simultaneously. In my dissipated thoughts lie images of a boat in the middle of the night at sea, with harsh waves and dark navy clouds. And a chilling wind. And a looming fear that

You

Are

Not

Okay.

While this is given, death feels transcendent of all realities. I thought I had lived this out for myself already, but I truly had not. Finding out that I had died, especially that I had died by my own will, wiped away many of my human priorities, yes, but only enough to where I "skipped school". None of that ever mattered.

When you *feel* as though you're about to die, you do not care for anything else. All that is prioritized mentally is your own life, and whether it will end.

When you *know* you are about to die, there is not a single thought in your head that matters. Living is not a priority as it is impossible. You become helpless and quickly understand that reality; accepting death or not, you understand that you are helpless.

I thought I knew what death was.

I had lived it before. Without remembrance, of course, but I still had lived it. And, somehow, that caused me to feel as though I knew death better than any other person. While there was melancholy in all of my doings, there was also a weird, misplaced sense of pride. I felt *better* than other people for thinking about these things, even though they were so detrimental to my health day-to-day.

I say these things while neuron activity still exists, but this passage feels like it's already been said before—there's a striking similitude between these thoughts and ones I feel that I have experienced. Underlying these words is a strong feeling of déjà vu that I cannot put aside. These same words must have crossed my mind when I first died—when I was falling from the building to my death.

That is weird to say. And now the feeling is gone.

I do not know where my mind is. I never believed in any afterlife, so I don't understand where these words are coming from. I'm out of anything "intellectual" to say—now I just feel transcendent, in a sense. Why is this lingering?

Part 4

Kaeda Bynum Saito

One

??????, ??????? ??, 2036, ??:?? ??

I wake up and feel my senses gather, following one another like a pattern. It's interesting.

Beyond my eyes, though, is a setting that strikes me as vaguely familiar, but I can't exactly describe how.

It looks almost like a lab.

SHANNEN GREENE

Author's Note

Dear reader: thank you.

Thank you for reading this book; thank you for turning the page. Never has another project had the longevity that this one—the project you've supported today—has had in my life.

Never has another project had the significance that this one has had—never has another project meant as much to me as this one.

Similitude has grown with me. When I first had the idea for this book and its plot, I indulged myself in the writing process with pure bliss. I was starting my first year of high school having only quarantine writing experience that was for pure enjoyment—since then, this book has evolved significantly. And, with that, I would like to thank you so, so much, for reading it.

This book has revealed to me countless intricacies of myself—it has been an outlet of emotional expression when I felt that I did not know what I was feeling; it has been a series of documents on which I've bled out my complex thoughts and feelings whilst sitting at a bedroom desk in moments of my life when those complexities were unintelligible in my mind. Unexpectedly but not unfortunately, Kaeda has, in the past two years in which I've been writing her character, taken on aspects of my personality which I did not entirely understand or even knew existed. In the beginning of this novel, I hardly knew myself as a human—I suppressed emotion and only emphasized the logic and rationale of my own self, not understanding how detrimental this was. If I could tell Shannen from the beginning of Similitude's creation one thing, I would advise her to be willing to change (and to not censor the parts of her book which she believes should be censored—to be authentic!).

I'd also like to thank everyone who has helped me along this journey—I don't think you understand how much motivation your encouragement towards this project has helped me, and I plan on working towards many other projects like this one in the future!

About the Author

Shannen Greene is a young writer of psychological fiction with a passion for creativity and the sciences. When Shannen isn't writing, she can be found indulging in photography, studying different topics of interest, and sketching! She was born and raised in Maryland, U.S.